TAKEN BY A MONSTER

EVERNIGHT PUBLISHING ®

www.evernightpublishing.com

Copyright© 2020

Sam Crescent

Editor: Audrey Bobak

Cover Art: Jay Aheer

ISBN: 978-0-3695-0198-1

TAKEN BY A MONSTER

DEDICATION

To all of my fabulous readers. Thank you for your love and support and making this dream possible. Also, to my wonderful publisher, for giving my stories a home.

TAKEN BY A MONSTER

TAKEN BY A MONSTER

In the Arms of Monsters, 2 of 3

Sam Crescent

Copyright © 2020

Chapter One

Another dead end!

Preacher stormed into his office, going straight to his desk. He stared down at the file on top, the last known picture of Robin, and threw the entire file across the room. Bear had already grabbed a bottle of whiskey and sat on his sofa, drinking.

"Now isn't the time for losing your senses," he said.

"Nah, well, it's a good start seeing as we've got absolutely nothing else to work on. We're dead in the water and we've even got Billy checking for bodies to match Robin's description." Bear tilted the bottle and drank deeply. "Let's face it, we're fucking screwed on ideas. We can't save her. She's gone."

"I don't believe that."

"When are you going to realize you can't save her? She's dead, probably at the bottom of some fucking lake, or even worse, she's been sold like a piece of cattle,

Preach. Robin is gone."

"I'm not going to give up on her!"

"It's been two years, Preacher. When are you going to realize we're fighting dead ends all the time? We can't find her. She's gone and you're crazy to think Reaper would keep her as some kind of plaything. Do you think she'd even want to be alive now?" Bear got to his feet.

Two years.

Two fucking years Robin had been gone and he couldn't find her. The moment Reaper disappeared, he hadn't been able to locate her. It was like Reaper disappeared off the map and Preacher had to call in many fucking favors to try to find her again.

"I can't give up," he said.

"I know." Bear looked down at his whiskey bottle. "Not a moment goes by that I don't regret what happened. I was so focused on my own shit I didn't see what Rebecca was doing. I figured she'd be happy being my old lady that I wouldn't have to care," he said. He snorted. "I should have known, really. She'd never loved me. Had only used me."

Rebecca had been Bear's wife and Robin's mother. Finding out she'd sold her daughter to O'Klaren to get rid of her, they'd ended Rebecca's life, but it hadn't been an easy death. Alongside O'Klaren, they'd tortured Rebecca. Both them had begged for their lives but he hadn't given in to them.

He'd waited, and only when he had to go on another lead did he allow them to die. They had both deserved what was coming to them. None of it had given him any real pleasure though. The pain of losing Robin had been too hard to bear. Until the end, O'Klaren and Rebecca had been useless to him.

Neither of them had known Reaper's plans. They

thought the rival biker had lost interest because Robin lost the baby, but like always, Reaper had other plans. Once again, he knew he should have killed that fucker years ago. It would have been too kind of a death.

Running his fingers through his hair, he realized he hadn't cut it in two years. He didn't want to think about the last time he'd gotten his hair cut. Robin had been the one to do it.

With Robin gone, he'd laid all his cards on the table to Bear. His best friend, his VP, he knew the entire truth of his feelings for Robin. Feelings he'd never gotten to tell her. She'd been gone before he'd even whispered *I love you.* So much time wasted. So fucking useless.

"I'm not going to give up on her. I can't."

"You're fighting a fool's errand, Preach. Robin is gone. You've got to learn to accept it." Bear grabbed another glass, filling it with whiskey. "Come, have a drink with me."

"I don't want to drink."

"You're going to throw useless files all around the room? Will it make you feel tough doing some shit like that?"

"It's not going to make me feel anything. I just … fuck…" He grabbed the glass from Bear and took a seat opposite him. Swallowing a mouthful, he relished the burn. For two years, he'd been spending every single useless mission at the bottom of a glass even though he vowed never to take another drop after what Milly did to him and Robin. Still, the alcohol didn't help him. It didn't even give him a chance to forget her. Robin was always there, a part of him. The women knew not to come near him. Most of the guys also gave him a wide berth. Between running the club, his usual business, and now finding Robin, he was stretched thin. He couldn't give up on the club to follow every single lead. He had other men do it, even though he knew they didn't want to.

"She's not gone."

"I hate to see you like this, man. You know it's not healthy. I tell you every single time not to allow yourself to be broken by what's going to happen."

"I know."

"And yet, you still continue to do it," Bear said. "You think this doesn't break my heart? My little girl is out there in the arms of a monster. We know what Reaper's like and he's been wanting to make you pay for a long time. Robin was your one weakness. You never should've let him see how much she means to you."

"Do you really think I planned this? That I wanted anyone to know how I felt about Robin? I thought I hid it well. Do you think this is easy for me? She was eighteen. After everything that happened, she should hate my guts, not want me. This was all new to me too," he said. "I didn't expect to want her, Bear. I'm not the kind of man to feature in young women's fantasies."

"I know. Robin's special. You've got to face the fact, though. She's gone and she's not coming back," Bear said. "You've got to stop looking."

"No." He would never give up. She wasn't dead. He knew deep in his heart, she was still very much alive.

"Come on, Preach. Look at us. We're a mess. We can't keep doing this to ourselves. I see the way you fill with hope. You are constantly going further away. You can't keep doing this. The club needs us here. We have to stay here. You don't think this makes us look weak, chasing after ghost stories of a girl we used to know? Robin, if she's still alive, would be twenty by now. She wouldn't want you to give everything up for her. She knows the club is important."

Preacher stared into his whiskey.

Bear had been wanting to give up over six months ago. They'd gotten a hit through Dog's crew about a sighting of Robin. When he went there, it had been a dead end, a dead motel.

People just wanted money, and well, Preacher was throwing it at people in the hope of finding out the truth. He was being foolish, he knew this. Over the last two years, he'd made plenty of mistakes, but getting Robin back wasn't a mistake. She didn't deserve whatever Reaper was putting her through. He couldn't even bring himself to think or to guess what it was. That man would hurt her just for the fun of it.

A knock at the door pulled his attention away from the dark amber liquid. The only time he didn't feel any pain was at the bottom of a bottle. He liked to be completely numb, to forget about his troubles and only focus on his burning need to have Robin, not that it really worked. There were times he'd dream about her and imagine her in his arms, where he could hold her, make love to her, even fuck her.

He was a forty-seven-year-old man and he was having wet fucking dreams about a woman who'd been taken from his life two years ago. A woman he loved more than anything else in the world but would never get the chance to tell her.

"Any news?" Bishop asked.

Preacher snorted.

"Dead end," Bear said.

"Another one?"

"Yes. Another dead end. No sign of Robin or Reaper. When I get my hands on him, I'm going to destroy him and it's not going to be pretty."

"First, you've got to get your hands on him." Bishop stepped into the room, taking a glass and holding it toward Bear for him to fill. After Robin was taken, Bishop moved out of his home, and he was really fucking pleased to see the back of him.

Bishop had been broken and bleeding, but Preacher still felt his son was responsible for Reaper taking her. Even as he thought it, he was struck by a little guilt for even thinking the worst when it came to his son, but he couldn't help it. Bishop should have done more to keep her safe.

If Bishop hadn't seen them kissing, would he have tried even harder to save her? Preacher would never know the answer, but he didn't know what to think of his son right now. Bishop had only come on a couple of their trips to find her. Considering he claimed to love her, Preacher doubted his son's true integrity. Staring at him now, there was nothing there. No fear, no sadness, nothing. It was like they were talking about the weather. Robin had been Bishop's friend since they were fucking born, and yet, nothing.

"Oh, I will," Preacher said. Getting his hands on Reaper was exactly what he was going to do, no matter how long it took.

"So you're not going to give up?" Bear asked.

"Give up?" Bishop looked between the two of them.

"Bear believes she's dead and it's not worth me constantly going out of my way to find her."

"Come on, Preacher, we would have found her by now," Bear said. "When are you going to realize the truth? She's gone. I'm a realist here. Even as it hurts me to say it."

He finished off his glass of whiskey, letting out a sigh as the burn traveled down his throat. "What do you think, Bishop?" he asked.

"Me?"

"Yeah."

"About what?"

Preacher laughed. "Finding Robin. Do you think it's a dead end or do you think I should keep looking?" He really didn't give a fuck what his son thought, or anyone else for that matter. The last person to talk shit about Robin as just being some pussy, he'd cut out their tongue and made them swallow it. Of course, he'd then killed the person but only after using the time to amuse himself hurting them.

He'd killed a lot of people in his search for Robin.

Too many.

Some, he just had to kill because they'd been so fucking stupid to let her go. In the first month, their leads hadn't been pointless. From one of the many hotel stops Reaper made, there was security footage. The man behind the counter had claimed it looked more like a father-daughter argument than a kidnapping.

Preacher had seen the footage and killed the guy behind the desk. Robin had been screaming for help. Begging the guard to call a guy named Preacher. Telling him the Twisted Monsters MC would come for her.

They'd never gotten the call. Reaper had paid the guy and left. Useless dead ends. Wasted time. It was what he had to deal with, constantly, never giving up hope.

"What do you want to do?"

"Don't you have a brain cell in your head? I know what I want to do, I'm curious about you."

"You've got to keep looking," Bishop said. "You know, in case you find her."

"And if she's dead, what should I do?"

"You can't do anything. She's dead."

"You know, considering she's your best friend,

you've been able to handle this really fucking well," Preacher said. "Don't you miss her?"

"Of course, but I can't allow myself to dwell. I know Robin wouldn't have wanted that."

"Preacher, she's my little girl. You know I want to find her more than anything. I miss her so much and I can't stand the thought of that bastard being out there with her, hurting her. We all know what Reaper is doing to her, but … we've got to learn to let shit go. It's no longer been a few hours or a few months. We're talking two years."

The anniversary of when she was taken had passed a few days ago. No one else had said anything or maybe not even realized it, but he did. Another day of his failing.

Holding out his glass for another refill, Preacher didn't argue with Bear.

Bear had given up long ago. There was no point in even asking his opinion. He truly believed Robin was dead. Why would he believe anything different? He didn't know Reaper like Preacher did.

"I've got to get laid. Excuse me." Bear took the bottle with him but Preacher didn't move.

Bishop took Bear's place but Preacher didn't look at his son. At times, he found it was harder to stare at the man who allowed himself to be beaten and his girl to be taken. What the fuck kind of man did that?

Robin, where the fuck are you?

"What did you ever do to Reaper for him to do this to you?" Bishop asked.

Staring over the rim of his glass, he kept on watching him. He saw parts of his younger self in his boy, but only parts.

Bishop had graduated from high school, only just.

Robin, she would have graduated and probably

even considered a college as well. He'd have helped her no matter what she wanted out of the future. She was smart. He had to hope that in some way, he could give her that.

"You don't have to answer me. I know it's hard for you to even look at me sometimes. I get it."

"You get it? You don't know anything, Bishop."

"Then tell me. Talk to me. Make me understand why my best friend was taken by Reaper. Why he really wanted to hurt you. Did you know each other a long time ago? Did it start in high school or something?"

"There doesn't have to be a reason, Bishop." He laughed. "Is that what you think? Reaper and I had some high school crush or some shit?" He shook his head, needing another drink. "Reaper and I, we're from different clubs. Our rivalry started because I'm better than him. He's weak and he knows it. He can't have what I do because no one will follow him. He's nothing."

"But if he's so weak, why does he still have Robin?" Bishop asked.

Preacher stared at his son, but he didn't have an answer, at least, not one he wanted to share with him or anyone else.

"I guess that's the best question. He never stays in one place long enough and wherever he goes, he leaves a trail of death and destruction in his wake."

"And you still can't find her?"

"This conversation is starting to bore me." He got to his feet and nodded at his son. There was no way he would leave his office open and exposed to anyone trying to find his secrets.

"What if Bear is right? What if she is dead?"

Preacher locked his office door before turning to his son. "You really should be careful what you say to me. Considering she's supposed to be your best friend, but so far you've spent every available moment telling me how useless it is looking for her, it makes me wonder exactly why that is. What do you have to hide?"

"I don't have fuck all to hide, Dad! I can't help but wonder if we're wasting our time here. She's gone and there's no way she's coming back."

"And that's why you'll never fucking find her." Preacher pocketed his keys and without another look back, he headed out of the club. He went straight to his bike. He hadn't drunk enough to even worry and he needed to clear his head.

Being at the clubhouse didn't help him to think or give him any positive clues. All it did was remind him how much he'd fucking failed and he hated nothing more than being reminded about how fucking clueless he was when it came to Robin.

He shouldn't have gone to torture O'Klaren. When Bishop found them, he should have stayed with her, or at least took her to the club.

After climbing onto his bike, he turned the engine over, gunning the machine as he took off through the metal gates. He no longer spent a great deal of time there. It was all work for him and when he did have time to rest, he went home.

He pressed on the gas and rode, sweeping each curve as it came, building up speed, trying to find a place where he no longer thought about Robin, or how fucking useless he'd been in his search for her.

There were moments he was sure he heard Robin plead for him to find her. It was fucked up, he knew that, but no matter how hard he fought, he felt her. She wasn't dead. He didn't know how he knew it, only that he did. If she was dead, he would've felt it, wouldn't he?

Love is for pussies.
The weak.

The useless.

He used to believe all those words. They were, after all, part of his inner mantra. Women were just for pleasure and business, never to actually care about. Bishop's mother hadn't been a good woman. She'd spread her legs for anyone willing to pay the high price, and when he stopped being willing to pay, even for his son, she'd turned on him. Reaper again.

That bastard had been a thorn in his side for as long as he could remember and there was nothing he regretted more than not squashing that bug when he had the chance. Reaper needed to die and one day soon, he'd be the one to drain the life out of him, to watch him burn.

He'd thought of all the ways he could hurt, torture, and kill the son of a bitch, but he wouldn't do anything until he knew where Robin was. Even if she was dead, he wanted to bring her home. She deserved to be laid to rest, but no, he wouldn't allow himself to think like that. Fuck. She wasn't dead!

A part of him knew Reaper wouldn't kill her, at least not intentionally. Not out of any obligation to keep her alive. With Robin dead, it stopped the pain. Whereas with Robin alive, he knew she was being hurt. Reaper was all about hurting him, fucking with him. Instead of coming to him, Reaper was a fucking coward and instead took a woman.

He didn't want to think about the life Robin had lived for the last two years. She'd always been a sweet girl and then turned into a beautiful flower, the love of his fucking life. He'd never seen it coming, never seen her.

He came to a stop near a parked police car. The lights on top of the vehicle weren't on. No flashing lights. No sign to show who it was.

He slowed down. Parking in front of the car and

turning off his ignition, he looked toward the man.

A flaming light and the scent in the air gave away his smoking.

"Smokin' will kill ya, you know?" He got off his bike, heading toward the man perched on the front of his car.

"Yeah, and so will an angry woman with a knife. I don't want to meet either and seeing as my woman doesn't like me to smoke, I've got to get my kicks somehow," Billy said.

Billy had taken over from that fucker O'Klaren. From what Preacher had been told, O'Klaren's disappearance had been accepted by all. With his wife's admission of his abuse and years of deceit, the cops who worked closely with him just wanted to put a bad case to rest and accepted everything they were told. After Dog released the information from the cell phone, along with the witness accounts, trying to make a huge case out of a crooked cop wasn't on a high list of priorities. Preacher had no doubt there would be some cop who would look into O'Klaren's disappearance. They'd never find a body though, and if they tried to take him down again, he'd be ready for them. Until then, he was clear to do his shit. Only now, he was more cautious than ever before. He wasn't willing to take too many risks, not with his freedom. Not with Robin being out there somewhere. Cops had always been on his back, but like he and Billy, they had an understanding. He wouldn't allow them to get too close.

"You and the wife having trouble?"

"When are we not having trouble? She doesn't like how much more time my job takes now. She likes to complain she never sees me, but for the pay raise, she loves me even more." Billy shook his head. "At least the kids are doing okay."

Billy had a wife and two kids, and one of them had been very sick, which was one of the many reasons why Billy took his money and helped him out. This man saw the bigger picture and even though he killed people, he never went after innocents.

Like Bishop's mother, she'd never been an innocent.

"How was your last lead?" Billy asked.

"I'm here talking to you rather than dealing with and killing the man who took her. What do you think?"

"Maybe you shouldn't tell me what you're going to do with the man who took Robin. I'm still a cop, after all."

"You're chief now. Don't forget that," Preacher said.

"Yeah, no one else would take the job and seeing as I was the longest serving man still on the force, well, I got the job. Let's face it, you do most of the work for me."

"So why aren't you at home with your wife?"

"I'm trying to help." Billy reached into his jacket and took out a small file. "It's not much, but the picture looked like Robin."

Preacher took the file. He held his cell phone above it, flicking it on to use the light. Inside was a single piece of paper and one picture.

Robin was there. Her long brown hair had been hacked off and it looked like it had been dyed red. In another picture a few months ago, it had been red.

All of her hair was gone.

He'd loved it spread out across his pillow. Of course, he didn't get many opportunities to admire it like that.

"When was this?"

"Camera's date is three days ago. I know it's not

much and they're probably long gone by now. He's still bouncing from hotel to hotel. He's in the country but hours away."

"How much do I owe you?"

"Consider it free of charge."

"Why would you do this?" Preacher asked. He never got anything free. He was the kind of guy who had to fight or pay his way to get shit.

"Robin wasn't a bad kid. I met her a few times and whatever she's going through, she doesn't deserve it. I don't like to think of her hurting and if I can do anything to help, even if it is something so small. I'm willing to do it."

"Without anything in return?"

"Preach, you pay me plenty. This doesn't change our other arrangements at all. It's the least I could do and I would hope that if it was my girl, someone would be there for her, offering me help like this."

Preacher closed the file and nodded. "Thanks."

"I should be getting back and you need to go home. I can smell the alcohol on your breath and you don't want to end up with your ass thrown in jail."

He laughed but nodded. He waited for Billy to leave before looking back in the file. This was one of the leads he'd already followed but he appreciated Billy trying. The closest person he'd ever had to a friend was Bear, but he was starting to believe there were others lurking around. He just needed to be a bit more open to accepting friendships, even if it did come from cops.

He straddled his machine, turning over the ignition once again, and this time headed straight for home. He didn't make any stops and kept well within the speed limit. The moment he got home, his floodlights kicked in. He parked his bike and went into his empty house, flicking the locks and heading down to his basement. His home was one of the hardest places to be in right about now. Without Robin around, all he had were memories.

Gripping the cord, he pulled, turning the light on. Inside were all the pictures, maps, and files of a man obsessed with finding the woman he loved. Every single dead end and false lead. Even some that weren't.

They were all laid out on the wall. Removing the file from inside his jacket, he grabbed a pin, and putting it through the single picture with the notes Billy had attached, he found the right spot for it on the wall and pressed it in.

Stepping back, he looked. Each image was like a separate clue.

In the beginning, the fire burning in Robin's eyes was clear to see. Even in the blurred pictures and the video footage, which he had a great deal of. With each passing day, week, month, and year, the fire had died a slow and painful death.

It was how he knew she was still alive but her fight had gone. Something had happened to her, and she'd given up, but she wasn't dead. In some of the pictures, he saw the bruises on her face. Again, in one of the video footages, he saw the marks on her arms and legs. Reaper didn't exactly make her cover up or hide his destruction of her. The son of a bitch was taunting him and Preacher knew he couldn't react. He had to bide his time. As the months passed, the bruises no longer appeared, though. It was like she was untouched by Reaper, but something had to have happened for the fire to go.

There had to be bruises, just ones he hadn't seen.

He should've found him by now. Reaper wasn't a strong man. He was a fucking loser, but over the years, he'd perfected the art of falling off the map, of disappearing, which was why it was so difficult to find her.

Taking a seat, he gripped the stress ball he'd picked up and hoped it would help him to think. To clear his head of all the troubling thoughts consuming him. There was no time for him to give up or give in.

Squeezing the ball, he looked at the latest picture. She'd lost a lot of weight. Her face looked gaunt. The way her head was tilted, he saw the marks on her neck. The kind that came from a man hurting her. Wrapping their fingers around her neck and squeezing.

He was going to get her back. There was no doubt in his mind he'd finally have her in his arms once again.

The only problem he saw was the mess she'd be in when he did finally get her back. Robin's body could very well be alive, but her soul, her heart, her mind, could already be lost to him forever.

Chapter Two

Three days later

The fight was brutal, bloody. Probably one of the worst fights Preacher had ever witnessed and considering how many he'd viewed and been a part of, that said a great deal. Two men, both of them naked.

One of them even had a rock-hard cock, but the wealthy female clients loved the show. A woman's penchant for death and blood had stopped surprising him long ago. He had no doubt some women hated blood, hated the violence. But others, they loved to see the raw animal instinct come forward.

A brutal sport of the best man winning.

The fight to the death never failed to lure people in and even though he'd been doing this for nearly twenty years now, the volunteers were endless. There was never a shortage of people willing to die all in the chance of winning. The money was always the one motivator. Their chances could be slim but to many, but they didn't care. The money was a lifeline for them.

Another punch that resulted in a tooth being spat into the crowd. The ones closest to the fight got splattered. There wasn't any anger, though. No, the crowd lapped it up. Loving the proof of what they were witnessing. Another spectator slipped on the slick floor.

"You'd think people would get tired of the same old shit," Dog said, coming toward him.

"You're on the wrong side. You're supposed to be supporting your guy over there," Preacher said, pointing toward the railing on the opposite side.

The warehouse was secure. The building was structurally sound and the cops who patrolled the area within the city had been paid a great deal to keep the law off their backs and of course to turn the other way.

"We both know my guy is a goner. I'm surprised he's lasted this long. Too bad. He came into my territory claiming to be one experienced fighter."

"He is, if he's beating up high school geeks," Preacher said.

The sound of a crack, deathly silence, and the fight was over.

Preacher stayed where he was while money and the body were being dealt with. Within two hours, he and Dog still stood together, alone.

Their men were waiting for them. Their cuts sat in neat envelopes on the table below. If anyone even dared to touch the money, they'd be shot on sight.

There was a time when Preacher got a thrill out of tempting people to steal from him. He'd hunt them down and take care of them swiftly. It had been a game to him, one he used to relish. Now, it bored him. His life, it meant nothing, and he knew why.

Robin.

"I heard about the dead end," Dog said.

Preacher kept silent.

He and Dog weren't the kind of people to talk about their feelings.

He'd asked Dog for some favors and paid him handsomely for it. It was why his envelope was a lot bigger.

The club hadn't liked his negotiation with Dog. They didn't feel their cut should have to suffer. Preacher had told any man who didn't like the way he ran the club could come at him, fight him for the crown, but so far, no one had come forward. They had left the running of the club to him, and well, he didn't see a reason to change his methods. They were all earning money through other means, and it was by far more than what they got through the brutal war of fighting to the death.

"Is there a reason you want to sit around and chat?" Preacher asked.

"Not a lot sitting going on."

"I find this all very touching, but I need to head back to the clubhouse."

"I've been hearing rumors," Dog said.

This made Preacher stop. He turned to Dog. The man was just as deadly, just as fierce since the first day he met him.

"Is this where you want me to offer up more of my cut? Maybe take the drug money from me? You think I'm going to offer you shit for the chance of some gossip?"

"You know I'm not the one who took her and I've been helping you when I can. It's not about the money. I can't believe I'm fucking saying this, but maybe after all this time, I see you as something a little more than an ally or my fucking enemy I'm in bed with."

"You want to be my friend?"

"Stop being a dick. We are friends. The only person who doesn't see that shit is you."

"Yeah, because friends shoot each other."

Last year, he'd been pissed off at a lead from Dog that had gone stale. The man had held on to it too long and rather than think of a strategy, he'd marched into Dog's territory with the intention of killing the man, only to get shot in the leg for his trouble. Dog had taken his gun.

"You and I both know you deserved that kind of treatment. We're friends, but I'm not going to let you take the piss. I gave you what you wanted. If it had been anyone else, their head would have been mounted on my wall."

"After you sat on that information for over a week. I could have gotten her if you'd given it to me."

"He had his entire club with him. They were armed, and believe me, this battle you've got with Reaper, I want you to win but not at the sacrifice of your life."

"Aw, are you going to tell me you love me, Dog? You want to be my little pet?"

Dog laughed. "I forgot how much of an asshole you can be. You already figured out that any ambush you make on the whole club would kill the woman you want. Her death would be on your conscience, and yeah, I've got a pretty sweet deal. I can handle anything thrown my way. I have done it for fucking years, but I don't want to have to deal with another MC president who thinks he pisses rainbows. I don't have time for that shit. We work together and we hate each other. It's how this shit works. Regardless of what you think, we're in this together. Since the moment you took the clubhouse in the abandoned garage, you've been setting down roots. Your club comes and goes, but it's like life. They're still bound to the club because once you make a vow, it's death that takes it from you."

Preacher sighed. "What do you want?"

"I don't want anything. Actually, that's a lie. When you get your girl back, I want to meet her."

"You're not going to tell me to stop looking for her?"

"Why the fuck would I tell you to stop?"

"Let's just say the advice I've been getting, they pretty much tell me to give up."

"Clearly you've been getting really shitty advice. I'm not going to tell you to give up. Fuck that. Giving up is for losers and you're not a loser. You'll find your girl because she's still alive."

"She is?" This was the first piece of good news he'd heard in a couple of weeks.

"Rumor has it the president of a moving MC has attached himself to a woman. She's got the highest protection but it doesn't stop her from running."

"Wait, how the fuck do you know this?" Preacher's heart started to pound.

"Like I said, these are rumors that come down the club. One of my guys heard it around a campfire three days ago. When he realized you were looking for your girl and I'd been following my own leads, he gave me the information. There's never a guarantee of where they are. They stay in one place for a couple of days, no longer than five, and move on. It might be worth following the news and getting your cop to check leads on dead women."

"Why dead women?"

"They take random women either from the street or kidnap the pretty ones, keep them during their stay, rape them, and discard them. There should be a trail of bodies. I don't know if it will help if there's some kind of path, pattern, or method, but it could lead you right to your girl."

Preacher ran a hand down his face. "Thank you."

"Any time and don't forget my invitation when you do find her."

"I won't. Why do you want to have dinner with others?" Preacher couldn't think of a single reason as to why Dog would even want to spend any extra time with him. They weren't close and neither of them shared any part of their lives apart from the fighting.

"I want to see what it is that made you become this obsessed prick. You got shot in the leg. I've never been able to put a bullet in your body before she was taken. I've seen what a crazy dick you've turned into. Call me intrigued by the woman who tamed the beast."

Preacher took off, heading down to grab his cut.

As he got to the table, he looked at Dog. "She keeps trying to escape?"

"So I've been told. Again, this is all rumor, Preach. Everyone has a price and well, Reaper clearly paid a lot of money to men that he wants to keep her close."

"Thank you."

"Don't mention it."

He grabbed the money and headed out. Bear was at his bike, smoking. He was surprised there wasn't a drink in his hand and this made Preacher stop.

After killing Rebecca, Bear had turned to women and alcohol. Was there a problem there he needed to take care of?

"Hold your hand out," Preacher said.

"Is this some kind of joke?"

"Hold your fucking hand out." Preacher waited.

Bear rolled his eyes. "Are you going to put a ring on my hand as well?" Bear held his hand out.

It was steady.

No shakes.

He put the money in his grip. "Take this back to the club."

"You thought I was in withdrawal, didn't you?" Bear asked.

Preacher sighed. "Can you blame me?"

"No, I can't blame you but it's a little unfair you think so fucking little of me."

"I don't think little of you, Bear. Drinking and sex, it's all you've got. You've given up on Robin. What else do you have to live for?"

"I haven't given up on my girl."

"Then why do you keep on suggesting I stop looking for her, huh? If that's not giving up, I don't know what is. I'm trying to find her. We both know she's alive, but you want to stop. Why?"

"Do you think you're the only one who breaks a little when you come back home empty-handed?" Bear asked. His voice was so soft, calm, it was almost impossible to hear, but he did.

"What?"

"The first twenty-four hours. That's what they say, isn't it? If you're going to find anyone taken, it has to be within those first few hours."

Preacher didn't have a clue what the saying was and he really didn't care. In his book, the only time to stop looking was when he had a body, alive or dead. "It's been two years. Each time we come back with the lead being dead, I die a little more inside because I've failed her again. You think each time is easy for me? I love my daughter and I failed her. I let her down by keeping her slut of a mother around and I should've seen what a toxic cunt she was. If I'd seen the truth, Robin would still be here."

"It's not your fault."

"But it is. I was so busy getting my own dick wet I didn't see the truth. I should've known Rebecca was up to something, but I couldn't stop her because I wasn't there. This is all my fault. You think I don't imagine my little girl begging for help? Wanting her daddy to come find her? Fuck. I messed up, Preach."

"This is what that bastard wants," Preacher said. "This is what all of this is about. To tear my club apart looking for her."

"You're playing right into his hands," Bear said.

"Not just me. All of us. I will find Robin. She's alive. Get that to the club. I'm heading in to see Billy. I've got some new leads."

"And what are you going to do if all of this is bullshit? She's dead and has been resting at the bottom of a lake somewhere. What are you going to do then?" Bear asked.

He knew she wasn't dead.

Right now, Bear's weakness was starting to piss him off, to the point he wished he actually had a drinking problem.

"Then I'm going to find Reaper and for however long it takes for me to find the truth of Robin's death, that's how long I will keep him alive to hurt him. You need to understand me, Bear. The moment Reaper took Robin, he signed his death sentence. Even if I find her alive, he's dead. I won't stop hunting him. I will find him. I'll fucking kill him and when I do, I'll make sure you're there to celebrate right along with me."

He got on his bike and left the warehouse. Once again, it was dark, but he didn't mind. The darkness helped him to blend in and to not be so consumed by the burdens chasing after him.

There weren't many people milling around on the streets. No chance of him mistaking any of them for Robin. It had happened a couple of times driving through the city. A couple of women he'd scared because he was sure he'd seen her. Again, the mind playing tricks on him, which was why he preferred to hunt for her at night.

His hopes and dreams were never squashed if he hunted for her at night. Bear would take the money back to the clubhouse and church would be called when he returned. He would hand out the money, take some from the safe as well to give them all their weekly cut, and update them on their businesses.

In a few weeks' time, he would have to cease all searches for Robin as he had a drug run which would take him from the docks and across state lines to delivery. This was another deal he'd struck in his search. The cartels monitored the docks and he'd organized a delivery deal with a reasonable cut in order to make sure that if Reaper tried to leave by boat, he'd be alerted. Unlike Reaper, he had the funds to keep the bastard on the ground. At least while he kept the cartels happy.

He also had men working for him at the airports. Actually, it was two computer geeks who had some outstanding warrants. He'd called in a few favors and they were no longer worried about getting their asses thrown into jail. They monitored the security footage for him, and any time an image showed Reaper or Robin, they called him.

So far, Reaper had been able to travel under the radar. There was no way for a computer to detect all facial features hidden behind a baseball cap and Reaper knew how to stay off the grid.

He arrived at Billy's house. After parking his bike, he walked up the steps and banged his fist on the door. The moment he did, regret filled him.

Billy's family would be there and he'd knocked like a fucking crazy person.

Billy opened the door. He wasn't dressed in his uniform. "Preacher, what are you doing here?"

"I need you to make some calls for me. Check your database and find any clues—"

"Who is this man, Daddy?" a young blonde girl asked. She stood behind her father's legs.

Preacher recognized her from some of the pictures. This was the young girl who'd been battling leukemia.

"I'm a friend of Daddy's," Preacher said, crouching down so he was at her level. He didn't want to scare her. "I'm Caleb." He held his hand out. He never gave his name away. To everyone else, he was Preacher, but this was a little girl.

"I'm Tillie and my sister's name is Catherine."

"Both of you have nice names."

"Are you the person my mommy hates?" Tillie asked.

Preacher laughed. "No, sweetheart. She hates my job. Not this man. Go and finish watching the movie."

"Billy, what's going on?" Billy's wife, Debbie, walked down the stairs, tying her robe.

This wasn't exactly what he wanted today. He just wanted to get his information and get out.

Debbie stopped on the stairs. "Oh," she said. "Hello, Preacher."

"I just want to borrow your husband for a few minutes."

"Taking him back to his work. I should've known I wouldn't get two minutes to have a bath and relax."

"If he's got a computer in his office, we don't need to leave," Preacher said. The last thing he wanted was a pissed-off woman who hated her husband being away and ran her mouth off.

He liked Billy and his kids needed a mother. He didn't want to have to take out his wife because she couldn't keep her mouth shut.

At his suggestion, Debbie smiled. "I can handle that kind of business setup. Come in, Preacher. Would you like a drink?"

"Nothing, thank you. I don't want to stay long."

"I'll deal with this and handle the kids," Billy said.

"Good." Debbie walked off.

"You notice how I didn't get offered a hot beverage?" Billy asked.

"Are you in the doghouse?"

"I'm in one kind of fucking house. I used to have time to let her have her mom time, but lately, I've been staying late at work."

"Should I be worried you're building a case against me?" Preacher asked, joking.

"I'm trying to find Reaper. There's nothing else going on in town and I've been trying to locate where he could be."

Preacher entered Billy's office. "I get you following up leads for me, but it shouldn't be taking you away from your family." Especially as he hadn't been paying the man for the extra work.

"I know. I'm … I have to do it. Not just for the money either."

"Then why?"

"You've seen Tillie and Catherine."

"So, they're safe at home."

"And one day, they're going to be out there in the big, wide world. I know you haven't had a daughter yet, but … I can't stand the thought of a man like Reaper being out there. I don't want to think of him ever getting near my daughters." Billy sighed. "I'm sorry. I don't mean anything bad about it. I just, I know to some I'm a fucking shit cop, but I've got to try my best, you know. I've got to at least do something."

"It's fine. Believe me. You don't want him anywhere near people you love." It's why he tried with all his might to keep him away from the fucking town. That day two years ago, maybe even longer now, at the diner, he should've told Robin to go somewhere else. To be nowhere near him.

"What exactly am I looking for?" Billy asked.

"You have some kind of database that allows you to look for possible clues or tracks of murder or homicide."

"You do realize how many of them happen per day, right? Some of them are cold cases. Some of them are suspected and are not always homicide cases."

"You're only looking for a small collection of women. One or two every so many miles."

"What are you thinking?" Billy asked.

"Reaper will take women, use them for a couple of days. They may show signs of rape, beatings, stuff like that."

"May?"

"Some women are agreeable to being used for the right money. The only thing is, Reaper won't pay them."

"Okay, can you be clear on what kind of search you want?" Billy started to type into his computer.

"Anything about one or two women. On the rare chance, there will be a guy thrown in, but I mean rarely."

"Do you want me to look specifically for prostitutes?"

"No. Reaper won't care if they're a working girl or not. He'll see a woman he likes and take her."

Billy began his search. "How are you holding up?"

"I'm in your house, chasing rumors and gossip. How do you think I feel?" he asked.

"Wow, honesty. I didn't think you had it in you."

"Oh, believe me, I do. People just don't like my idea of honesty."

Billy laughed but it sounded forced. "Okay, what do we have here? This could take a couple of hours, but we do have a hit about thirty miles out of town and that was only a couple of weeks ago. Oh, wait, it was a drowning."

"Are you sure it wasn't him? Some of them could look like suicides and deaths."

"No, she was drunk and walked into a lake. At least that's what it's saying as a reason. They've got security footage that shows her doing this. The lake is near some kind of protected real estate. Sorry."

"Keep looking." He leaned over Billy's shoulder, but the database didn't look familiar or in any way make sense. "How did you become a cop in Knight's Bridge?"

"You mean because I've got the ability to be a city cop?"

"Pretty much. You'd have been promoted a long time ago."

"Yeah, because they'd overlook me helping you," Billy said.

"You're a good cop."

"I do what I can to protect people and the town. It doesn't make me a good cop. It makes me a really good person. That's all." Billy kept on clicking away. "We all have our faults and I don't want to be a city cop. Never did. I wanted to make a difference in a small town and that's what I do. I make a difference where it counts and to me, here, this is where it counts. Nowhere else."

"Fair enough."

"What's the deal between you and Reaper, anyway? You've got some kind of shared past?"

"Something like that. Believe me, you don't want to know."

"One day, I expect it will be a story you can share with me. Wait, I think I have something."

Preacher's phone began to ring. He glanced down at the screen to see an incoming call from Randall. "What the fuck does he want?" He ended the call and looked over Billy's shoulder only for the screen to make no sense. There were a bunch of names, numbers, and what looked like reference points. His cell phone rang again and he saw it was once again Randall calling.

"Clearly, whoever that is wants to speak to you. Answer it. I don't mind."

Preacher cursed and answered. "I'm a little busy right now—"

"We have her," Randall said.

"Excuse me?"

"Robin, she's in the hospital."

"You're joking."

"I'm not. It's her. She looks different but it's her. I'd recognize her anywhere, even with the hair. You need to come to the hospital, Preacher. It doesn't look good."

"What do you mean it doesn't look good?"

"You'll understand when you get here, but you need to come. Quickly." Randall hung up the phone.

Billy had stopped typing. "What is it?"

"That was Randall. He says Robin's in the hospital but it doesn't look good. Wouldn't you have gotten a call?"

Just then, Billy's cell phone rang and both men looked at it.

Billy picked it up. "Hello." He didn't say anything, just listened. "I'm on my way." Billy clicked on the computer and within seconds, it was dead. "We've got to go. That was the hospital. Robin Keats is in the hospital. She's in a coma and the doctors don't know if she's going to wake up. She's been beaten and they need me to go down to take a look."

Preacher wasn't sticking around to hear the rest. He was out of Billy's house without a look back. Was it a trap? How could he have not found her for the last two years only for her to suddenly end up at the hospital just as he'd gotten another lead?

Chapter Three

"I swear to you. I wasn't even going that fast. Like maybe thirty. I had to get home to the wife and she wasn't in the best of moods since I took her only non-fat yogurt and she loves those things. She swears by them and believes she's losing weight because of it."

"Get back to the girl stumbling in front of your car, please," Billy said.

"Right, so I was driving down the stretch of a dark path. There's no lights and there really needs to be. You don't know what kind of things that will jump in front of you, and the next second, she was there. She went up over the top of my car, her head hitting the window. There's a crack, I think. I don't know. She slumped back to the ground. I didn't think. I stopped the car, got out, went to her, and she was out cold, but there were so many bruises. I don't even think she could see. I didn't think. I picked her up and brought her straight here."

Preacher stood out in the hallway, staring into Robin's room.

It didn't look like her, but it was. The hair, the length was gone. It was short, blonde, and it didn't suit her. Her face was a bruised, angry mess. She was small, thinner than she'd ever been.

Her eyes were swollen shut and there was a machine helping her to breathe. One of her ribs that had been cracked punctured her lungs. His hands clenched into fists. Randall had already told him if she hadn't been brought in when she was, she would've been dead.

One of her feet was also smashed. According to Randall, it looked like a hammer had been brought down on it. He didn't even want to think about it. It creeped him the fuck out.

"Thank you, sir."

"I've already had blood tests to confirm I wasn't drinking and I know I wasn't."

"It's fine. You've done everything that has been required of you."

"Thank you."

Preacher didn't look to see Billy leading the man away. He had no intention of harming him. Even though his car did hit Robin, the man didn't leave. He'd picked her up and brought her to safety. One day soon, the man would find his reward for bringing her home. Preacher always kept his promises and Billy had the man's address.

"How are you holding up?" Randall asked, joining him.

He'd yet to go inside and see her.

He'd called Bear but the man was too drunk to make it to the hospital. He hadn't even bothered with Bishop. Right now, he didn't want to see his son or make him aware she was here. It would all happen soon, anyway. There was no way this would stay a secret. At least he'd have tonight with her. He couldn't fucking believe it. She was right here. After two years, she was at the hospital, within arm's reach.

"I'm going to have a guard on her door at all times. You need to be aware of this."

"The staff have already been alerted to this."

"Good." He didn't want to think right now, only look at her. "How did you know it was her?"

"Look at her, Preacher. I've been seeing this girl all my life. I would know her. She's a good girl."

"This coma, how bad is it?"

"It's … it's not going to be easy. You can go in there. Talk to her. Offer her some company. There's brain activity, so you could bring her out of this."

"She's sleeping."

"There's been research that shows some patients can hear their visitors and relatives. Obviously, I don't know how it completely works, but you can have faith."

"I lost my faith long ago."

"As a doctor, I don't. I like to believe in miracles. I know to some that is deluded and unfounded, but I believe we all have a higher purpose, one reason we're sent down to this earth to seek out."

"Don't start spouting the Bible at me, Doc. I don't want to hear it. Me and the big guy lost our faith long ago and I'm not going to get it back." He was tired of this conversation and he really didn't want to have a religious talk with anyone.

Sitting in the room with Robin was the lesser of two evils. It was still high up on the scale of problems he didn't want to face.

After stepping into the room, he closed the door. At first, he just stood there. The sterile room sickened him, but the woman who lay unmoving, looking like she was dead in the bed, she was still Robin.

It had been two years since he'd been in this position with her. He didn't want to think about the last time he saw her. Her worries about Bishop as he brushed them aside and still went and did what he wanted to, without a care in the world. He'd been dealing with a lot of guilt over his decision. If he'd stayed, he might have been able to stop all of this from happening.

Running fingers through his hair, he heard the machines. Their persistent beeps, which should have been a comfort, only they pissed him off. Angered him, even. He didn't want to think about their constant sounds. They at least gave him hope, didn't they?

From the look of her, he didn't think it would be possible for her to return to him.

He had to be close to her, so he took another step into the room.

Her face was completely bruised and her foot had a cast on, as well as her wrist. There was also a bandage around her middle, but he didn't see that, just knew it was there.

"I don't think you'd be happy with the way you look right now," he said. He grabbed the seat, lifting it up and placing it close to the bed. Machines were on one side, giving the reading of her heart rate and blood pressure.

"I hate seeing you like this." He laughed. "I know wherever you are right now, you're probably annoyed at me stating the obvious. Sorry to do that, you know, state the obvious." He ran a hand down his face. "I'm so sorry." He reached out, about to take her hand, but he stopped himself. "I'm not used to talking like this or being with anyone like this. I don't do feelings. You know this. I'm trying. I want to do what's best for you, but I … I'm struggling. Damn, Robin. I've been looking for you for two years and I know when you wake up, you're going to have a whole lot to say."

He stared at her. "I can't wait to hear your voice. I've been thinking about you all the time. Every decision I make, it's in the hope of finding you. The club's pissed at me because I've made some really shitty deals for information. I guess to some, I've been a bad leader but it was all to bring me closer to you or at the very least, to try and find you." He wanted to hold her. It killed him inside to know he couldn't take that step to be near to her, to touch her, to hold her. For now, he had to hold back.

Clenching his hands into fists, he sat back in his chair, trying to be calm. Trying to get his shit together and find some source of control, but it wasn't helping.

He finally had Robin, but she was as lost to him as she first was.

****

"It's her?"

Preacher jolted awake at the question. He turned to see Bear in the doorway of the hospital room.

"Yeah, it's her."

He stood up. He couldn't remember when he'd fallen asleep but he'd been out cold. Running a hand down his face, he tried to clear the sleep from his eyes.

"I came as soon as Grave gave me the message."

"Was Bishop with you?"

"Nah, I haven't seen him for a couple of days. I don't keep track of him." Bear stepped forward. "What's going on?"

"The doc says she's in a coma."

"When will she wake up?"

"When she's ready. She walked into an oncoming car. It's how she got here. I'm going to grab some coffee. You want some?"

"Yes, I want some." Bear took the seat he'd been sitting in and Preacher left the room. He chanced another look at the woman he loved before pulling himself a way to go and grab some coffee.

The doctors, nurses, and medical staff gave him a wide berth and he really didn't give a fuck what they were thinking or how worried they were about him. They needed to stay the fuck away from him right now because he really needed to get his shit together in one way or another.

He made his way to the cafeteria, which had already opened for breakfast but it was now lunch. Seeing as Bear would need to have some alone time with Robin, he ordered himself a sandwich and coffee. He sat near the window, eating and not really tasting, looking out at the world and waiting for some kind of feeling to wash over him.

He'd found her.

No, someone else had found her, but she was now back in his care.

Only, he didn't know what he was dealing with or how to fight it. Seeing her all beaten up and helpless, he couldn't do anything about it. How had she gotten away? Was Reaper waiting somewhere to take her back? Was this a game? He wouldn't put it past the son of a bitch to already have a plan in place or wanting to do something else to hurt him.

"I figured I'd find you here. Bear's having a hard time of it upstairs," Randall said, dropping his tray on the table and taking a seat.

"I didn't say you could sit here."

"Come on, now. We're old-time friends and you look like you could use a chat."

"Because I talk to you at the best of times."

"I'm the only person you've got who understands what's going on with Robin."

"You don't have a clue. Me and you, we don't know the kind of shit life she's had the past couple of years."

"You're right, we don't, but I do know what she's going through on a medical front. I know her injuries are severe. She may never walk again, and she certainly will struggle to run. The bones in her foot were shattered. That's going to hurt like hell and she's going to need some therapy. Then of course, we don't know what else she's gone through, or what kind of pain she's dealing with on the inside. I've got the resources to help her. I know the best people and I can help guide you. We can bring her back to us, together."

"I can pay the best, Randall. Money makes the

world go round, remember?"

"You can't buy respect."

"No, but I can buy loyalty."

"Which someone with a bigger price can also offer."

Preacher sat back, looking at Randall. All his life, he'd always had the bigger cash flow and if money didn't help, fear was a great secondary tool.

"Why would you want to help me, Randall? I know you've worked for the club for years and I can trust you, but I also pay you. Why are you willing to help me now?"

"It's not about you, is it? This is about Robin. I helped bring her into the world. I was there when Bear and Rebecca had that huge fight twenty years ago now. I was the one who held her in my arms when Rebecca turned her away and Bear was too drunk and scared to hold her. She was screaming, scared, hungry. I held her. Fed her. For three days, no one wanted her until Bear, he finally came and when he did, he held his daughter for the first time, and I knew she'd be safe, but I bonded with that kid. Whenever she had a cut or graze, or just felt ill. I was the one she came to. I care about her, Preacher, and it's not because of who you are and what it is you do. Robin's a good girl. Always has been, and she's going to need those who love and care about her close."

"You love her?"

"She's like a daughter to me and even though I've never heard you say the words, I know you love her too."

Preacher didn't say anything. He ate his now-cold sandwich and stared across the table at Randall, who had started to eat.

"Where do I need to look first in taking care of her?" Preacher asked.

"First, we get her healthy and we hope she wakes up."

"If she doesn't, will Bear have to make a choice?"

"We can talk about that problem when we get to it."

"I say we talk about it right now seeing as I'm thinking about it and I need to know my options."

"Okay. If there is even a chance she won't wake up ever, or her brain activity diminishes, then yes, the choice will be up to Bear as to whether or not he turns off life support, but she has to get to that stage. Right now, we're assisting her breathing purely because we don't know the true extent of the damage. And after the surgery, we're giving her a chance to relax before we go in on any possible invasive surgery. Does that help?"

He sat back down and breathed a sigh of relief. "Yes, it helps. I'm sorry."

"Welcome to the world of being human, Preach."

"I … I don't know what to do right now." It was the first time he'd ever openly admitted to being out of his depth.

"Thankfully, this is something I can in fact help you with. First, you will finish your breakfast. Then you'll get a cup of coffee to Bear because I've spoken to him and he stinks like a brothel. Then you'll go home, get washed and changed. I'm going to be at the hospital with Bear. He won't let anything happen to her and neither will I. You're going to need your strength. Robin's not waking up today."

"Any indication when people do wake up?"

"Do you want me to really answer that for you?"

"I need to know."

"Fine. Sometimes it can be a couple of days, a few months, years, or never. I can't give you some kind of miracle date here, Preacher. That's not how it works. She's either going to wake up or not. You can't lose hope, though."

"Yeah, but it sounds a lot to me like you believe she won't wake up," he said.

Randall sighed. "I can't tell you for definite she's going to be the same woman. She may never be the same person you knew, Preacher, but I have to believe she'll come back to us because I don't want to think of the last time I saw her as being the last. You're not the only person who wanted her back." Randall finished his lunch and left.

Preacher shoved the last piece of his sandwich into his mouth, forcing it down. He drank the cold coffee and got himself another and one for Bear. When he returned to the room, Bear was there, holding her arm.

"I can't even hold her fucking hand," Bear said. "Look at her. She's back and I'm too fucking drunk to even make it. I'm a useless father."

"You're here, aren't you?"

"Yeah, and look what good I am. I can't … I'm a fucking mess."

"None of us knew what was going to happen, Bear. You can't beat yourself up."

"You were here, like always. You were ready." Bear took the coffee. "I think I've got a problem."

"With what?"

"With drinking. I think I need to go to rehab or, I don't know, detox."

"If that's what you feel you need to do, we can get you admitted to one as soon as Robin's better, or you can go this afternoon."

"I don't know if I have a problem. I don't drink every single day and I don't knock myself out all the time. I'm not desperate for a drink. Fuck, I drink because it passes the time and last night was the first time in a couple of days."

"It's up to you," Preacher said. "When Robin wakes up, our focus is going to be on getting her well, not on thinking about us or what we need."

"I know. I know. I will. Even if I don't have a problem. I'm going to do it. I need to get my shit together. Robin doesn't even have a mother to rely on anymore. She's got us."

"That's still a lot of people she can trust," Preacher said. "She's not alone and she will never be alone again." He sipped his hot coffee, relishing the burn as it sank down his throat. He hated to think of Robin on her own. He didn't know what she'd been through and how she'd survived.

Had she begged for him?

"Are we still going to hunt for Reaper?" he asked.

"Oh, yes. He's not getting off easy. I'm going to hunt him like the fucking dog he is and he's going to wish he'd never looked in Robin's direction." Preacher wasn't going to stop hunting for Reaper. The time would come when he'd find him and when he did, he was going to serve justice in his own way.

****

A couple of days later

"How come I didn't get the memo?" Bishop asked, stepping into the room.

"I don't go chasing you around," Preacher said. He was reading a book. It was some kind of crime novel, but he hadn't really taken in the story. It was just a bunch of words on the page. He was more interested in watching Robin, but after a couple of days, there was still no change. Randall said it was a good thing. Even though there was no change, it meant she wasn't getting worse. He'd been told many times he had to start seeing the positive, but no matter how often he was told, it didn't make it any easier, in fact, he found it far worse. He was growing tired of waiting, but at least she was here, with him. All he had to do was reach out and touch her to know she existed, that he wasn't losing his mind. He hadn't told Bishop. What was the fucking point in telling his son anything? Robin belonged to him, no one else.

"I'm her best friend and you didn't think to tell me she was safe?"

Preacher looked up from his book to stare at his son. "How many times have you joined me on the leads I've been chasing?" He waited but Bishop didn't give him a reply.

"Last time we spoke, you told me how pointless it was to pursue her. I should just give up because she was clearly dead. Again, you told me that. Tell me, Bishop, why the fuck would I tell you anything? Especially when you've spent every single available minute I've needed you avoiding the issue."

"You think this is easy for me?"

"I think, like always, you're a selfish little prick because you only think of yourself. Like now. Look at her, Bishop. Look at your best friend. The one you care so much about. Tell me she means anything to you when all you can think about is how you've been wronged Look at her!" He put the book down, pissed off at Bishop's interference. He wanted to hurt his son, which was a feeling that grew every single day and had started to wear a little thin.

"I'm looking."

"You see the bruises? The casts? Do they not mean anything to you? She's been through a lot, so no, I wouldn't call you. Not when the only important person in your life is yourself!"

He was done with this. Bishop annoyed him,

pissed him off. Getting to his feet, he was about to throw the little prick out, but Randall chose that moment to enter.

"How are you today, gentlemen?" Randall asked. He walked up to the bottom of Robin's bed, clipboard in hand, and began to make some notes.

"We're fine," he said, taking a seat again. He wasn't here to give his son an ass whooping. He'd come to relieve Bear so he could get a shower and some food.

They were all taking turns. In a couple of hours, Grave would be by. Bishop, with his complete lack of regard to his authority and the club, wouldn't be allowed to be alone with her. He didn't care how much it pissed him off. Preacher's word was law.

Picking up his book, he ignored Bishop when he left and returned minutes later, holding a chair. He sat down, and Preacher continued to read his book, waiting.

Of course, it didn't matter how long his son and Robin had been friends or even what he'd been doing. The only thing that mattered to him right now was taking care of his woman. It had been two years since he'd last seen Robin, but she was still and would always be his woman. He loved her more than anything in the world and always would.

Running a hand down his face, he tried not to think of the loneliness and fear that had consumed him in the last couple of years. All he could think about was Robin. He'd made some tough choices for the club in order to call in as many favors as he could, but that was all over now. He only needed to focus on Robin getting better.

"I'll be back in a couple of hours," Randall said, leaving him and his son alone.

The minutes ticked by. The only sound to fill the room was that of the machine beeping, letting him know she was alive and would continue breathing. He didn't want to imagine a world without her.

"You could have at least sent me a text."

"Really, what would that do?" Preacher asked. "You rarely answer your texts. You do your own thing now, Bishop. What more could you possibly expect from me?"

"I don't know. Something. Anything. I don't want to lose her."

"You haven't lost her. Not yet," Preacher said. "She's right there."

"But what if she doesn't wake up?"

"You know, I'm growing tired of your negativity. She will wake up and when she does, we'll know the kind of hell she's been through." Preacher stayed seated as Bishop got up.

"I can't watch her like this."

"I didn't tell you to."

"I'm out of here."

Once again, he watched as Bishop left.

"I don't know what to say about him, sweetheart. He claims to love you but spends a great deal of time walking away or thinking of the worst when it comes to you." He didn't touch her but placed his arm close to hers, not wanting to let her go, just be near her.

A few hours later, that was where Grave found him when he came to take over.

"Keep an eye on her. Don't let any nurse or someone pretty distract you."

"I won't."

Preacher left the hospital, drove home, and took a quick shower. He didn't bother making himself a cooked meal and settled on a quickly thrown together sandwich. Before leaving the house once again, he made his way upstairs to Robin's old room.

Nothing had changed.

Before Bishop had left home, Preacher had caught him once, trying to clean up the room as if she'd left and wasn't coming back. It had pissed him off to the point he attacked his son and ordered him to put everything back in the right and appropriate places.

This was his home, not Bishop's, and Robin's stuff stayed. Sitting on the edge of the bed, he noticed that the scent of her had long faded but her stuff was still there. One of her English books was on the counter, open at the last page she'd been reading.

Some of her notebooks were spilling out of her backpack, and he didn't have the heart to move them. He didn't have the heart to move any of it. She belonged here. This was her home and he missed her so fucking much.

With Robin back in his life, when she did finally wake up, he'd bring her here. "You'll be back soon."

After getting to his feet, he walked toward the nursery. Opening the door, he stared into the room. Again, he hadn't changed anything. The picture of the tree she'd asked him to draw was on one side of the wall. She'd loved his design.

Even when everyone kept telling her she didn't need to keep the baby, she'd been determined to do exactly that. She had fought against everyone, and yet, she'd lost the baby. Then, too soon, he'd lost her. He didn't need to keep remembering those first few days. The helpless feeling had never gone away. This was one of the reasons why he'd never allowed himself to fall for a woman. The control they had was too great, but he couldn't stop his feelings for Robin. From the moment he let her in, there was no letting go.

****

The days turned to weeks and then into a month.

Preacher divided his time between his club, his businesses, and Robin. It was hard not to put her first. The club, they shared in keeping an eye on her. Bear was at the hospital constantly, and so was he. He only picked the men he trusted to keep her safe.

The bruises began to fade on her face, and one day as he sat there, Randall stood over her, lifting up her wrist, staring at his watch.

Preacher watched her, waiting.

All of a sudden, she opened her eyes.

It was like magic.

One moment, they were closed and the machines were doing their merry little show of keeping everything intact and in place. The next, they were beeping. Going crazy as her heart rate sped up.

She sat up in bed and started clawing at her face, trying to yank her breathing tube out.

"I need some help in here," Randall said, calling out to be heard. Nurses and doctors rushed into the room.

Preacher stood up, wanting to help. He saw the panic in her eyes. The fear.

Anyone would be able to see it if they only took a few minutes to stare at her. She was trying to claw at her face, but with one hand bandaged, she struggled.

His heart was pounding.

What should he do? There was nothing he could do to help her. He wasn't a doctor and seeing her like this, it broke his heart. The panic, the fear, it was tangible.

"What's going on?" Bishop asked. He held a small bouquet of flowers, tulips and Preacher smelled the other women on his body.

Not caring about his son's selfish ways, he stared at his woman, amazed that she had woken up. He'd seen her eyes open and it was beautiful to witness. He never thought he'd ever been so freaking happy than he was at that moment.

"Robin, I need you to calm down. I'm going to take the breathing tube out. You're going to be in pain. You've been in an accident."

As Randall took charge, making her listen to him, she stopped trying to fight the machine. Preacher struggled to watch as they removed the tube and she gasped, taking in deep breaths.

"Water?"

Her voice was croaky but just hearing the sound of her voice was sweet bliss to his ears.

Randall handed her a glass. "Okay, Robin. It's good to see you. This is good news."

The nurses and fellow doctors were all nodding and confirming their agreement. It was fucking brilliant news.

Robin kept on drinking until she finally stopped and turned to look at Randall.

"Who's Robin?" She frowned.

"Robin?"

She nodded.

Randall looked toward him.

"Do you know who I am?" Randall asked.

"You're a doctor."

"Yes, but who am I?" He hid his nametag and she kept on frowning.

"I don't know who you are."

"What's your name?"

Robin opened her mouth and closed it. "I don't know."

"Do you know who these men are?" Randall asked, pointing toward him and Bishop.

"No. I don't. I don't remember."

"Do you remember where you were a month

ago?" Randall asked.

She looked down at the bed, and he watched her try to come up with an answer, but nothing was there. "I don't remember."

One of the monitors started to beep erratically again.

"I don't remember. What does that mean? I don't understand. Why can't I remember?" she screamed, starting to cry.

Preacher wanted to comfort her. But how do you comfort a woman when she didn't know who he was? He couldn't just go and take her into his arms.

Randall cleared the room. Nurses and doctors left, and finally he and Bishop stood at the door.

"She doesn't remember anything?" Preacher asked.

"I need to have a few minutes with her. I need to understand the extent of her amnesia. If it's everything she knows or just facts," Randall said.

"Wait. What does this mean?" Bishop asked.

"It means she's very sick and is going to need a lot of help. I will know more soon, but for now, you're going to have to wait." Randall closed the door.

Preacher looked through the window and saw her staring right back at him. Her head was tilted to the side and he watched her.

He'd never been so fucking nervous in all his life.

"What the fuck does this mean? What does any of this mean?" Bishop asked.

"It means she's very sick," Preacher said. "We're going to have to wait for Randall to fill us in on the details."

In one moment, he'd felt so much pleasure and relief. She wasn't dead or hurting, but now, he didn't know what was worse—her not knowing who he was, or the long-term damage this could have caused.

"What do we do?" Bishop asked.

"We do what we have to. I'm going to have to call Bear."

"I can go and get him. It's not far. You should stay here," Bishop said.

"I will."

Bishop left and Preacher took his cell phone out, sending a quick text to Bear. His son had a one-track mind, and Preacher didn't want something as important as this to be forgotten.

Preacher sat out in the hall. He watched as the hospital continued to move. Patients were seen. Doctors and nurses hurried up and down the hallway. Code blues were yelled. Patients were brought in. He saw it all, heard it all, but none of it mattered to him. He was completely oblivious to it all. Preacher didn't know how much time had passed before he caught sight of Bear running toward him.

"I came as soon as I got your message." He stood at the window.

"Randall's checking on her to see the full extent of the damage."

"We don't know what is going on?"

"Nope. We don't know anything."

"What did she know?"

"Nothing," he said. "She knew Randall was a doctor, but not his name. She didn't know who I was, or Bishop for that matter. He's seeing what she does and doesn't know."

"This can't be happening. We can't get her back for her to be gone again. I don't want to … no, it's not going to happen."

"If you go in there, you're going to freak her out," Preacher said.

"Freak her out? I'm her father. What the fuck does that mean?"

"You didn't see her trying to get the breathing tube out of her mouth. She was so scared. I'll never forget it."

"You're so fucking calm about this."

"I have no choice, do I? I either let this get to me and lose control, or I accept I finally found her, and now, I've got to wait a little longer until she's well again. Either way, this is good for us, and I'm not going to give up."

Bear took a seat beside him.

They both waited for Randall to leave the room, which he did a short time later.

Preacher stood up.

"So, what's the verdict, Doc?" Bear asked.

"She doesn't remember anyone or anything of her past. She can read, write, understand everything on an academic level, but her life, she's a blank canvas."

Preacher took a deep breath. "So what do we do?"

"We give her time. The brain works in mysterious ways. She could remember in an hour, tomorrow, next week, or as in some cases, she may never recover her memory."

"What does this mean?" Bear asked.

"It means we have to take our time with her. Sometimes, she may feel a little overwhelmed. It would be good not to bombard her with too much information but to see how she reacts to people and situations. She may need therapy as well, and I do want to get her started on some exercises for her foot. Robin is going to need us now more than ever."

Chapter Four

Who was she?

Why was she in the hospital?

How did she get all these bruises?

She looked over her arms and saw some ink wrapped around one wrist, almost like a chain. Beneath the bandage on her other arm, she wondered if a replica tattoo was there, but she couldn't see it. She'd asked the doctor, but he hadn't been able to help her.

There was more ink on her body, but again, she didn't know why.

The pain in her side was from a cracked rib. She had to take it steady or she'd hurt herself even more. Every single part of her was hurting.

Picking up a strand of hair, she saw it was blonde, the kind out of a bottle. How did she know all of this but not her own name?

The machines around her, why?

Her foot hurt a great deal. Her face was swollen. She could only see out of one eye, but the doctor had told her it was getting better, and a month ago, she wouldn't have seen anything.

Great, just great.

Her hands shook a little. Her heart raced. She felt a little sick.

Nerves? Worry?

Why would she be worried?

It wasn't every single day a woman woke up and couldn't remember her own life. She knew the doctors were medical staff, as were nurses. Chairs were to sit on, and beds to lie down on. She didn't know anything else and it was really starting to bug her.

The door opened and in walked the doctor. Two other men she didn't recognize stepped into the room.

Both men were wearing leather cuts. Again, no warning bells went off. No recognition.

"Did I do something bad?" she asked.

"Why would you think that?" Randall asked.

"The face. The broken bones. The head-on collision with a car you told me about. It kind of makes me think I did something wrong."

"You don't need to worry. These men, they're not here to hurt you."

"Hey, baby," the one on the right said.

"Baby?"

"You're my daughter."

"Oh, hello ... Dad." The word didn't sound right on her tongue.

"The name's Bear," he said.

"If you're my dad, does that mean you know my name?" she asked.

Should she feel anything? Some connection to this man? Nothing made any sense to her, and it freaked her out.

"Can I tell her her name?" Bear asked.

"I don't see why not. She needs to know it."

"I'm sitting right here. I want to know my name," she said. What she didn't like was being spoken over as if she didn't exist. She was right here for them to see. Hello!

"I know, sweetheart, but it's also important for us not to overwhelm you."

"I need to know my name, though, right? I need to know what to respond to." She hated not knowing. She rubbed at her temple, feeling the start of a headache.

"Are you okay?" Randall asked. "What kind of pain do you have?"

"I ... it's fine. I can handle it. I need to know everything."

"Let's start with your name."

She wanted to tell him no, to tell her everything, but she settled on her name.

"Robin, your name is Robin Rose … Keats."

"Why did you hesitate on my last name?" she asked. Something was going on, she knew it deep in her soul.

Again, Bear looked toward the doctor.

"I'm sitting right here." Tears filled her eyes. "I just want to know what is going on. Do you have any idea what this is like?"

"I know, sweetheart, but you've got to give this time. There's a lot that happened to you. We haven't seen you in a long time."

"How long?"

"A long time," Randall said.

She wiped the tears away and sniffled. "I … I'm sorry."

"You're not to blame." The man who hadn't spoken until now stepped forward.

She lifted her head, staring at him, hoping for some kind of memory to trigger. In the back of her mind, it was like she was desperate to know the truth. It was important to her to know every single little detail of what happened.

"Who are you?" she asked.

"I'm Preacher," he said. He held out his hand and she stared at it.

It was a big hand, firm, strong-looking. She lifted her hand, not the injured one, and took his hand.

No memories surfaced but as he touched her, she felt … safe. Was it possible to feel safe with a man she'd never known?

"My name's Robin Rose Keats. You're my dad, and you're my …"

"I'm your friend," he said.

"Friend?"

He nodded.

It didn't feel like a friendship, but she kept her mouth shut.

Looking from her dad to her …friend, she knew something wasn't right.

"What about a mom? Do I have a mom?" she asked.

Bear and Preacher looked at each other then at her.

"Your mom passed a long time ago. You don't need to worry about her."

"Why would I need to wor—"

Someone gasped at the door and she turned to see a young man. He looked a little like Preacher but not entirely so. He smiled as he stared at her. "Robin, it is so good to see you awake."

"Bishop, I don't think you should—"

"Who are you?" she asked, talking over Preacher.

"I'm your husband," Bishop said.

****

Preacher wanted to beat the living shit out of his son. Robin didn't get up from the bed and run to him, nor did she look at Bishop as if he was a gift from the gods. No, she stayed in the bed and looked at him.

"We're married?" she asked.

"Yes. You and I, we're married and have been for about three years now," Bishop said, stepping closer.

He wanted to warn Bishop, but he couldn't say a fucking thing. Yes, Bishop and Robin had been married but only to keep him out of jail and to avert a fucking crisis. Robin didn't love Bishop.

Does she even love me?

No vows or promises were whispered to each

other and now, he felt like a fucking prick for not telling her he loved her.

Robin stared down at her hand. "I'm not wearing a ring."

Bishop reached into his pocket. "I have it here. We had a bit of a fight."

"Did you cause this?" she asked, pointing to her face.

"No, I would never hurt you. You know this."

"I don't know anything. I don't know who you are." When Bishop took a step toward her, Robin jerked back. "Don't come any closer."

"We're together. We've been friends for life."

"I don't know who you are."

"You can trust me."

"Please leave," she said.

The machines beeped.

"Bishop, leave," Bear said.

Preacher stayed perfectly still, watching his son. Bishop's shoulders slumped.

"One day, you will recognize me and know that I love you and you love me, so much." Bishop put the wedding band on the bed and left.

She didn't make a move to pick up the wedding band.

Randall picked it up and placed it on the cabinet beside her bed. "I think it is best we let you rest," Randall said. "Rest will help you."

She looked toward Bear and Preacher. "Am I married to him?" she asked.

"Yes," Preacher said.

"Do I love him?"

He honestly didn't know how to answer that.

"You and Bishop have been friends for a really long time," Bear said, taking the lead.

"That doesn't answer my question."

"It's hard to answer. You and Bishop have always had issues. You love him in your own way. I honestly don't know what else to tell you."

She didn't trust him. Preacher saw it.

"Bear, I'm going to need you to come and sign some paperwork," Randall said.

Preacher stayed perfectly still, very much aware of his son not too far away.

Robin watched the other men go and she finally turned her gaze back to his. "You've been really quiet."

"I'm just pleased you're okay."

"Were we close?"

He stared at her, not sure how to answer.

"I guess I'm going to have to get used to people keeping secrets from me, aren't I?" she asked.

"It's not a secret. We can't overwhelm you." He took a seat, watching her.

"I … I don't know who that guy is who's claiming to be my husband. I feel a little sick and I don't understand why. Can I trust my body? My mind?" She laughed. "My mind, it's totally gone." She leaned back against the bed.

"You're tired. You need to rest."

"I want to remember everything. Can't you tell me every single little detail?" she asked. She reached out, trying to grab him.

Preacher took her hand. "You're going to be fine, Robin. One day, you will remember everything."

"What if I don't? What if I never remember anything and you all are waiting for me to remember important details and facts?"

"None of us are expecting you to remember anything. We all just want you to get well. Sleep for now, Robin. I will be watching you and taking care of you."

"Promise?"

"Promise."

She let go of his hand and settled back on the bed, breathing out a sigh of relief. "That's good. That's really good. I can handle it. I can handle all of this."

He watched her fall asleep before finally leaving the room. He pulled the door partially closed and leaned against the wall. He breathed in deeply then expelled his breath. He did this several times, thankful she was at least alive and that he didn't have to go on hunting for her or worrying about what was happening. She was back home and that was all that mattered to him. Above everything else, she had to be safe.

He couldn't think about anything else right now, just keeping her alive, away from Reaper. That son of a bitch, he would kill him when he got the chance. His hunt wasn't over.

"I bet you're feeling pretty smug about all of this," Bishop said.

Preacher looked at his son. "And why would I feel smug?"

"She doesn't remember me or that we're married. Or how much she loves me."

He laughed. "I really fucked up when it came to you, didn't I?"

"She's mine."

"Last time I checked, son, she didn't have a fucking brand on her to state she was anyone's. She has no owner."

"She doesn't remember me and she doesn't remember you. You're not going to get her back."

"Son, all I want from her is to be healthy. I want her to get her life back. This isn't some kind of fucking competition where one of us is the victor. She's not a trophy. She's a real human being and maybe if you got your head out of your ass, you'd see it."

"Oh, she will see it. You took her from me once, but you won't do it again."

Preacher stepped up to his son. "The only reason I haven't smacked you down like you deserve is because you're my son, but all I ask from you, Bishop, is to keep on going down this selfish path and I will make sure no one can ever identify your body."

The threat was there.

For Preacher, there were only so many excuses he could make for his son before he realized he had to take him out. He'd only just gotten Robin back, and he couldn't allow for anyone, not even Bishop, to take her from him. He didn't know how he was going to deal with Bear either.

Without another word, Bishop turned on his heel and walked away. Soon, he would revoke his ability to enter the club. Preacher was getting tired of his tantrums and entitled ways.

Taking a seat, he stared across the hall once again, watching the comings and goings of the staff.

This was where Bear found him when he returned. "It's a fucking fortune to be ill."

"Do you need any money?" Preacher asked.

"Nope. It's all taken care of." Bear groaned as he sat down. "Seeing Robin like this, it makes me want to kill her all over again."

"Rebecca?"

"Yeah."

"Me too, and O'Klaren. That piece of shit got it easy."

Bear laughed. "Neither of them got it easy."

"That's right, and they never will. I hope they're rotting in hell somewhere." He ran a hand down his face, trying to clear his thoughts. He was so fucking worn out. "I'm going to find him."

"I don't expect anything less. Reaper will have what's coming to him. I know you'll take care of it."

"Oh, believe me, I'm going to do more than take care of it. When I finally have Reaper, I'm going to have him begging for death and praying to every single god there is."

"I'm going to enjoy watching his torture. I'll even join in. What are you going to do about Bishop?"

"Nothing. He'll show his true colors. I want the word out with the club. Bishop no longer gets a free pass. His leather cut will be returned to us and I'm going to give the little shit an ultimatum."

"Is this because of Robin?" Bear asked. "He's your son."

"Yeah, and he better start acting like it because so far, he's no son of mine."

****

Robin didn't know if she hated hospitals or if this was her newfound disposition with them. She hated the food, the clothes, and the sounds. The machines drove her crazy and the constantly changing faces freaked her out. One nurse saw her in the morning, another at lunch, a different one in the evening, and then another at night.

The only constant was the doctor, Randall. He always seemed so happy and chipper. His happiness was infectious, and she looked forward to his visits.

She also liked spending time with her father. He snuck her cookies. According to him, chocolate chip was her favorite. She didn't know if it was true but didn't see a reason to doubt him. Bear was serious most of the time. She saw how sad he was, his nervousness around her. He wasn't being himself and she hated not being able to put him at ease. He didn't bring her any clothes and he'd told her she'd lost quite a bit of weight.

Between the cryptic words and meanings, she had come to see that she'd been gone from their lives for two years. She hadn't gone of her own free will but someone had taken her. For two years, no one found her until she stumbled in front of an oncoming car, beaten, bruised, and broken. They don't even know if the collision with the car was what caused her amnesia. They were all trying to be careful, to avoid overwhelming her.

She hated it but also appreciated their concern.

Then there was Bishop, her supposed husband. If he was married to her and they cared about one another as much as he said they did, shouldn't she feel something? She didn't hate him, at least, she didn't think so. Whenever he did visit her, she found him exhausting. He wanted to constantly talk about himself, their future, and she didn't even know their past.

He'd demanded she wear the wedding band, and she refused. He got a little angry at her refusal, but she didn't care. She wouldn't wear something because he demanded it. He wasn't her keeper, at least, she hoped he wasn't.

All of it was a little confusing to her. She wanted to find her life again, and Bishop, he didn't seem like he cared to even know the past with her.

His kisses, she found them a little uncomfortable as well. Was that her fault? Was she the one feeling the wrong kind of things when it came to Bishop? He kept looking at her with hope, as if she had some kind of magical answer, and the truth was she didn't have anything. She was as clueless as him. There was no way for her to change anything that had happened to her.

Why are you even worrying about him? You're the one in the hospital bed.

Then of course there was Preacher.

He didn't speak a whole lot and he never brought up the past. For the most part, he didn't even seem to be in any kind of rush to make her remember the past. He was happy to just sit and talk to her. She enjoyed his company the most.

There was stuff she knew had happened between them but again, it was more a gut feeling than actually knowing.

"Do you read a lot?" she asked when she woke up to find him sitting with her. There was always someone with the Twisted Monsters MC cut near her. She didn't mind. The one who stuck in her mind apart from Preacher was Grave. That guy was scary, but he never made her feel anything but safe. The patch did that, for some strange reason. She'd asked Randall about it and he'd told her to wait and to allow certain memories to materialize all in good time.

She hated waiting.

"Nah, I don't read a whole lot, but it seems I've taken it up while waiting for you to wake."

She let out a little stretch. "I hate staring at this room."

"You want to go for a walk?"

"I don't feel like walking." Twice a week, she was instructed to walk even with the cast, and it was proving difficult. Her pain medication had been reduced and she'd been expected to deal with it. If the pain was more than she could take, they would give her more drugs, but she didn't like how groggy they made her feel.

"I'll get a wheelchair. We'll go out for a stroll." He put the book beside her bed and left the room.

She lifted the book up and a picture fell out. She lifted it. It was one of her and Preacher, smiling. She looked happy.

Was this the clue she was struggling to find? Was

there some kind of hidden message she should have? A clue?

Nothing came to mind and she had a sudden overwhelming need to hit her head. Before she could do that, Preacher returned, and she slid the picture back into the book. She'd ask him about it another time.

She didn't need answers today, or even next week. She simply didn't need answers at all. At least not yet. If she was married to Bishop, what was her relationship with his dad? Why did she feel more comfortable with Preacher than she did with her husband? None of it made any sense to her.

"Are you ready for your trip?" Preacher asked.

She pushed the blankets from her and Preacher moved closer. "Hold on to me."

She wrapped her arms around his neck, and he lifted her with ease, carrying her to the chair. His closeness sparked something within her. A pleasure she didn't know she possessed. It felt good to be in his arms, natural.

He put her in the chair and then started to put the blanket around her. "I don't want you to be cold."

He moved behind her and they left her room. The moment she was outside her hospital room … something changed. She was no longer confined to that one bit of space and she could finally breathe easier.

"Are you okay?"

"I am. I feel so much better." She tilted her head back, offering him a smile. "You can stay with me, can't you? We can do this?"

"We can do whatever you want. We're not bound by one place." He moved onto the elevator and no one else shared it with them. She watched the floors change as they descended.

"How are you feeling today?" he asked.

"A little tired. Do you think I'll ever get out of the hospital? I don't need to stay here overnight all the time, do I? I'm not in danger or anything. I could go home, right?"

"Do you remember your home?"

"No. I don't. Do I live with Bishop? Do I live with my dad? I'm twenty years old, so does that mean I married at seventeen? Why did I marry so young?"

"Those are all good questions. What I will say is after you married Bishop, you lived with me."

"Will I be staying with you again?"

"Bishop doesn't live with me anymore."

"I don't think it's a good idea if I stay with Bishop," she blurted out. Should she have kept her nerves and doubts to herself?

"You can do whatever it is you want to do."

The elevator doors opened.

"You're not angry with me?"

"Why would I be angry with you?"

"Bishop's your son."

"I know."

He didn't give anything away, which was so frustrating.

"Did we have a good marriage? Everyone is being so secretive."

"You need to remember everything in your way. We can't give you clues."

"But clues can be fun."

"And you're not going to get them."

"This is so not fair," she said.

He chuckled. "I don't recall you being so impatient."

"I don't want to waste my life waiting for some clues as to what it all means. I know I'm not making any sense."

"You're making perfect sense."

They were silent as they left the hospital, heading out to a synthetic garden. It didn't look natural to her. He didn't stop even when they came to some benches. Some people were smoking, others eating.

"The two years I was gone, did I leave of my own free will?" she asked. No one had told her the true extent of her leaving.

"What do you mean?"

"I get the feeling there's something you guys aren't telling me. Something big and it does scare me a little. Should I be worried?"

"You've got nothing to be worried about," he said.

"Something bad happened, though?"

He came to a stop near the end of the garden. There was a bench toward the far side and he put the brakes on the chair, moving in front of her and taking a seat. The air had a chill but she didn't want him to take her inside.

"Do you want the truth?"

"Yes."

"Okay. The truth is someone took you."

"Did I know this person?"

"No. You'd seen him but you'd never met him."

"Oh."

"There's a lot that went on between then and now. This is the first time I've seen you in over two years."

"Were we close? You and I?"

"We were, in our own way."

"You're very cryptic."

"I'm not going to give you the answers to all of your questions. You've heard what the doctor said. Some stuff you really do need to figure out on your own."

She blew out a breath. "So not making it easy for me." She smiled.

"This isn't something you need to rush."

"But it feels like it."

"What do you mean?" he asked.

"It's like … I don't know how to describe it. I feel like I have to figure everything out as fast as I can otherwise something bad is going to happen, and that scares me. I know I'm not making any sense. Even I don't understand it."

"The club, your dad, me, and even Bishop, we will protect you."

"Right, Bishop." She sighed.

"What's he done now?"

"I don't know. He's impatient. Sometimes I don't even know if I would even like him. My head is messed up. I clearly liked him enough at one point to have married him."

"Things will all become clear one day."

"And what if they don't? I heard what the doctor said. All of this stuff takes time and there's even a risk I'll never remember. I don't know if I ever want to live with that feeling."

Preacher took her hand. "There was a time you would believe everything I said. I'm telling you now that I'm not going to let anything happen to you and I will take care of you."

"Why do I always believe you?" she asked.

Chapter Five

"I've got my guys checking out all the hideouts from the list you gave me," Dog said.

"Is this going to cause any trouble with your crew?" Preacher couldn't give a shit about Dog's crew or his hierarchy, or how he controlled his men. He had a lot of other problems to deal with, but he didn't want to have to worry about his men watching their backs.

"They're all good. They all know I'll take them out if they even dare to speak out against me. This is what I tell them."

Preacher nodded and Dog grabbed his arm as he was about to walk away.

"You okay?"

"Yeah, fine."

"Look, I know you and I, we're supposed to be enemies and shit, but I'm still your friend. I'm still here for you if you need me."

"I'm good."

"I heard what happened. If you need any added protection, my boys and I will help."

Preacher stared at Dog. He'd never really considered the man a friend before but he was offering his services as if they were. "What's in it for you? I can't give you the dinner date you wanted," Preacher said.

"I've heard all about what happened to your girl. I'm aware the terms have changed."

"There are no fucking terms."

"You can get pissed at me, we can fight it out, or you can accept the hand of friendship I'm offering."

Preacher didn't know what to make of this turn of events. "The last time I checked, when someone wanted to change the rules of friendship, they had something to hide."

"I've got nothing to hide. I know our partnerships haven't always been … agreeable, but we're friends, in our own way."

"I appreciate it." Preacher shook his hand.

"There's a rumor," Dog said. "One you're not going to like."

"And why should I believe rumors?"

"It got you to find the trail Reaper and his pests have been on, hasn't it?"

Preacher folded his arms. For the first time in his life of knowing Reaper, he could safely say the other man had the upper hand.

"I'm listening."

"Good. My boys are hearing whispers of it being an inside job."

"I know he had help from O'Klaren."

"No, we're talking about someone within the club. You cannot deny it was way too much of a coincidence that Reaper could avoid you as much as he did. I heard you and he had a lot of history, but you've always been able to best him. If that was true, you should have found your girl long before now." Dog held out his hands. "I don't know who it is or who it might be, but you may want to consider who you put as a guard on your girl's door."

Preacher took the advice, shook hands again, and left. The latest form of business was complete. Dog had demanded an entire shipment of guns. He didn't ask for the whys. In business, he didn't care so long as he got paid and they had an agreement none of his gang war shit would touch his club or the town he was near. A town he very much wanted to protect with Robin now being back.

Straddling his bike, he took off toward the hospital.

When he arrived at Robin's room, he saw Bishop

was already there. Rather than taking the chair, his son sat beside her on the bed, eating her food, and he wanted to strangle him.

"Hey, Pops," Bishop said.

"He was just telling me a story about how you chased us all around the clubhouse when we were kids."

"Dad, do you remember the summer we were four and we'd opened the beer cans into the inflatable pool? There was nothing for you guys to drink and you were so pissed?" Bishop asked.

It was a memory he'd forgotten about. Around the time Rebecca was taking care of the kids and bringing them around. It was before he'd killed Bishop's mother. A lifetime ago when his life hadn't gotten complicated and when he didn't want to kill his son for invading his life.

"I remember."

"It's safe to say I don't remember. Wow, we must have been so sticky with the beer."

"It was your idea," Bishop said. "You wanted to go for a swim. Your parents wouldn't take you out to the lake and the only best thing was the beer. We snuck down into the basement and brought up so many cans, and no one was paying attention to us. Until they wanted their beer."

She chuckled. "It's great to see you again, Preacher. Can I offer you some dessert? I think it's a chocolate cake."

"The food is there for you to eat to gain strength."

"They feed me so much. I feel a little sick. Bishop was helping me finish everything." She wrinkled her nose. "Did you have a good morning?"

"Productive. You?"

"Ah, I'm doing fine."

"And therapy?"

"It was … painful. They took another x-ray of my foot this morning. It doesn't look good."

"Randall says it may not heal right," Bishop said. "I'm going to grab me some coffee. Do you want anything?"

"A hot chocolate sounds good."

"Just like always." Bishop got up, leaned down, and kissed her head.

Preacher's hands clenched into fists.

It's not good to hit your son.

If Robin hadn't been struggling with her memory, he'd have taken the son of a bitch out. Instead, he had no choice but to watch, force a smile, and wait.

Bishop took her tray and left the room.

Preacher took a seat.

"I missed you," she said.

He noticed her cheeks heated.

"I don't know why I even said that."

"I missed you too."

"Oh, good. I mean, I think that's good. I hope it is."

He stared at her, wanting to ask her so many questions.

"Bishop was here when I woke up. He took me for a walk and then he was there with me in therapy. It was hard with him there."

"It was?"

"Yeah, he's very … encouraging. I don't know. My physical therapist has been telling me to take my own pace, you know, gradually build up until I'm ready."

"You need to listen to your therapist."

"I know. With Bishop there, I feel he wants me to get better as soon as possible. If you guys visiting me at the hospital is a great inconvenience—"

"It's not."

"If it ever is, I would understand. You could tell me and I can deal with it. I hope."

"You're always going to have someone with you, Robin. You won't be alone again, I promise."

"I believe you." She tucked some hair behind her ear. "So he was with me through therapy and stayed for my lunch. Now you're here. He'd only told me about the beer pool story."

"It was a fun story."

"I don't know. I bet we really annoyed you when we were kids."

"Nah, it was good to have you around."

She licked her lips and glanced around the room.

"What is it?" he asked.

"I don't suppose ... no, forget it."

"I can't help you if you don't tell me what it is. I've got more chance of being able to give you what you want."

"I want to go home. I know I need to do therapy and everything the doctor has ordered, but I don't know where home is. Do you think I could go home?"

"I think that sounds like a wonderful idea," Bishop said, joining them. "You can come back to my place. I'll be able to help you. I'll get you to all the necessary appointments."

"Oh, I don't know," she said.

"Don't know what?" Bear asked, arriving.

Preacher was pissed off. He'd wanted to have the morning to himself and instead, he was sharing her with Bishop and Bear. Now his son was trying to get her to move in with him.

"I want to go home. I really appreciate all the staff and the hospital, but I don't want to stay here, not for longer than I have to. It's not that I'm ungrateful or anything."

"You can have your old room," Bear said.

"No, she can stay with me. She's my wife."

"Bishop, you know that's not a good enough reason for her to stay with you," Bear said. "You're rarely around and she's going to need someone to take care of her."

"I'm fine, really," she said.

"And I can take care of her. I have all this spare time on my hands now. I don't need to answer to anyone. I'm my own man."

"Really, I don't want to put anyone out," she said.

"Let's take this outside," Preacher said, getting to his feet.

"I honestly don't want to cause an argument."

"You won't. I'll handle this." He gripped Bishop's shoulders and forced him out of the room, closing the door behind him.

"Let's not have this conversation here." Preacher spotted Randall.

He signaled the doctor toward him.

"How can I help?" Randall asked.

"Can Robin go home? To any home she chooses?" Preacher asked.

"So long as she keeps up her physical therapy, rests, and takes it easy, she can do whatever she likes. Make sure she doesn't overdo it. I trust you'll keep her safe, Preacher."

"Awesome. You talk to her about the kind of activity she can do while us boys talk about her living arrangements."

He shoved them toward the bathroom, which was empty. If it hadn't been, he'd have kicked out whoever was there out. He was tired of playing these bullshit games.

"What the fuck do you think you're doing?"

Bishop asked, pulling away.

Bear leaned up against the sink while Preacher stared at his son.

"I'm trying to find out what game you're playing."

"Yeah, I'd like that as well. You're not a member of the club, nor do you live close by. My daughter needs someone who's a lot more attentive than you. The moment you want to get your dick hard, everyone else fails to exist in your world. Why the fuck would I trust her with you?"

"Like you'd trust her with my dad?"

Bear said, "He's not trying to manipulate her."

"Oh, please, he's not showing her his true colors. She doesn't know he's a cold-blooded killer."

"You want me to show her your rotting corpse when I'm through with it?" Preacher said. "You're playing into a lie."

"What? About her being my wife? Last time I checked, she was my wife, or do you want me to forget about that tiny detail? She's my wife and I should be the one taking care of her, not you."

Preacher shook his head about to speak but Bear got there first.

"No matter how much you try, Bishop, you can't rewrite the past. Robin didn't love you. Her feelings for you weren't there. You can try to fight it all you want but it's not going to change the fact it didn't happen. She wanted Preacher."

"Yeah, and you don't think that's a little sick? He's the same age as you. You and Robin never should've been together."

"You're right. Between me and Robin, it shouldn't have worked. We're complete opposites, but it doesn't change the fact we happened. Robin picked me."

"Why weren't you with her that night, Dad? Oh, that's right, you were too busy killing a cop."

"You keep speaking up, I'm going to have to cut out your tongue," he said.

"Go ahead. It will only mean she'll know what you're really like."

Bear sighed. "Robin knew what he was really like, Bishop. You're acting like a child and I'm not going to let my little girl go with you. In fact, she's not going to go with either of you. I'm going to take her home with me. That's final. You can fight with me all you want."

"What about Rebecca? What are you going to tell her about that?" Bishop asked.

"Your son is a pain in the ass."

Preacher had heard enough. He left the bathroom and walked down the long corridor to find Randall talking to Robin. She was smiling. He must have told a joke. She was so beautiful. Staring at her, it made him ache to hold her once again.

She looked up toward him and lifted her hand, waving.

Randall got up and came out toward him. "Did you decide on anything?"

"She's going to live with Bear."

"It's probably a good thing. I was talking to one of the brain surgeons. Robin has experienced a trauma before the amnesia, and she also has the loss of her unborn child. He believes both traumas, unless unleashed separately, could have an adverse effect within her body."

"He wants time."

"I'm afraid so."

"Everyone always wants time to explore." He rubbed at his eyes, feeling the beginning of a headache. "Is there a chance anything could go back to normal?"

"You know I can never give you guarantees."

"I know."

"I can only hope for you." Randall looked back into the room. "I've seen the x-rays, the scars on her body. I know she's been through a great deal in the last two years. Her body is all the evidence you need to tell you a tale. She didn't have it easy."

"I gathered."

"She needs you, Preacher. I know you're having a hard time and Bishop's trying to insert himself as part of her life, but it's all lies and you need to recognize it."

"Oh, I do, believe me, I do. I'm going to take care of my son. Don't worry about him."

Randall slapped him on the arm. "It will turn out good. I can't guarantee the when or the how, but I have a feeling it's just around the corner."

Preacher watched him leave but he didn't feel convinced. With Reaper still out there, she would never be safe. With Reaper at large, he'd never trust her alone.

Bishop stormed past him, sporting a bleeding nose, and Bear joined him at the window.

"Do I want to know what happened there?"

"If you're going to punish me for putting your boy in line, then no, you don't need to know."

"Did he deserve it?"

"Yes."

"Fine."

"I don't want him alone around her," Bear said. "He's got an agenda. I don't know what it is and I don't like it."

"It's simple. He wants me away from her because he believes I manipulated her into belonging to me, instead of seeing the truth."

"And what's the truth?"

"Robin picked me, not him, and no matter how

hard it is for him, he can't stand to think about how he lost." He shrugged. This wasn't gloating or taunting. Until Robin confessed her love to Bishop or even to him, there was no game over.

****

"This is your room," Bear said.

After struggling up the stairs, Robin had hoped to see her room and to have every single memory come crashing back over her.

Nothing.

Her room was bare.

"Where's my stuff?" she asked.

"Oh, I'm getting Preacher to gather some of our things and drop it back over. You took a lot of it with you when you went to stay with him."

"Oh, I went to stay with him?"

"Well, you lived with him and Bishop."

"Wouldn't Bishop have taken my stuff when he moved?"

"You and Bishop didn't share a room."

"Because we were so young?"

Bear paused for a second. "Something like that."

"Why does it feel like you're not giving me the whole story?"

"I'm giving you what you need to know," he said. "It's complicated."

She moved into the room. Holding the crutches in one hand, she lowered herself to the bed. "Complicated seems to be an understatement. I moved everything out."

"What you didn't take with you, your mother sold or threw out."

"Was I close to my mom?"

"No. You hated the bitch."

"Bitch? I guess you weren't exactly friends with her."

"Your mother and I, we had a … complicated relationship."

"Like Bishop and me?"

"No. You were the best of friends."

"And we married each other. Why would we marry?"

"How about we just accept that you guys are married and it wasn't always easy. It's not easy."

She tucked her hair behind her ear and nodded. "Not easy. Got it." She blew out a breath. "I like the room."

"Good. It's gone through a lot of changes. When you were first born, I painted the walls yellow."

"Yellow?"

"We thought you were going to be a boy."

"Wow, that must have been a bit of a disappointment."

"Nah, not really. I loved you from the moment I held you. You've been my little girl and always will be." He sat down beside her, wrapping his arm around her. "It changed to this pastel pink when you were a girl. You wanted to be a princess and this was your castle. Of course in your eyes, I was always the fierce knight who protected you."

She chuckled. "I like the sounds of these memories. They sound nice."

"They are. We didn't always have a good time, Robin, but I tried."

She rested her head against his shoulder. "I can imagine you did a whole lot of the time, and I really do appreciate it. All of it."

He laughed. "Even if you don't remember it all?"

She smiled. "I wish I did."

"I wasn't the best dad, though. When you do get your memories back, you're not going to like some of what you remember."

She glanced down at her jeans- and shirt-covered body. "I've got a feeling there's going to be a lot I eventually remember you're not going to know about."

Bear held her hand, but the cast was in the way. Instead, he put his arm across her shoulders once again, and this time, he kissed the top of her head. "Just know whatever the memory, I'm here for you. Me and Preacher."

"Not Bishop?"

"Preacher's the one I trust."

She closed her eyes and the doorbell rang.

"I'm guessing it's the man himself. You stay here. I'll have him bring up the box or boxes. You want something to eat?"

"I'd love something. Anything. I'm starving."

"Food is coming right up." He kissed her head again and she watched him go.

Just another moment in a whole list of them to confuse her.

Running her hand down her thigh, she stared at the ink, the chain wrapped around her wrist. Bishop had told her she didn't have any ink on her body when she left. Not only did she have the ink around her wrist, but there was also a rose trailing up her waist, and across her back was the name *Reaper's Bitch.*

The moment she caught sight of the ink at the base of her back, she'd been overcome with a wave of sickness unlike anything she'd ever experienced. She didn't know if she should tell anyone.

When she showed it to Randall, asking him if it had been a joke, he'd told her it was in part of her memories where he wasn't in her life.

The two years she'd been taken, where her body showed the evidence of the abuse that her mind couldn't.

She rubbed at her temple, wanting nothing more than to cry. It would be so much easier to give up. Everyone kept looking at her as if she was some kind of strong woman or something. The truth was, she was close to falling apart, holding on by a thread.

"Are you okay?" Preacher asked.

She lifted her head and sighed. "I don't know." She sniffled. "Do you like my room?"

He carried a large brown box. "It'll look better with some of this." He put the box on the floor in front of her.

"Please, don't go," she said. "I don't want to be alone."

"Do you want me to take you back to the hospital?"

"Hell, no. I'm sorry. I mean no, I don't want to go to the hospital."

"Will you be okay here?"

"I think so."

"Any memories?"

"Nothing. Not even an inkling of one. It's more like … a feeling. I do know this place. It's right there but not close enough for me to be entirely sure what I'm looking at. I know, I'm going completely crazy, aren't I?"

"You're not going crazy at all."

"I feel like it. This is my bedroom. Apparently, my mom hated my guts and sold everything I didn't take with me."

"There's a lot of stuff in the box for you to see. It might help."

"Or leave me in a never-ending pit of despair."

"This is new," he said.

"What?"

"You being negative all the time. I'm not used to

it. It's not a good look for you."

She chuckled. "I wonder how you'd feel about losing all of your memories and not getting anything back. With everyone constantly looking at you and expecting there to be a spark. Some kind of magical button that will awaken you from this deep sleep." She pressed her lips firmly together.

"No magical button?"

"I've got nothing to be able to wake me up. It … sucks." She shrugged. "It could be worse, I suppose. I could be staying with my husband who I don't know and everything feels odd with. Sorry. I will start to think more positively."

"You can have your meltdown, it's fine."

"Is it, though? I feel insane."

Preacher reached out, putting a curl behind her ear. "It is what it is. I'm grateful you're alive, and I can see you."

"There you go, saying all the nicest things."

He chuckled.

"I guess I better look and see what I was all about." She opened the brown cardboard box. The first item was a pillow. It had a dog on it, a cocker spaniel, she believed. "I like it."

"It's your favorite dog."

"Do I have a dog?"

"No. You never asked for one."

"So if I asked, I'd get it?"

"I tended to make sure you got everything you wanted."

She paused as she reached into the box. He was talking about him being the one to give her things, not Bishop. If Bishop was supposed to be her husband, why was it Preacher making her life easier? None of it made any sense. Rather than ask him about it, seeing as he liked to be very secretive, she went back into the box.

There was a small jewelry box. Each item she took out, he put in the places she asked him to. When she got to the final item, it was a photograph album.

She rested it on her lap and Preacher sat beside her. "Do you want to open it?"

"I don't know. Do I?"

"Remember, there is no rush to know everything. This is all for you. You can take your time."

She nodded her head, but she didn't believe it. She didn't know why she was so freaking nervous about all of this, only it felt important to her to remember everything.

Opening the book, she frowned as a picture fell out.

Bending down, she picked it up. "Is this an ultrasound photo?"

"Yes."

"Is this me?" She tilted her head to look at the picture and something twisted in her gut. "It must be me." She put the image back into the book and started to look at some of the other pictures. Instantly, she saw most of the photographs were of her and Bishop.

"I guess we were really close, huh?"

Preacher didn't say anything.

The sound of the door opening again interrupted her thoughts. There were none of her and Preacher in the book, which made her sad. She thought they were friends at least.

"Dinner's here," Bear said.

She snapped the book closed and placed it on her bed. "I'm starving. Are you staying for dinner?"

"Yeah, of course."

She got to her feet and nearly plunged forward. Preacher grabbed her and she held on to his body, staring up into his blue eyes. They were really beautiful.

"I had brown hair," she said.

"You remember?

"The pictures. In each one, I had brown hair."

"Of course, you did. It's your natural hair color."

"And now I dye it?" she asked.

"The hair is new to me. I've never known you to dye your hair."

"So it's not normal?"

"I guess we'll see." He helped her downstairs. It was difficult on the crutches but she somehow managed to do it.

"You're a strong person, Robin. You're going to get through this, no matter how hard it may seem right now."

Chapter Six

Two years ago

Robin climbed off the back of Reaper's bike and before anyone could stop her, she made a run for it. She had to get back to Preacher. He had to learn the truth. There was no way she could allow Reaper to kill her. She hadn't even told Preacher she might love him. She cried out as she was shoved to the ground. Tears filled her eyes as her head hit the hard, dirty ground. This couldn't be happening to her. Not after everything she had already gone through. She wanted Preacher. He would protect her.

"You know, I'm going to enjoy keeping you around," Reaper said.

He held her back down to the ground, smearing her cheek on the dry dirt. She couldn't control her screams as the sharp rocks dug into her cheek. The flesh too soft to handle such harsh conditions.

"Please," she said.

"What is it? You want to say sorry?" he asked.

"Yes, yes. I'm so sorry." She wanted to spit in his face, kick him in the balls, and run in the opposite direction, but she couldn't do either of those options. She had to be a good girl, at least for now.

Reaper didn't let up on his hold. "You know, this time with us could go either good or bad. It really is up to you."

"Fuck you," she screamed as he gripped her ass tightly. His hold would leave bruises on her tender flesh in the morning.

"One day, you're going to stop giving me sass and realize this is your life now. You belong to me, and there's nothing you can do about it." His lips were next to her ear so she had no choice but to listen to him.

The pain in her cheek and on her ass was intense.

Don't cry.

Please, don't fucking cry.

Tears leaked out of her eyes and she sobbed. "Please."

She didn't want to ask this man for anything or beg. Didn't want to give in to him. Preacher would want her to be strong and so would her dad. She wasn't weak. She was a strong woman and could face anything and anyone, only, she felt useless.

Reaper laughed. "Don't you worry, sweet girl. By the time I'm done with you, you're going to learn begging is a skill you're going to need."

His weight was off her and he grabbed her shoulders, pulling her to stand up until she faced him.

Her heart raced at the cruelty she saw within his gaze. This wasn't a nice man. He was a mean, vile, disgusting man, and right now, she was at his mercy. For how long, she didn't know. There had to be some way of getting messages back to Preacher for him to know where she was and what was happening.

Looking around the open ground, she didn't have a single clue where she was. If she hadn't held on to Reaper, she would've fallen off the bike. Even though this was the last place she wanted to be, dying wasn't an option.

Blood dripped down her cheek and as she swiped at it, she cringed at the sight. It was all a little too much for her at that moment.

Reaper stared down her body and smiled. "I can see why he likes you."

"Let me go."

"Not going to happen. Robin, you and I are going to have some fun."

****

Present day

Robin woke up to the sound of knocking at her door. The nightmare at the fringes of her mind tingled down her spine but as she tried to think of what the dream meant, it faded into nothing.

"Morning, sunshine," Bear said, entering her bedroom, carrying a tray.

"Breakfast in bed? Did I do something good?"

"You came back to us," he said. "You're healthy and we're going to get through this."

"Healthy? My foot is shattered. I can't remember anything, and I've got a husband who feels like I betrayed him because I'd rather live here than be with him." She winced. "Sorry, that feels like an overshare."

"It's good."

Sitting up in bed, she grabbed a pillow and placed it over her lap. "Nah, it's not. I probably should spend some time with Bishop. He might help me jog my memory."

"Remember, at your own pace. Don't be overwhelmed or anything. Take your time."

"I don't have time." She cut into one of the pancakes. "At least I don't think I do. It's all confusing to me."

"All in good time."

She put the bite of pancake into her mouth and chewed. "It tastes good."

"I'm glad."

"After therapy, is there anything you'd like to do today?"

"Yeah, I think I'd like for you to take me out. You know, give me a chance to see the neighborhood."

"You want to try and force your memories?"

"Yeah and no. I want to see if there's anything around here that will help. Don't you think it's worth a shot?"

"Anything you want to do to help you get back to where you want to be is a shot. Eat breakfast and I'll take you to therapy, and afterward, we'll have lunch."

"Where's your breakfast?"

"I ate it downstairs."

"Did we do this often? You and me, eating breakfast together?" She watched as he looked away. "I take it that's a no."

"We were close. I'd like to think we were but with your mom here, I never came home."

"Where did you stay?"

"At the clubhouse most of the time."

"Twisted Monsters?"

"Yes."

"I see."

"You don't see, but it's okay. The old you understood."

She nodded and took another bite, not really tasting the pancake anymore.

"What did happen to her?" she asked.

"She had to pay for her sins. Karma has a way of catching up to her. If you want to take my advice, don't mourn her."

"Don't you think it's a little cold for me not to mourn my mother?"

"She didn't mourn you being taken from us, Robin. She's a waste of your time. Don't allow yourself to dwell."

She finished off her pancakes and Bear left her alone. After pushing the blanket off her legs, she swung them around, reaching for the crutch. Lowering her foot to the ground, she was careful as she lifted herself up.

"I can totally do this."

With the use of one crutch, she got herself steady

on her feet before taking the second step. She slowly made her way into the bathroom, turning on the light as she entered. She did her routine, using the toilet, washing her hands, brushing her teeth, and then rinsing cold water across her face.

Lifting her head up, she jerked back as her reflection changed, showing long brown hair and a smile, but then she was back to the short, badly cut, dyed-blonde hair. She touched her hair. She was seeing herself. It had to be.

There were no such things as ghosts. She reached out, touching the glass.

"You're going to be my little plaything. I can't wait for Preacher to know just how much I like playing with what is his."

The words were gone as quickly as they appeared. The voice, though. It sent a dark shiver down her spine at the memory of it.

Wait?

Memory.

Rubbing at her temple, she tried to find more, to think of more, but it disappeared. Holding back. Clenching her hands into fists, she wanted to scream at the injustice of it all.

Returning to her room, she changed into a pair of jeans and a large, baggy, plain black shirt. She really didn't care about the way she looked, not to go to therapy. She had a bag already packed to change into shorts and a tighter shirt.

She hated her lessons. As she ran a brush through her short hair, the photograph album caught her attention. Lifting it up into her arms, she stared at the cover of the book. It didn't tell her anything, and so she opened it up.

The ultrasound picture was the first one and she held it close, trying to get a good look at it.

No memory. Nothing.

If her mother was such a bad person, why did she keep this?

Why did she have it?

Questions with no answers and Bear wouldn't help her figure it out.

Turning the page, she smiled as she saw her and Bishop. They were lying down on the grass and it looked like Bishop held the camera as she snuggled up against him, but they were both laughing. She had her tongue out as if she was going to lick his cheek. She looked happy, and so did Bishop.

There were so many of her and Bishop. There was no mistaking the connection and love she felt for him.

Why didn't she feel it now?

Did they fight?

Why hadn't he taken any of her stuff if he missed her as much as he claimed to?

All valid questions, but when she tried to ask him about their past together, he closed up, ignoring her.

Snapping the book closed, she got to her feet and made her way to the top of the stairs. Lowering herself down onto the top step, she put both crutches beside her, and slid, slowly, step by step, down until she got to the bottom. The instant her butt got to the next step, she held on to the railing. Once she was halfway down, her father appeared at the bottom of the steps.

"I can help you with that."

"I know, but I'm quite capable of doing this," she said. "Besides, you're not going to always be available. I don't need a babysitter. You know, I find that frustrating."

"What?"

"I know everything. I know what a babysitter

means, and the days of the week. I have all this common knowledge but anything relating to personal me, I'm coming up empty. It sucks."

"Stop trying to force it." He grabbed the crutches for her and she lifted herself up, taking them from him.

"I never knew you to be so impatient."

"You didn't?"

"You had your moments, but you were always such a hard worker. Nothing ever fazed you. You were ready and waiting for anything. Now, you look … scared. I don't like it."

"I don't mean to be scared. I can't seem to help this feeling twisting in my gut that something bad is going to happen."

"You're home. If something bad is going to happen, we'll deal with it like we deal with everything. Together."

They left the house and went out to the truck. As she stood there, waiting for Bear to open the door, the hair on the back of her neck seemed to stand on end. The nerves weaving through her stomach went into overdrive.

Looking around, she tried to think of what could be close by, but there was nothing.

No one was watching them. No one was waiting to scare them.

"Are you okay?" Bear asked.

"Yeah, I'm fine." After sliding into the car, she put her seatbelt on and wished for the nervous feeling to disappear. It was worse because she didn't know what she was afraid of, and that was even scarier than anything she'd ever faced before.

****

After therapy, exhausted, aching, and hating all things physical, Robin sat in a chair out in the waiting room with everyone. It was organized chaos. Doctors came and went. Patients checked their watches, clearly pissed at sitting around waiting.

People grew anxious.

Kids ran around the chairs, trying to entertain themselves.

She sat off to the sidelines, never participating, just watching. She wasn't part of it all. Her appointment had come and gone. Bear was supposed to be picking her up, but he was running late.

"It's all a little busy, isn't it?" Randall said, taking a seat beside her.

"Hey," she said. "Be warned, I smell."

"I talked to your therapist. He believes you're making excellent progress."

"That's good, right?"

"It's very good."

"Awesome. It's what I want to hear." She smiled at him. For some reason, Randall always made her feel at ease, calm.

"You do know you'll never be able to run again, and your foot may also have pain."

"I thought doctors were supposed to install hope. You know, kind of like a computer update."

He laughed. "I'm afraid I'm a realist. I want to help my patients, but I don't want to give them unrealistic expectations."

"I can totally relate to all of that. I think." She didn't even know why she said some things she did half of the time.

"How have you been feeling?"

"I've been home a day, and everything is good. I've been looking through old photos, so I know this is totally not me." She lifted a strand of hair. "I'm going to change it as soon as I let it grow more. I've also lost a lot of weight. Again, I don't know why." She thought about the bathroom incident and then the voice. "Can I ask you something?"

"You can ask me anything. I don't know if I'll be able to answer, but I will certainly try my best."

"Memories. Do you know how they will come back?" she asked.

"I honestly don't know. Each case is different, like I've said before. The mind, it works in mysterious ways."

"I totally get that, but, what if it does it in flashes, or like whispers? Can I trust them? Or should I just wait for the big wake-up?" She hated how vague she sounded.

"Have you remembered anything?"

"I wouldn't say I've remembered anything. It's more like a … feeling." She thought about the whispered words. "Yeah, I think that is what it is, a feeling. I mean, I was staring at my reflection and one moment I looked like I do now, and the next second, over the top, it was like I was staring at old me. I know, creepy."

"You've got to take your time. Don't force anything. I want to warn you, your life here was good, but there were still problems with it. There's heartache waiting to find you, Robin, and I don't want you to have to go through it again."

"I'm sorry," Preacher said, drawing her attention.

Her heart raced at the sight of him and the pit of her stomach tightened. It wasn't through fear, either.

"Preacher," she said, with a smile. "Where's my dad?"

"He's doing club business. Thank you, Randall, for keeping her company."

"Always a pleasure. You take care, Robin, and if there's anything you want to discuss, come to me."

"I will. I promise."

She got to her feet, and Preacher helped her as

they left the busy hospital. Being outside in the cold air was refreshing and she breathed it in, stopping to inhale and exhale.

"Was it a hard session?" Preacher asked.

"It was intense, as they're getting to that stage now. There's always something to do."

"How is your foot?"

"Still attached to my leg but he advises me it's a good thing."

Preacher chuckled. "Bear let me know five minutes ago you wanted to drive around town."

"Or walk."

"You want to go to old places, see if they help you remember?"

"Something like that."

He closed the door of the car, and the scent of him surrounded her, making her feel protected and warm. Seconds later, he got behind the wheel of the car, turned the ignition, and they took off. To get out of the grounds, he drove slowly, making way for people passing. Out of the corner of her eye, she couldn't help but watch him. He looked so powerful and commanding. His entire presence strong, resilient.

"How was your first night away from the hospital?" he asked.

"It was good. You know. I got breakfast in bed, which was totally cool. I happen to really like eating, so it's a bonus. I like being around Bear. I mean, he's my dad. You know what I mean."

"All of this is new for you. I'm sure it's overwhelming."

"Yeah, it is." She thought about Bishop. "What's Bishop doing today?"

"I don't have a clue. Unless it affects the club, he's his own man."

"You and him aren't close?"

"We never were. He's my son, and I was a bad father. I wasn't ready to be a dad and I don't know the first thing about taking care of a kid."

"He's alive, so you can't be doing that badly."

"There's more to raising a kid than keeping them alive."

She didn't recognize where they were going. Preacher wasn't speeding, and the silence in the car wasn't uncomfortable.

"Are you busy today?" she asked. "I know I want to go and see places but if you're too busy…"

"I'm fine. Believe me. There's nothing else I'd rather do. This is what you need."

"Great." She kept on staring at him.

"I'm freaking out a little with the constant staring. Why are you trying to read my mind?"

"I'm not trying to read your mind. I'm just trying to figure out why it is you're always trying to make my life better."

"You've known for me a couple of weeks, Robin."

"And you're always there, helping me, making my life better. You're making the right decisions. It's not a complaint."

"Then what is it?" he asked.

"I'm wondering why you're doing this and not Bishop. If he's supposed to be my husband, why are you at the hospital, not him? Why didn't he come by yesterday?"

"Did you want him to come by?" Preacher asked.

She opened her mouth about to say of course she would, but she closed her lips. Being near Bishop was a little uncomfortable and she tried to keep her distance from him, even when he visited at the hospital. Was that even normal to feel so cut off from a guy who was supposed to be her husband? She didn't know if it was just her memories, or the lack of that was affecting her.

"I'm sorry," he said.

"It's not your fault. It's mine. I don't know anything, not really."

"Well, this might help." He parked outside a large building proclaiming itself to be a high school.

"One day, we're going to look back on these days as the worst ones of our lives," Bishop said.

"Please, it's supposed to be the opposite. These are supposed to be the best days."

"We can't all have everything."

"I went here with Bishop?"

"Are you remembering something?" he asked.

"I don't … no, I don't think it's a memory. A vague conversation." She rubbed at her temple. It meant nothing to her. Everything was just a load of nothing.

She stared at the building, and before her eyes, it flashed to ambers and reds, and back to the fullness of greens. She'd seen the school throughout the different seasons.

"Did I graduate?"

"No. You were taken before you were able to do so."

"Wow, that sucked. So I'm twenty years old, have no graduation diploma, and I don't even know if I was a good student."

"You were a good student. Smart."

"I was?"

"Yes. You always made time for studying. You had a very tight schedule. You didn't know what you wanted, if college was in your future, but you loved to learn."

She looked back at the school but once again, it

was nothing more than a blank. "I wonder if I'll ever remember."

"If not, I'll be here, and so will the club."

"And Bishop?" She noticed his hands clenched around the steering wheel and he didn't seem particularly thrilled with her question.

"He'll help where he can."

"It says a lot that I haven't seen him."

"I'm not going to give you any warnings here, Robin, if that's what you're trying to get me to do."

"No warnings. I promise. I guess I just really want to know who I am. If I'm a good person. What I'm capable of. You know, all of the important stuff."

"It'll come to you," he said.

"And if it doesn't?" she asked, repeating the same broken record. She felt all she kept doing was going around in circles, coming back to the same original problem.

"Then like your dad, I'll be here to help you out."

She sighed. "I'm starving." She'd hoped for at least one memory. Not a bunch of nonsensical words that meant absolutely nothing to her. "Can we go get something to eat?"

"Of course." He pulled away from the high school.

"So you're the president of the Twisted Monsters MC?" she asked.

"I am."

"Do you like it?"

"I do."

"Do you do bad things?"

"I'm going to wait to see if you remember anything."

"I don't mind. I won't tell anyone." She frowned. "O'Klaren."

Preacher tensed up.

"Why do I know that name?" she asked. The word itself didn't exactly evoke any other feeling than contempt and hatred.

"He was an old problem. You don't have to worry about him anymore. The last time he was seen, he was heading out with some woman younger than him."

"Oh. I have no idea what that was. It entered my head. I guess I better get used to all of these things happening."

"You're not alone. You'll always have us."

"I know. Thank you."

****

The days turned to weeks, and Robin continued her physical therapy. Preacher received regular updates from her therapist on how she was progressing. She also liked to talk to the therapist about random memories she was having. Most of the time, they didn't mean anything. She recalled falling off her bike the other day, and Bishop being the one to carry her home. What she didn't remember was how pissed Bishop had been with her when they were kids. He'd shoved the wheel of his bike into hers, forcing her off and nearly breaking her arm. Instead, she'd gotten a cut that required stitches. They'd only been kids at the time, but he'd been pissed.

Late Saturday night, he sat in the office at one of the titty clubs he owned. He stared down at the facts and figures but he didn't see anything. He had a lead he intended to follow the moment he dealt with a current problem. One of the girls was offering free services on the side. The men, they were after the cheap pussy, and well, Preacher didn't allow that kind of action in his club. There was another service the woman could use, and he wasn't about to have this establishment dragged through the dirt because of a greedy whore.

The women had lodged a complaint. There were a lot of powerful and rich men who visited the establishment, which he'd placed in a rather sought-after area in the city. He rarely came to the city. Most of his businesses were taken care of by a select group of people he trusted. He only came when there needed to be muscle, and with his search for Robin, everything else had fallen by the wayside in his pursuit of finding the woman he loved. Tapping his fingers on the desk, he waited for Grave to get him the woman responsible for slowing him down.

Frost stood in the corner, waiting, while Rider was on the sofa, looking through a magazine.

"You have to give the bitch credit," Rider said. "She's got some balls to break our rules."

"It doesn't give her balls. It makes her fucking stupid," Frost said.

The door opened and Preacher stared at a semi-clad woman. Her tits were hanging out and it looked like her panties had been pushed to one side.

"What's the meaning of this?" she asked, growling at each of them.

Preacher raised his brow, sitting back in his chair and staring at the woman who dared to make him wait.

"She had one customer fucking her and was blowing another." Grave put a piece of paper on the table. "She makes them pay upfront by check."

"Check, that's a rather old payment method."

"Yeah, well, they can't click a button and keep their payment once it's done."

"They can still stop checks, and they can even be writing you a duff one," Preacher said. "Give me a damn good reason why you're breaking my rules or Grave here is going to start breaking bones."

"Wait? What?" Since she'd entered the office,

she finally looked afraid.

"Darla, is it?"

"Yeah, what's it to you?"

"Oh, it's nothing to me. I'm just wondering why you think you can steal from me without any repercussions. It takes someone with a big old set of balls to even contemplate doing that, and yet, here we are and you're shaking. Scared."

"I … I thought we were allowed to make a little extra money."

"Not in this establishment. You see, the men who come here, they have a certain bankability about them. Blackmail is such a dirty word, but if I want shit done, I have the right places to get it. You and your dirty mouth and cunt are going to draw attention I neither want nor need. Now, I'm going to give you a choice. Either you go and work at one of my other more selective places of work, where you don't get to pick the cock you ride, or you walk out of here now. No pay. Nothing."

"That's not a choice." She cried out as Grave grabbed her hair, holding out her arm. She tried to struggle, but she was no match for Grave.

Preacher walked behind the desk and stared at her. "You were warned. I've been made aware of the three warnings you were given about the way we conduct business. This is not your first offense. You didn't listen and now you pay the price. What will it be?"

She cried out as Grave hurt her a little more.

He grew even more tired. "I'll pick for you."

"I'll work for you. Please, don't break anything. I don't want to be in pain."

"Excellent choice. Rider here will escort you to where you need to be."

Grave shoved her in the direction of Rider, who didn't catch her, so she stumbled to the floor.

"I've got business to attend to. Give me an update when this is taken care of," Preacher said, leaving the bar. He had no interest in the women or what they had to offer.

Once outside, he got onto his bike, turning over the ignition and relishing the purr as it did. His bike never failed him, but other people, they had a way of disappointing him.

Pulling away from the club, he took off in the direction Billy had given him. It was the last known location of Reaper, or at least, it hinted at it. An old abandoned factory.

Two women were found, raped and murdered, no trace of the club, but there had been sightings of Slaves of the Beast there.

Thinking about Reaper always brought him to Robin. She was making progress, but her memories had yet to return. Nothing had come back to her about O'Klaren even though she mentioned his name once several weeks ago.

The cast on her foot would also be coming off in a matter of days. The therapy was working well, and she didn't appear to be in as much pain either.

Bear was struggling. He tried to devote his time between his daughter and the club. For Preacher, Robin would always come first, and all the guys knew how important it was to him to keep Robin safe. She was his number one priority. Always.

Even with Bishop lurking at the edges of her life. So far, he hadn't tried to take over and visit her all the time. He'd arrived a few times while Preacher had been there, but Bear assured him she was never alone with him.

He shouldn't even care, but something told him to keep Robin safe.

Pushing the thoughts of his son to the back of his mind, he instead focused on the building up ahead. There were no bikes parked and Billy had assured him it was empty. He had contacts within the city's police force who let him know it was completely clean.

Parking his bike, he looked up at the old building and wouldn't doubt for a second that Reaper had been using this place. The other biker rarely settled down, and it was strange for him to have stuck around near Knight's Bridge for so long. It was a mistake Preacher had paid for.

"There's the police tape," Grave said. "They were here."

"Two bodies were discovered. We don't know if we can trust our contact, so keep your eyes peeled. Don't leave anything to fucking chance. I don't trust these assholes and neither should you."

Preacher got to the main door and twisted the doorknob. It opened easily. Billy had told him finding locksmiths or keys on buildings cost a fortune and most of the time, police tape kept people out. It was either the homeless or squatters they had to worry about.

Bending down, he stepped inside, pulling out a flashlight. He looked left and right and saw no signs of anyone. There was silence as he first entered.

"What exactly are we looking for?" Grave asked.

"Any indication of where they went. Even if it's just a receipt." He stepped forward into the building. It was an old factory. Dust covered every surface and some pieces of old equipment were still in the room, but he didn't know what the factory did before it closed down.

There were six floors. "Split up. I'm going to head up to the top. Yell if you see anything," Preacher said.

In his experience, Reaper always liked to use the

top floors. It never made any sense to him because at the top, you had to come down. Reaper once told him it gave him a chance to get away.

For Preacher, the ground floor was the best get away, with at least three exits. If there was a front or back, always have a side entrance no one knew about. It was how he always got away without anyone following him. By the time they realized he wasn't there or if he was, he was gone.

He found the back stairs and he made his way up each flight. When he got to a floor, he'd stop to check inside each window that overlooked the floor.

No one was there. Not a single sign of anyone.

Moving up, he finally came to the sixth floor and stopped. He heard music. It was faint.

Turning off his flashlight, he looked toward the window of the door. There in the center of the room were several computer screens, and someone sat behind them. Opening the door, Preacher slid through and listened. The man in question had music on so loud through headphones on his head, he couldn't hear a thing.

The man was typing at the keyboard at such a speed it would have easily given him a headache.

He didn't signal for his men.

It looked like he'd somehow been able to use a portable battery in order to fire up the computers without giving off a signal the building was in use. He'd have to let Billy know his contact didn't know jack shit about checking out the building to see if it was empty or not.

Preacher stood for several minutes, watching what the man was doing. From the looks of it, he was looking for Robin. He didn't know for sure, but he saw her name and then of course there were a couple of pictures of her from the hospital.

He'd seen enough. Stepping forward, he grabbed

the man's head and slammed it forward.

A cry filled the room. Preacher fisted his hair and pulled him away, spinning him around, and he slammed his fist against his face, hearing the crunch of bone. The sound sent a thrill down his spine.

He wanted to hurt someone and this man, he may never have met Robin, but something in his gut told him he was working for Reaper to get her back. Anyone who worked for Reaper was on his shit list, and they had a very short life span once he got a hold of them.

Hitting him again, he used his head to slam against one of the computers, smashing the screen.

"Please, stop. Please, stop."

Preacher shoved him back down in the seat. "I'm guessing you weren't expecting any visitors."

The man lifted his hand to his face and cried out. "You broke my nose."

"You shouldn't be worried about your nose. It's the least of your worries."

"What are you going to do?"

"What am I going to do? It's a loaded question, really. There's a lot I really want to do, and I kind of need you to tell me what you're doing looking at this girl on your pretty flashing screens." He pointed to the picture of Robin.

"I've been asked to keep an eye on her. That's all. I'm just following orders, I swear. It doesn't mean anything."

"Who's telling you?"

"Reaper. He wants to know what the girl is up to at all times. It's important to him. I'm supposed to let him know when I see a chance for him to take her again."

Preacher hit him, once, twice, and a third time. No matter how many times he hit the man, the pleasure didn't come. He wanted to feel something, to help ease this rage within him.

The man cried out. "Please. I'm only doing what I'm supposed to do."

Grave and Frost arrived just as the man's cell phone rang.

"That's him. He wants an update. I swear I don't know what all of this is about. I'm new to all of this. I owe him a favor and this is what he asked of me. I don't want no trouble. I promise. I'm a good guy."

Preacher didn't believe him. A good guy didn't sit in an abandoned old factory with a bunch of computers, hunting for a girl he didn't know.

Taking his cell phone from him, he clicked on *accept call* and put the device to his ear.

"What do you have for me, Milo?"

Preacher would recognize that voice from anywhere. It didn't matter how many years ago it had been, or how long. That voice he'd been hunting for a long time now.

"Hello, Reaper," he said, putting the call to speakerphone.

"Preacher, I should have known you'd find my contact."

He pulled on Milo's hair and the guy screamed. "Did you promise him you'd protect him? I've got to say, Reaper, you're not very good at keeping promises, but then as my memory serves, you never were. You were the kind of guy who dumped people into shit and ran."

"You've got Robin back."

"I do, and if you hold on just a moment—" He drew his knife and slashed it across Milo's neck, killing him. The death didn't give him any kind of solace at all. "I've just ended one of your sources of contact. If you think you can get to her again, you're sorely mistaken. There is no way in hell I'm going to let you or any piece of shit near her."

Reaper laughed. "You know, you and your little crew are all running around trying to save her. To protect her. Have you ever considered she doesn't want protection? I've had her for two years and she didn't try to get away. Don't you think she wants to be back with me?"

"You think I haven't seen the mess she's in? I know what you did to her. The monster you are."

"It's a funny thing about monsters, Preacher. It takes a one to know one."

"I know, which is why I know you're not getting near her."

"One day, I'm going to have Robin back and I'm going to look into your eyes as she picks me over you." The cell phone went dead.

After throwing it to the floor, Preacher crushed the device beneath his boot. He grabbed the computers and smashed them, destroying any evidence of Robin. Once he was done, all he wanted to do was go home and fucking hold her.

He couldn't do that, though. She wasn't his to hold or to have.

"Are you okay?" Grave asked.

"I want to make sure there is a guard with Robin at all times. Even when she's in her house, I want someone with her to protect her." He ran fingers through his hair.

With Reaper seeming to be one step ahead of him, he had to do something to stay back in control. "I need to go see Dog."

"Wait," Frost said, standing up. "We all know what you're going to do. I understand you trust Dog, but this has got to be a club decision to bring him in."

"He's not going to be a member of the club,"

Preacher said.

"Yeah, but you're drawing our two worlds together and the guys need to vote on that before you do it. We'll call church tomorrow, but you can't just go and organize shit that will affect all of us. Having Dog's crew in town or near us, it will bring heat with it, and the boys, they don't want to deal with a whole lot of heat if they don't need to. Got me?"

"I want church tonight. Not tomorrow," Preacher said. "I don't give a fuck what the men are doing or who they're doing. Tonight." He turned on his heel and left the building.

Frost was the last to leave and he closed the door behind him.

Straddling his bike, he turned over the ignition and pulled away from the curb. He needed speed, the open roads, and to clear his fucking head once and for all. He couldn't keep reacting to Reaper. This was where he was making too many fucking mistakes and it wasn't good for him or the club. He had to keep his shit together. If for no one else but Robin. She deserved a fresh start and he was going to make sure she got that at least.

Chapter Seven

The time with Reaper

One month she'd been with Reaper now. Robin stared at the calendar on the wall in a brand-new hotel room. They were always moving. Never in one place more than a couple of hours. She hated sitting on the back of a bike. She also hated the great unknown and each day that passed with her life in Reaper's hands, her life, her very existence, and how long she would be alive, were unknown. At first, she thought Reaper was going to kill her. Hurt her, torture her, punish her, but kill her. She'd expected to be dead long before now. She wasn't dead, though. Very much alive with all her body parts. No missing nails or fingers or toes. Even her tongue was in contact.

The first week had been the hardest of all.

Every time he came close to her, she expected pain. The first day, he'd hurt her so badly, she hadn't been able to see. He'd raped her as well. The worst part of the ordeal wasn't even the rape.

He'd taken her multiple times and he didn't share. Some of the men she heard talking said it was unusual for him to not share. She didn't know if she should be happy about that or scared.

If he wasn't sending her out to his men, what did he want from her?

After the first week, only when he was really angry did he hit her.

Now, four weeks into her ordeal, what she hated the most was when he tried to make love to her. She didn't know for sure if that was what he wanted to do, or if he was trying to break her down.

Either way, his lips on hers, and the way he stroked her, caressed her, she found that harder than anything else.

She sat on the floor at the edge of the bed, knees drawn up, arms wrapped around them, waiting.

In the distance, she heard a woman scream. They'd ordered some prostitutes to entertain themselves. She hoped they would all drink and drug themselves into comas so she'd be able to find an opportunity to escape. She was always looking for a chance to leave. Always. She was determined to get out of there, one way or another. They would get sloppy.

She'd never known anyone at the Twisted Monsters to hit the drugs. They had a lot of parties but there was always someone keeping an eye on things. They never turned their back on danger.

Did Preacher miss her?

Resting her head on her knees, she tried not to feel sick about what could be happening. For all he knew, she was dead and he was waiting for her body.

The door of the hotel room opened.

"Figured you'd want something to eat," Reaper said.

She stayed silent as he closed the door. This was a new experience for her. He liked her company when he ate. She tried to give him the silent treatment and it never seemed to bother him.

"How do you feel about Chinese food?" he asked.

Again, silence.

He grabbed her chin, tilted her head back, and forced her to look at him. "You will learn to answer me or the only thing you're going to be eating is my cum. I'll shove my dick so far down your throat, you'll choke on it."

She tried to pull back but he wouldn't let her go. "Chinese is fine," she said.

He let her go and she expected a blow to the face,

but he didn't deliver it.

She waited.

One second.

Two.

Maybe a minute?

She didn't know, but when no pain came, she opened her eyes.

He stared down at her. "Are you done? I'm not going to hit you unless you deserve it."

"And you think any woman deserves to be hit?"

"I know some women do need a good slap," he said.

She hated him.

"Now, you're being stubborn and I'm just doing my best to try and make your time go more easily."

"Then take me back home."

"Not going to happen. You're going to have to get used to this place being your home. Now, eat up. I want you to stay big and strong."

Would it be so hard if she plunged the spork into his eye?

Figuring she wouldn't get far, and that she had to plan her getaway stealthily, she opened the first carton of Chinese food and started to eat.

"See, that's not so hard, is it? You take a bite, enjoy, and we can both be happy."

She didn't say anything else to him but kept on eating her food.

He opened a cartoon and she watched him scoop up some noodles. The moments like this, where they were both normal, they were the hardest for her. She didn't know if her life would be a lot easier if he beat her up, hurt her.

"This is good, no?"

"Yeah, it's good."

"See, this isn't so hard. So, before all of this, what did you plan to do?" Reaper asked.

"Why do you care?" she asked. There was no attitude to her question. She was simply curious to know why he would even want to know.

"Call me curious. I'm not just a big kidnapping thug. I have feelings as well, you know." He smirked. "I'm guessing graduating would have been at the top of your list?"

"Yes. I won't graduate now."

"Doesn't mean you won't ever," he said.

"You're planning on sending me back?"

"Hell, no. I think what you need to realize, Robin, is that I'm not letting you go."

"If this is all revenge or whatever for Preacher, why do you think it'll work keeping me around? I'm nothing."

"We both know you're more than nothing to him." He laughed. "I think it's fun to keep shit from him, especially when it's something he really wants, and you, Robin, you're far more precious than a jewel. Right now, he's looking for you. He'll use up favors and drain away people's patience in his search for you. Only, you're never going to go back to him. When the time comes, you're always going to pick me."

"You're crazy," she said. "I will always pick Preacher."

"Aw, poor old Bishop. He never did have a chance with you, did he?"

"Don't you dare mention his name to me," she said, hatred unlike anything she had ever experienced before consuming her, and it was all directed at her best friend.

No, he wasn't her best friend. He would never be her best friend.

"A little touchy there, I see. One day, you're going to have to face the reality of how you're feeling."

"Fuck you."

"You've got a sexy mouth. I wonder how you'll sound when you're begging me for more." He grabbed the back of her neck, tilted her head back, and before she knew what was happening, he was kissing her. His tongue plunged into her mouth.

She didn't kiss him back nor did she try to bite him. The last time she'd done that, it had ended badly for her, and she was a fast learner. She had no reason to do something that would cause her pain.

"You see, Robin, when the time comes, you're going to always come to me because I'm never going to wear a condom with you, and you're going to have my kid."

****

Present day

"We don't have to do anything," Bishop said. "We can just hang out and get to know each other again."

Robin stared at her husband and waited for the feeling of anticipation to wash over her. It didn't happen. She was nervous and she didn't know why. Whenever she was near Bishop, she had this weird sense to run, to get as far away from him as possible. It was crazy.

"Er, sure, it sounds like fun." Bear had to go to an emergency meeting with the club and Bishop had arrived as her father was leaving.

Now, they were heading out to have some fun. Her cast had been removed, and the bones were healed. She still had some aches and pains, but the doctor had advised her to take it easy and explained she'd need to keep walking and using it. Only when the pain got too bad was she to give herself a break and ease up.

This was her easing up.

"I can't ride on a bike."

"I brought my car."

"Ah, you did. Okay. Yes. Let's go and have some dinner and dance. I like that." She grabbed her cell phone and jacket, locking up the house and following him to his car.

He held open the passenger side and she climbed in. She'd buckled up her seatbelt as he started the car, leaving the safety of her father's driveway.

You're fine.

"How have you been?"

"Oh, you know, boring my dad. He's taken me around town and I've had some memory recall or vague recollections. Nothing big. My foot has been the biggest improvement. I'm healing up nicely."

"I imagine it was staying in the hospital for all that time. It helped."

"Yeah, I bet." She looked out of the window. "Was it always weird for us like this?"

He laughed. "There would have been a time you wouldn't have pointed out the obvious."

"I guess."

"No, it wasn't always like this. We're, you know, different." He reached out, touching her wrists. "Like this."

When her bandage came off from her hand, she'd seen the tattoo encircling the second wrist.

"Yeah, it has been a whole big change." What she tried not to do was show Bear, Preacher, or anyone else how scared she was. She'd flick through the photograph albums and try desperately to conjure up an image or a memory.

It was useless.

She was useless.

Nothing worked.

Even driving around town didn't spark anything.

The only place she hadn't gone to was the room she had at Preacher's. Being around Preacher was even scarier. Where she felt awkward and nervous with Bishop, with Preacher, she felt this overwhelming attraction that hadn't diminished. It sparked within her and refused to go away for even a moment. She would find herself staring at Preacher's hands and imagining them on her body. What unnerved her was the way she could picture them on her stomach, holding her. Then of course there were his lips. She found herself aching for him to kiss her. To have those lips between her thighs, and she'd woken up many times wet, shaking, and filled with a hunger for him.

Again, whenever they were together, she never brought it up. The very thought of her cheating on her husband with his dad scared her. Was she the kind of girl who cheated? Was that why Bishop didn't come around all that often? That deep down, he despised her and didn't want to show it?

Was she overthinking everything once again? She seemed to do it a lot, and there was no reason to do so.

"We had comfortable silences. I'd spend a lot of time complaining about my dad. You'd listen, and we'd move on. It was kind of our thing to do, you know, moving on. Talking."

"So we were really close?"

"We used to share a crib together, and I married you, so yeah, it's easy to assume we were very close."

"Only assume?"

"We were really close, Robin. I hope we can be again."

He lifted her hand to his lips and pressed a kiss against the knuckles.

"I'd like that as well. I ... I missed you." The lie

fell easily from her lips.

"I missed you too."

"I've been looking at pictures of you and the two of us together. I find it a bit weird having my own ultrasound picture, but you know, I guess I must have had some narcissistic tendencies."

"Ultrasound photo?"

"You know, of me in my mom's stomach. Do they have another name?"

"No, it's fine. Yes, it's you. I guess your mom was going to throw it out." Bishop let go of her hand and she watched as he gripped the steering wheel tighter.

"Have I upset you? If you want, you can see the photo."

"Nah, it's fine. I don't need to see it. You and I got to know each other outside of the stomach."

She frowned. He was acting weird.

"Here we are," he said, pulling up outside of a converted barn, given the signpost declaring it a bar.

"It's busy," she said. "Did we come here a lot?"

"No. You've never been here. I think we need to stop looking into the past and start focusing on your future."

"I like that."

"Me too. Everyone wants you to remember, and you will. All in good time, but for now, let's go and have some dancing and fun."

She climbed out of the car and Bishop took her hand, practically running toward the door. Pain shot through her foot, but she ignored it, following him.

There were so many people. None of whom she recognized, and her heart started to race. She pushed all her feelings to one side and forced a smile to her lips, trying to be happy with Bishop. It was the first time since she'd been back that he actually looked happy. His smile was infectious.

He pulled her onto the dance floor and grabbed her hips. Where she was a little unsure of how to hold and touch him, he took over and led the dance. He put her hands around his neck.

"Hold on to me. I'll show you how it's done."

She laughed as she danced her around the barn. If they bumped into couples, she'd apologize along with Bishop. They would ask her how she was doing. Bishop would remind them she had amnesia and they'd back off.

After an hour, she was way too thirsty. "I need a drink," she said.

Taking off to the bar, she found a spot and waved her hand at the barman.

He nodded at her but she had to stand around and wait. Perspiration dotted her brow.

The music seemed to fade around her as her mind wandered. She was still in the same room, only now it was different.

"All of these people, they want one thing. You're kidding yourself if you don't see the lust in their eyes, burning for each other. It doesn't make them monsters, Robin. It makes them people. Fucking, taking, begging for it. It's not wrong to want it. It's not wrong to want me, and I know you do. You don't think I feel a difference within you?"

She came out of the memory, shaking, feeling sick.

The barman was in front of her, but she shook her head, needing fresh air. Without another word, she left the bar, stumbling outside. She bent forward, heaving, throwing up all that she'd eaten that day.

"Are you okay?" Bishop asked, coming toward her.

She didn't get a chance to ask as she vomited

again.

Her entire body was cold. The memory, it didn't seem bad but there was something about it that twisted her entire body up. "I want to go home."

"You're going to need something to eat."

She shook her head. "No, I really need to go home. I need to rest." She saw stars before her eyes.

"For fuck's sake, Robin, you've been a little sick!"

"Why don't you listen to her and take her the fuck home?"

His voice.

Preacher's.

Robin lifted her head.

Preacher and Bear, as well as Grave and Frost were a few feet away from them. She noticed people walked away, heading back into the bar.

"What the fuck is the problem now? You don't want her having fun?"

"I want her to have whatever it is she needs and if she wants to go home, take her fucking home," Preacher said. "Do you want to go home?"

Before she had time to answer, Bishop stepped in front of her.

"I'm her husband. Why don't you answer to me?" Bishop asked.

"You think you're big and tough because you're standing in front of her? Do you really think you're safe?" Preacher asked.

The threat was there, lurking beneath the surface.

Maybe if she hadn't been throwing up her guts, she would've been afraid, but as it was, she was throwing up everything, and well, Bishop wouldn't listen. She needed to get home.

"I know I am. I know what you're capable of and

I know what you won't do."

Before she knew what was happening, she heard the sound of flesh hitting flesh, and when she looked, Preacher and Bishop were punching each other.

She didn't know what to do, but she stepped between them. As she did, Bishop threw another punch, landing one right against her jaw, after which she fell in a heap on the ground.

"Ow," she said, hand to her face, trying to focus. Her vision went a little blurry from the impact.

"Fuck, shit. I didn't mean to hit you."

"You shouldn't have been fighting," she said. "I want to go home. It's not up for discussion, nor does it need to be some kind of fighting contest."

Preacher held out his hand and she took it.

"I'll take her home," Bear said.

She didn't argue. Now with the sick feeling, she had a painful jaw and a headache. That was what spending time with her husband would do for her. She would have to reconsider who she hung out with.

"Robin, please, you know I didn't mean for anything to happen. You have to believe me."

She sighed and turned toward him. "I do believe you, Bishop, but, you wouldn't listen. I know we've got a past, I can sense it, but I at least need you to … let me breathe and hear me when I speak." She paused. "We'll talk soon."

She turned on her heel and walked back to her dad. She had no choice but to climb on the back of his bike as he took off, heading home.

When they arrived, neither of them spoke. She went for a shower, to clean up and get out of her clothes. She wanted to wash the scent of the night from her body and rid her mind of everything that had happened.

Most of the bruises she'd gotten months ago had

long since faded and now it looked like she had a new shiner, courtesy of her husband.

After she washed and changed, she made her way downstairs, where she found Bear in the kitchen, leaning over the counter, sipping a mug of hot chocolate.

"You look … serious."

"I am. I don't want you being alone with Bishop again," he said.

She folded her arms across her chest. "Why not?"

"I need you to trust me to know that I'm doing what is best for you."

"Don't you think this is a little strange?" she asked. "He's supposed to be my husband and yet, you don't seem to want me to be near him. None of it makes any kind of sense to me."

"Do you trust me?" he asked.

"Yes. You know I do."

"Then know this, he doesn't always have your best interests at heart. He's always been a selfish prick and tonight, you got to see what he's really like. This is not just tonight. This is what he's like all the time. Only ever looking after himself. Never considering the bigger picture."

"And it scares you?" she asked.

"Your safety is what I'm worried about. Not Bishop's. He can take care of himself as he's been doing a pretty good job of it so far. Don't believe everything he tells you. Bishop has his own agenda."

"Okay. I won't." She didn't know if this made her feel happy or sad to know she couldn't trust the one man she was supposed to.

****

"You just can't stand it, can you?" Bishop asked, spitting blood onto the floor.

"What is it I can't stand?" Preacher asked.

When he'd gotten a call that Bishop and Robin had been spotted at the bar, he didn't want to believe it. He'd hoped Bishop wouldn't be so fucking stupid as to take her to a public place where Reaper could get to her.

He didn't know the full extent of Reaper's reach, but when he did, he would make the bastard pay. Until that time, he had to be content to sit around, waiting for shit to happen. This wasn't what he was used to. In fact, the very idea itself was fucking insane. Following leads was all well and good, but it took him away from the business he needed to contend with, which was by far more important than anything else.

"The thought of Robin remembering me with her. Of her thinking about me. I know you think you won her over, but I know my girl, and Robin, she belongs to me."

He grabbed his son's jacket, pulling him close. "You think she belongs to you, but you can't even listen to a simple request. Do you even know why she was sick? Vomiting? She'd been perfectly healthy, but after a short time in there, she's ill. Do you think she remembered something she couldn't stand? Maybe the truth about your marriage being a complete and total fucking lie." He shoved Bishop away from him. "You think you know what's best for her, but at every single turn, you're hurting her. You did it when she was pregnant, and you're doing it now."

"You were never supposed to have her."

"You think these feelings were planned? Prepared? Are you really that fucking stupid?"

"Fuck you."

He hit him again. Preacher wanted to do a whole lot more, but he held himself back, only for Robin. He didn't want her to feel guilty in case she saw Bishop's face and felt it was her fault.

Bishop earned every single beating he got, and

Preacher was going to make sure his son knew it.

"Look what happened the last time you and Robin tried to make a go of it. Reaper came and tore you apart. It's time you let me have my best friend back. She knows me. She's comfortable with me. You should have seen the way we were dancing tonight. It was like the past meant nothing. You call me selfish, look at yourself. You're old enough to be her dad and you're not letting her go. Maybe it's time for you to take your own advice and leave her the fuck alone."

Staring at his son, Preacher didn't say a word. He didn't need to. There was no point in prolonging this.

Without saying anything, he went back to his bike and rode straight to Dog's crew. On the edge of the border, he stopped, parked his bike, and climbed off, leaving it running. One of Dog's crew shouted out and seconds later, a door opened.

Every single time he came to Dog's turf, he was close by. It was like the son of a bitch had a radar or some shit for knowing when he was going to stop by.

"Well, well, well, to what do I owe the pleasure this time?"

"He's watching her. He's got eyes all over the place," Preacher said. "So I want to make a deal with you."

"You do?"

"Yeah, whatever you want, so long as it's reasonable, it's yours. In return, I want you, your men, and your group helping me to keep an eye on Robin. I'm willing to pay. The fighting ring, it's all yours if you want it."

"Wow," Dog said, looking over his shoulder. "And your boys voted for this?"

"They voted to bring down Reaper and Slaves to the Beast in any form possible. This is what I'm doing to achieve that."

"But you need eyes on your girl in order to achieve that."

Preacher thought about his son. The way Bishop was able to take her dancing without him knowing until it could have been too late. He didn't know how far away or near Reaper was when he took out Milo. For all he knew, he could be really fucking close, and he didn't like the thought of that son of a bitch getting close to his woman.

This was a game he really didn't want to play but everyone was pushing him to. "What do you say? Do we have a deal?"

Dog looked over his shoulder again. "Walk with me."

"I'm going to have to tell my boys to stand down."

"Go ahead. You can keep your weapons. I don't care. I'll kill you before you can even use them."

Dog waited as Preacher returned to his men, letting them know he was walking with Dog.

"I don't like this," Frost said. "I don't like any of this."

"I know what I'm doing."

"I hope so," Grave said.

Preacher left his men and walked back to Dog. Side by side, they headed forward. Preacher didn't know what he was going to find or why Dog wanted him alone.

Dog's men didn't follow, and when they got to the end of the street, Dog took off into the woods.

Without questioning the motives or why he was following him, he took off with him.

They ran for twenty minutes before Dog finally stopped and sat down on a fallen tree.

"You want to tell me what all of this is about?"

"Clearly, one of us has a leak in our crew. I've yet to find anyone who would even have the guts to step out on me, which leaves your crew. Someone is giving Reaper information. It's how he has always stayed one step ahead."

"Until tonight. Reaper didn't have the first clue I'd found his little cave." He updated Dog with the information he'd seen, including Reaper's desire to get her back.

"Then all I ask you, Preacher, is who wasn't part of your club. Who didn't have the first clue what was going on?" Dog asked.

Preacher sat back and looked at Dog.

"You know the answer and so do I."

"My son," Preacher said.

"And who was with her the day she was taken?"

"You're telling me you think my son is the person who's been helping Reaper stay one step ahead?"

"At first, I thought it could be a coincidence. You know, some men get lucky, but not this guy. Even I don't get that kind of luck and I make my own luck. I thought about it after our last conversation. Bishop doesn't want her to remember, does he? What if old Robin knows something new Robin doesn't?" Dog looked around. "You need to be careful with him."

"He's my son."

"And I don't think he's a big fan of yours, is he?"

Preacher shook his head. "No, but I don't … he didn't like that me and Robin were in a relationship, that's all."

Dog shrugged. "You've got to put pressure on your boy, Preach. I'm telling you, Bishop's the guy when it comes to Reaper."

Chapter Eight

The time with Reaper

Robin wanted to close her eyes, but she couldn't do it. Holding on to her legs, she tried to stay as still as possible.

One of the men working at the hotel where they were staying had dared to lay a finger on her. She didn't know what to expect, but it wasn't to be dragged into the middle of nowhere, placed near a fire, and watch as Reaper worked his magic, his exact words, on the man.

Now, the man in question had cupped her ass and told her she would need to ride a real man one day. Reaper had taken offense. She didn't know if he was doing this because of her honor or because he was upset by his lack of respect. Either way, the man currently didn't have a tongue and was being butt-fucked by a bat.

She felt sick.

In all of her years near the Twisted Monsters MC, she'd never seen anything quite so vile in all of her life. She wanted to throw up, cry, scream, and beg him to stop. His men were loving the show, telling him to make the guy take the bat even more.

She stared into the flames, holding herself tightly, wanting to be anywhere but here. The days had started to meld together now.

Another scream filled the air, and she flinched as Reaper pulled the bat out and proceeded to beat him with it. The sound was a crunch, and the deathly silence filled the air. Seconds later, cheers erupted. His men were more than happy with the death and carnage that had occurred while she wanted to weep for the man.

Did anyone deserve that kind of treatment?

Out of the corner of her eye, she watched as Reaper washed his hands and face and threw out cans of beers to his buddies.

He stepped close to her, gripped the back of her neck, titled her head back, and kissed her. Catcalls rang out as he deepened the kiss. Finally, when he was done, he let her go, and she held herself even more tightly, wanting to escape.

"What's the matter? Didn't enjoy the show?" Reaper asked, opening his beer and drinking. He drank a great deal but never did drugs. Compared to his men, Reaper was in shape.

"Did you really have to do that?"

"I've got to set an example to my boys. Business will mean I'll have to leave you alone. If they think they can touch you, do you really think witnessing that guy getting what was coming to him is the worst of your problems?"

"Why don't you just send me home?" she asked. "Then no one would have to die and I wouldn't have to worry about you going crazy on everyone."

"Nah, not going to happen. Where's the fun in that?" he asked.

"I want to go..." She wanted to say home but instead, asked to go back to the hotel.

Reaper surprised her by agreeing. He walked her back to his bike, and a couple of his men followed. The others stayed at the fire. She didn't ask what they were going to do about the body. The less she knew about them and what they got up to, the better. She would already have nightmares for weeks to come after what she'd just seen and heard. That man, she hadn't wanted him to touch her, but she also didn't want him to beg for death or feel so much pain.

Arriving back at the hotel, she realized she was getting used to riding on the back of his bike. Her legs no longer felt like jelly. She rushed toward the hotel room, needing to clear her mind and head. Rather than stop at the bed, she went straight to the bathroom, needing to rid herself of the very memory of what just happened. Turning the shower to cold, she stepped beneath the water, wanting to do nothing more than forget. Her thoughts, as they always did, turned to Preacher. Was he still looking for her? Time wasn't on her side and she'd never in all her life felt so lost and alone.

She stood beneath the spray of the water for what felt like hours, but for her, time did seem to move differently. Minutes felt like hours. Hours more like days.

After turning off the water, she wrapped her body in a towel and left the room.

Reaper was on the bed, naked.

When she appeared, he got off and brushed past her, going into the shower. There was no point in trying the door. If it wasn't already locked, there would be a guard outside. She knew because she'd tried it several times.

She dried as fast as she could, grabbing a nightshirt, any shirt, and quickly climbing into bed. She turned onto her side, facing the wall, closing her eyes, and hoping sleep would find her.

After what she'd just witnessed, sleep would be a long way off.

Still, she tried.

Failed.

Reaper returned from the shower without saying a single word. The light was turned off and the bed dipped with his body. She held on to her pillow and within seconds, his arms wrapped around her.

"I know right now you hate what you saw, but one day, you're going to see I don't let anyone put their hands on my woman."

"I'm not your woman." She whispered the words, wanting him to see the truth.

"You are." The hand at her stomach moved down to between her thighs.

She squeezed her eyes closed, hoping above all else to not respond to his touch. She was stronger than him.

Only, her body didn't believe that. Not as he started to kiss her neck. He hadn't used his fists in a long while. She had no doubt he was capable of hitting her. There was a time he would laugh as he hurt her. Reaper had decided to hurt her another way, by getting her body to betray her. He knew what to do to make her ache.

He kissed down her back and there was no way to stop him as he spread her legs.

"I want you to come all over my face, baby," he said.

Robin cried out as his tongue flicked across her clit, sending a spiral of fire between her thighs, moaning his name, begging for more. Never wanting him to stop.

He grabbed her ass, pressing his face against her pussy and licking her up as if she was some sweet treat he couldn't get enough of. The pleasure was too much, and even as she hated herself, she came all over his face. Now that he'd gotten the satisfaction of getting her to orgasm, she knew what would come next.

He'd make love to her.

****

Present day

Bear had become a little more protective of her since the night Bishop took her out. The memories weren't back, but she'd have flashes of feelings. Bear also wouldn't leave the house or her side, and so for the past week, she'd been more like his personal prisoner.

Robin had needed a break, and so after she'd

gone to her room for the night, she climbed out of her window. It wasn't hard to do, but it did scare her.

She hated heights. She didn't know if this was a newfound fear or one extending from her previous life.

Dropping to the ground from where she'd used the tree as leverage, she went onto her hands and knees, crawling past the windows, heading down to the driveway. When she was sure she was clear, she got to her feet and ran. At least she tried to run, which was impossible. The pain was too much and she couldn't run properly. She ended up in a fast-paced walk.

She wasn't afraid but once as she got as far as possible, she finally slowed down. She'd been around the town a few times now and so she recognized it.

Tucking her hair behind her ear, she folded her arms, suddenly feeling a little afraid. If something bad was to happen to her, she had no way of contacting anyone to come and help her.

Glancing left and right, she took a deep breath.

I can do this.

I'm a strong woman.

I've been through a lot.

I just don't exactly know what I've been through.

It's all a little fuzzy, but I can handle it.

She kept on walking until she got to the police station. For some reason, she found herself stopping and staring at the building. There was a single light on but she didn't go inside. The cold was seeping into her bones, and she waited.

When a man came out, she recognized him as the cop who'd come to see her at the hospital. Billy something.

"Robin," he said the moment he spotted her.

"Hi, sir," she said.

"It's Billy. I imagine with everything going on in

your life right now, remembering names isn't high on the list."

"I don't really know what is high on my list of things to remember." She took a deep breath in.

"Do you want me to call someone for you?"

"No!" She held her hand out as if to stop him. "I mean, please don't."

"You're out on your own?"

"Something like that. I don't want to worry anyone. Bear's being a little protective."

"Your dad always has tried to be. Especially when it comes to you."

She nodded but didn't question it. She ran her hand from her neck down to her chest, feeling her own pulse. Glancing around, she noticed a couple of people walking their dogs.

"Would you like me to take you somewhere?"

She was about to decline when she thought of something. "Would you take me to Preacher's house?"

"Yeah, of course." He nodded to the passenger side of the car. "Jump in."

She got into the car, putting the seatbelt on and staring forward. "Are you any closer in finding the person who took me?" she asked, not liking the silence within the car.

"I'm always chasing up leads. I'm sure Preacher's doing his own research when it comes to you."

"He cares a great deal."

"Yes, when it comes to you, he does." Billy took off, heading out of town.

"Where are we going?"

"Preacher doesn't live close. It's on the outskirts of town, away from all the trouble."

"Oh."

"How's the memory coming?"

"It's … not." She turned to look at him. "Can I ask you a question?"

"Of course."

"Bishop and I, what were we like as a married couple?"

"I don't think I should talk about things you don't know."

"You don't?"

"Your and Bishop's marriage was complicated."

"Did we love each other?"

"In your way, yes."

"Then why don't I feel anything for him?" She pressed her lips together. "Forget I said that."

"You and Bishop were married, but you didn't have a conventional marriage."

"We were best friends?"

"Yes, and he was with a new girl every single chance he got. You didn't care, though."

"About his cheating?"

"I guess you could say it was like you didn't care at all back then. You expected it."

Even now, hearing the news of his cheating, she didn't feel anything. Rubbing at her temple, she felt the beginning of a headache.

"Here we are. Would you like me to stick around?" Billy asked.

"No, that's okay. I'll be fine." She wanted to be alone with her thoughts. Unbuckling her belt, she tried the door and Billy touched her arm.

"If there is ever anything you need, anything at all, please, contact me. Don't hold back. Let me know what you want, and I'll be there."

"Thank you."

"Anytime."

She climbed out of the car, closing the door. The large floodlight turned on and as it did, she covered her eyes.

"You can do this the easy way, kid, or the hard way. I really don't care. That bitch is coming with us and you're surrounded. There's no way for you to stop what's happening."

"I'm not letting you get her."

"Then it's your funeral. I did warn you."

She stumbled but caught herself as Billy drove out. Giving him a wave, she looked back at the house, a sickness twisting inside her.

As she took a step, another memory flashed in her mind.

"Yeah, daddy dearest will be pissed, but come on. What's asshole really going to do? Complain that he can't keep me in line? I'm sick and tired of being PS. I'm one vowel away from being PMS!"

Only this one wasn't outside of the house.

Bishop was present in both memories, and only the voice of that man. The one she kept hearing in the back of her mind that made her think something was important.

She moved to the porch steps and sat down, resting her head in her hands. A spiral of sickness worked its way up her body, threatening to spill out. She took several deep breaths, wanting to remember.

But again, her thoughts wouldn't come.

Staring at the ground, she wondered what she should do when she heard a bike roaring down the driveway. Getting to her feet, she stepped into the darkness, wanting to hide from any impending doom.

There was nothing for her to worry about as the floodlight came back on and she saw Preacher.

"Don't you think you should wear a helmet?" she

asked.

"I haven't worn a helmet in a long time. Do you want to tell me what's going on? Billy called me. He told me he dropped you off here. Imagine Bear's surprise when I asked him and he went to check on you. He's worried." Preacher threw his cell phone in her direction. "You're going to have to call him."

She stared down at it. "I … I just needed to get out of the house. That's all." She handed him back his cell phone. "No other reason."

"Yeah, well, your dad worries about you. Let him know you're safe and I'll look after you."

She turned his cell phone on and found Bear's number. "You really should protect your phone with a password or something."

He chuckled. "I rarely use the thing. Believe me, there's nothing worth shit on that thing."

She followed him into his house as she put the cell phone to her ear. The moment she stepped through the threshold, she felt like she'd come home.

"Preacher, do you have her?" Bear asked.

He did sound slightly panicked, which immediately made her feel guilty. "Hey, Dad, it's me."

"Robin, what the fuck were you thinking? Do you have any idea how scared I was? I thought someone could have taken you. It's not safe."

"I know. I'm sorry. I just needed a bit of a break. You've been very … protective."

She didn't want to hurt his feelings. It was the last thing she wanted to do.

Bear sighed. "I caused this?"

"No, no, of course not. It's nothing. Believe me. It's all my fault and I'm so sorry." She cringed, hating how ungrateful she sounded. "I just needed to walk and I'm with Preacher. He'll keep an eye on me. I promise.

Next time, I won't climb out of my window."

"You know you've never done that before, don't you?"

"Done what?"

"Climbed out of a window. Damn it, Robin, you've got to be careful."

"I will. I promise."

"Put Preacher on the phone."

She handed Preacher his phone and took a seat as he pointed at one. Lowering herself into the seat, she waited as Preacher nodded, doing some humming and then hanging up.

"Has he always worried like this?"

"I think it's now his new hobby to worry about you. He just wants to take care of you." He shrugged. "Surely you can understand?"

"Yeah, of course, I do." She looked down at her wrists, seeing the chains wrapped around her wrists.

She caught Preacher looking at them and she pulled her wrists close, folding her arms.

"You wanted to come here?"

"Billy asked to drive me and this is the only place I haven't been to. I hope I'm not intruding."

"You're not. This was your home once. Has Bishop been in touch with you?" Preacher asked.

"Not since the night at the bar. He hasn't even stopped by. Why?"

"He's out of town. I was wondering if he told you where he went."

"I don't have a clue. When it comes to Bishop, I have a lot of questions."

"I'm sure you do. I'm not going to give you any answers."

"Why don't I feel anything for him?"

Preacher shrugged. "I've spoken to Randall. I

won't be feeding you any answers. Are you hungry?"

"A little bit. Can I go and see my old room? You said I stayed here with you for a short time. I'd like to go and see it."

"Of course." He took the lead and she followed close behind him. He opened a door. "There's your room. The only things that have changed are the items I've brought to you. Everything else is the way you left it."

She stepped into the room and noticed the light floral colors and the lemony scent. "This is how I left it?"

"Yes."

She sat down on the edge of the bed. "It feels comfortable."

"I'm going to go and cook. I'll let you know when dinner is done."

She watched him walk away even as she wanted him to come back. He closed the door behind him, and she stayed in her old room, with her thoughts.

Staring across the room, she saw a vanity table. It was plain white, but she noticed there was no makeup, just a box. She stepped closer and realized it was a black box with a lock in place.

She tried the catch, only for it to not work. The box didn't remind her of anything.

Walking around the room, she went toward the closet, then back again, pacing the length of the room. Again, nothing jumped out at her or screamed for her to know what was going on. None of this made any sense to her.

I want my memories back.

Leaving the bedroom, she came to a stop at a door.

Again, this feeling washed over her, and she tried the door handle, opening it. She stepped inside, and on instinct, she found the light switch, flicking it on.

It was a neutral nursery.

There was no baby.

The curtains were drawn closed.

She spun in a circle and saw the large drawn tree with wild animals from deer to bunnies on the far wall.

"Dinner is done," Preacher said, coming to a stop within the bedroom.

"Did I have a kid?" she asked, looking at Preacher. "Is that why I don't love Bishop? He and I were having a kid? Where is he or she? No one told me about a baby." She touched her stomach. "I don't understand what's going on."

"You need to calm down."

"I am calm!" She yelled the words. There was no way she was calm. In fact, she was freaking out.

She'd been pregnant and for some reason, she wasn't pregnant anymore. Why wasn't she pregnant? What had happened to her baby? Why wasn't she pregnant?

"You're having a panic attack. I need you to breathe."

The world started to get fuzzy around her. She couldn't breathe.

Where was her baby?

What was happening?

Where did it all go wrong?

Everything suddenly went black.

****

"Is she okay?" Preacher asked as Randall came out of her bedroom. He hadn't called Bear as he didn't want him to worry.

"She will be."

"What happened?"

"She had a panic attack. The memories, possibly.

I don't know. I've given her a mild sedative. There won't be any lasting damage but clearly, a child, it changes things for her."

"I've never seen her act like that. Not even when she lost our little girl."

"It will be hard for her at first. There's a past you don't know about. A lot can happen in two years. We're all just going to have to be patient with her, give her time. Let her come to all of this."

"How long will she be out?"

"Only a couple of hours. Long enough for her to rest. Call me if you feel she needs anything else."

Preacher showed him out. "With her reaction to the nursery, does this mean she'll remember?"

"It's a possibility. Again, I can't stress enough how powerful the human brain is. Everyone reacts differently. You can never give two patients the same outcomes. It just doesn't work that way. Robin's strong. I only hope she's strong enough to deal with whatever pains her. There is pain there, Preacher. You must be aware of it."

"I am. Thanks for coming." He closed the door and stared up at the stairs. His food was long cold but after seeing the way she reacted, he wasn't hungry. He took the steps two at a time and went into her room. She was still out cold but at least she looked peaceful.

He grabbed the chair from the corner of the room, bringing it closer to the bed, and took a seat. There was a lot of stuff he could be doing, like hunting his suddenly elusive son, but there was nowhere else he wanted to be than with this woman right now.

The love he felt for her was strong. Stronger than anything else he'd ever experienced. He'd been with his fair share of women over the years, but none of them had ever made him commit like this. It was … fucking magical.

Only, he'd been given a taste of it and hadn't been able to have anything else. Reaper had taken the one person who mattered to him more than anything and to know he'd done so for fun sickened him.

Running a hand down his face, he stared at the ink on her wrists. He had no doubt she'd been forced to get the ink, and he'd also seen the one with Reaper's name at the base of her back. Her body told so many different stories, and none of them she could remember. He didn't know if he should even let her remember them.

The minutes ticked on by, turning to hours before she finally sighed and started to move. She opened her eyes and looked up at him.

"Preacher?" she asked. "What happened?"

"You had a panic attack. It's okay now. You're fine."

"The baby room? I was pregnant, wasn't I?"

"Are you hungry?"

"Was it Bishop's baby?" she asked.

He stared at her, wondering what he should say. "I don't think you're ready to know the truth. I'm going to go and warm us up some food."

"Was it yours?" she asked. "There is only one reason everyone is keeping stuff from me. The ultrasound picture I have, it's of my baby, isn't it? Not me. My baby girl?"

Preacher turned to look at her. "You don't want these answers."

She was crying and he didn't want to hurt her. "If there's no baby then that means I lost it, right?"

He moved toward the bed, pulling her into his arms and holding her. "You don't need to remember this."

"But it doesn't feel right, thinking of having

Bishop's baby. I don't feel anything for him but when I'm with you, it feels right. Why does it feel right? Were we cheating? I don't know what's going on."

The pain in her voice was more than anything he could bear. "We ... we did make a baby together. It's a long, complicated story. We didn't start out by cheating. In fact, I don't even know if you liked me all that much when we first met."

"You don't?"

"I was Bishop's dad and you've seen me do a lot of bad things."

"But I started to have feelings for you?"

"Robin, I can't tell you what you felt. We were together a short time before you were taken, that's all I know. We didn't get into the details. There was an attraction there, but I don't know what else to say after that."

He ran his fingers through her hair, holding her close, never wanting to let her go.

"Did you love me?" she asked.

Preacher didn't respond. Randall hadn't given him these kinds of instructions for these difficult questions and he didn't know what to fucking do with them. "I ... yes, I loved, love, you."

She tilted her head back. "Do you love me still? Or did you find someone else when I was gone?"

Chapter Nine

Her time with Reaper

Another move. Robin couldn't remember the name of the last hotel or even where it was. They moved so often, the scenery blended into one. She hated moving more than anything and craved being back at Preacher's house.

There still hadn't been a sign of him, but she believed on several occasions now, he'd been close, so close. There had been only two times Reaper had moved in the middle of the night and she knew it was because Preacher was closing in and he had to try to be one step ahead.

She flicked over the page of the latest romance book he'd bought for her. He'd probably robbed a bookstore or killed whoever worked there. She wouldn't put it past him to do the unspeakable to get what he wanted. She hated him so much.

Do you hate him?

Robin tried to cut out the memories of them together at night. Reaper was a force to be reckoned with and he knew what he was doing with his body. It had stopped being rape even though she didn't want his touch.

Each time Reaper took her to bed, it would start out with her not wanting his touch. She hated to respond to him and what was worse, Reaper knew she couldn't resist. He'd touch, caress, and tease her into submission, and there was nothing she could do about it.

He was the one who held all the power while she held nothing.

The only power she had over him was when she responded. She knew he was desperate for her to feel things for him. Robin had already figured out that along with trying to get her pregnant, Reaper was also trying to make her fall in love with him. It was his final piece of revenge for Preacher. If she loved Reaper, then if the time ever came for a showdown, would she allow Preacher to kill him?

Right now, she didn't think it was possible to love him.

He'd stopped hitting her. There was no pain from his hands, and he also seemed to like her company. Whenever she asked him for something, he provided it, and he'd been a nice guy to her.

Of course, there were times she couldn't get away from who he really was. The monster who'd killed many women during their travels. She heard the women's screams, but she didn't dare to venture out. Reaper had told her to never come out when she heard those screams as it would always end badly for her.

She didn't need to be told twice to follow instructions.

"Are you enjoying the book?" Reaper asked, coming out of the bathroom.

"It's okay, I guess."

He sat down on the edge of the bed, pulling on a pair of jeans, followed by some socks that had holes in, and boots. There was a knock at the door and she tensed up. She hated to hear those knocks. It either meant something had gone wrong or it was time to move.

Reaper opened the door.

"He's here."

"Excellent. Get him set up. I'll be out in a minute."

"What's going on?" she asked, closing her book and paying attention. Whatever was about to happen, it wouldn't be good.

"There's someone I want you to meet." Reaper

grabbed his shirt, pulling it over his head. "Come on." He took her hand and she followed close behind him as he walked her out toward a man, who was setting something up in the parking lot of the abandoned hotel. "This here is Trick. He does the best ink all around, and well, I wanted to prove my commitment to you."

"What do you mean?"

"Stay there." He let go of her hand.

She didn't try to run. His men would be given the signal to stop her, and well, she knew what battles she wanted to fight and those that were pointless.

Folding her arms, she waited, wondering what all of this was about.

"You do know ink is for life," Trick said.

"There's treatment to get it removed," she said. "It's a hard and painful procedure." She didn't have a clue what it entailed.

"I'm not getting rid of it. You know what I want," Reaper said.

He winked at her, and Trick got to work, inking something over his heart. She didn't like this one bit, and as he finished, she didn't know how long it took, but it was a red heart, not a garish color either, one that suited the rest of the ink. Almost a dull red and in the center, was her name.

"This will show you, baby, I'm committed." He stepped up to her, tilting her head back and kissing her. Again, she never responded to his attempts to woo her, but that didn't seem to stop him. If anything, her determination not to respond only seemed to spur him on. Reaper wasn't going to give up. Not until he got what he wanted. She didn't know why he was so determined to win her over when she knew she could never love him.

He'd hurt her. Taken her from the man she loved.

"Now, it's your turn."

"What? No. I don't want to get any ink. Please, don't make me."

She tried to fight him, but he wouldn't let her go. He held her down with the help of his men and Trick began by inking the base of her back. She cried the moment the needle touched her skin. She wanted it all to stop, but there was no way, not when Reaper forced her.

He was going to get what he wanted one way or another.

She had to be strong.

The ink wasn't done at her back, though. No, he got Trick to ink both of her wrists so she would know for now and all eternity she was chained to him for life.

****

Present day

Robin's heart raced as she waited to hear the truth from his lips. Did he love someone else? Was there ever going to be a chance for her?

Pressing her lips together, she looked up at him, wanting to touch him, to hold him, to love him more than anything. Her memories weren't back yet. She didn't know if she ever wanted them to be back.

"I didn't find anyone else. There is no way I could ever want anyone but you." He stroked her cheek.

He was a large man, full of muscles and strength. Yet, each time he touched her, she was shocked by how sweet and gentle he was with her. It was like he couldn't bring himself to hurt her, and well, she wasn't going to complain about that.

She offered him a smile. "There's no one?"

"There's no one."

"Then why haven't you been with me? Why haven't you tried to help me remember?"

"I don't know what you went through with Reaper, Robin. There are memories that are going to be unleashed, and they're not pretty. Randall has warned us. The room upstairs, there's more to that tale. It's not easy."

"You know what I've come to realize?" she said.

"What?"

"Life isn't easy and it's not supposed to be. I don't want you to run from me or hide anymore. I'd like to get to know you." She took his hand, locking their fingers together. "Can we have a chance to be together? You and me with no one else trying to take it away from us?" She licked her dry lips.

"There are times I forget you don't remember."

"Is that a good thing?"

"It's the best kind of thing," he said. His hand stroked down her cheek, moving to the back of her neck and she waited. He pulled her close and when his lips met hers, it was everything she had hoped it would be. She let out a little moan, gripping his shirt and moving so that she straddled his waist.

The hard ridge of his cock pressed between her thighs, and a hunger she couldn't even recall consumed her. This was what she wanted. Needed.

"Robin," he said between kisses.

"Please, don't stop kissing me."

"We're moving too fast."

She pulled back. "I'm not panicking. I'm not scared. I want this, Preacher. I ... I've been near Bishop and there's nothing there. I don't know why I ended up married to him, and quite frankly, I don't care. Don't you feel this?" She put her hand on his chest. "I can't give you everything you want. I don't know if I'll ever remember what happened between us in the past, but I can give you my future." She kissed his lips. "You said we didn't have a whole lot of time together, so why wait?"

"A few hours ago, you couldn't breathe because of a panic attack. We should take it slow."

She rubbed her pussy against his dick, not wanting to take it slow. For some reason, she felt like there had already been too much time wasted already. She was tired of waiting for something to happen.

During her short twenty years of living, she'd become pregnant, married her best friend, been taken by a monster, lost her memories, and now she was this person who she couldn't count on anymore.

"I don't want to take it slow. I'm tired of waiting around." She kissed him, sliding her tongue across his mouth until he opened up, and she released a moan, feeling connected to him once more. "Don't you want me?"

"It's not a matter of want. I'm trying to do the right thing here and to give you a chance to recover."

She pulled away, staring him in the eye, really seeing him. "And what if I don't ever recover? What if these feelings will never return? I don't know what the future holds and to be frank, I'm scared. What if I never know what happened to me or who I can trust? My entire life is a mystery to me and all I care about right now is if you'd kiss me. I want you to kiss me. To feel you inside me. Is that so bad?"

He groaned, running his hands up and down her back, gripping her ass tightly. He didn't move or say anything for several minutes. She held her breath, waiting until he finally pulled her down and her lips crashed against his. She wrapped her legs around his waist, not wanting to let him go as she sank her fingers into his hair.

She released a giggle as he turned her to the bed, but she wasn't laughing for long as he lifted her shirt. His fingers danced across her skin. She held her breath as he grazed across the underside of one breast.

"Tell me to stop."

"No."

She pulled him down, kissing him again as he cupped her tit. A fire spiraled between her thighs and she took his other hand, placing it between her thighs so he knew what it was she wanted, what she craved.

He broke from the kiss, trailing his lips down to her neck, sucking over her pulse before moving down even further, going to her chest.

"I want this off." He tore at the shirt, pushing it up over her head and tossing it to the side. "Beautiful."

"Have you seen me naked before?" she asked.

"Yes, and you're just as beautiful now as you were then." He pressed her tits together and she watched as he flicked his tongue across each bud.

She moaned as the pleasure rushed straight through her body, going to her core. He sucked on each nipple, using his teeth to graze across the surface, nibbling and biting.

Preacher didn't linger for long as he started to kiss down her body, going lower to her stomach. What she didn't want him to see was the ink across the base of her back. She didn't know who Reaper was, nor did she ever intend to see him again.

When he got to between her thighs, he opened the catch of her jeans and pulled them down her thighs. She spread open her legs and he tugged on the panties. She heard the fabric tear and she giggled, smiling up at him.

"I've never liked you wearing underwear."

She cried out as he slid a single finger in her.

"You're so wet."

He pumped his digit in and out, driving her crazy with more need and then his tongue slicked across her clit before he nibbled on the delicate bud.

She felt the start of an orgasm. It built up and quickly washed over her, taking her by surprise from the sheer pleasure of his touch.

"I'd have to say that was a personal best for me," he said.

She giggled. "I guess I can say I like your mouth on me." She wrapped her arm around his neck, pulling him down. She tasted herself on his lips but didn't care about anything else as he put the tip of his cock to her entrance.

Preacher broke the kiss first, staring into her eyes as inch-by-inch, he sank inside her, filling her up. He kept on going, even when she didn't think she could take much more, he didn't stop, and she didn't want him to. It felt amazing. Wrapping her legs around his waist, she cried out as he slammed in the last inch, making her jolt. Pain and pleasure mixed together, driving her toward him. He took her hands, pressing them above her head, pinning her to the bed.

The instant he held her down, she felt her pleasure increase. She lifted up for his thrusts, and he pounded inside her.

She stared into his eyes and as he moved, they both looked to see his cock disappearing within her. His dick wet from her own arousal.

"Do you have any idea how long I've waited? How long I've wanted to be close to you?"

There were no answers because they both knew the truth. She didn't have the first freaking clue about what was going on between them.

He sped up his thrusts and she felt another orgasm coming. This one wasn't as intense as the first, but it was up there. Preacher pulled out of her and lifted her ass up. She watched him as he put his mouth on her pussy and began to lick and suck at her. He circled her clit, slid down to her entrance, and she closed her eyes as he began to fuck her with his tongue.

She gripped the sheet beneath her, trying to find anything that would keep her grounded. Of course there was nothing close by, but it didn't matter, she didn't want to be grounded. With the magical use of his tongue, she wanted to fly and no longer stay still.

He drew his tongue back up, going to her clit, sucking on it hard before going back down.

Robin begged him to let her come, but Preacher, he had her dripping. Her arousal leaked out, going down her crack, but she wasn't afraid. No, it only served to make her hungrier for more.

"Please, please," she said.

"Come for me."

He finally sucked, flicked her clit, driving her to a third or fourth orgasm. She couldn't remember which one as she'd lost count. The moment her orgasm hit, Preacher pushed her to the bed, spread her legs, and fucked her hard. Her release kept on going, milking his cock as he fucked her harder. The pleasure made her wild, and she scored her nails down his back, begging for more.

When he came, she watched as he let go, filling her with his cum until he finally fell against her, completely spent. They were both panting.

Lifting up, she saw he still had his jeans around his ankles and she couldn't help but laugh. "Well, that didn't take long."

"With you, it never will." He kissed her again, hard, and she knew this was what she wanted. This was what she failed to have with Bishop, and nothing was ever going to take her away from Preacher again.

****

"Tell me about your family," Robin said a couple

of hours later. They'd moved to his bed, and both of them were naked. Preacher had made love to her a second time, and he'd fed her. So far, no more panic attacks, and he'd already spoken to Bear for him not to worry again.

Still no sign of Bishop, but his son would turn up eventually. His main priority was to find Reaper and his MC. The moment he dealt with them, Bishop wouldn't be a problem.

Would he kill his own son?

He stared down Robin's back, catching sight of the Reaper tattoo marking her skin.

Yeah, he really would. He would do whatever it took to keep her safe. He'd already failed once, and he wouldn't fail again.

"I don't have any family."

"Did I know anything about your parents or your life before my amnesia?"

"No. You didn't know anything."

"Why not?"

"There was nothing to tell. My family, they weren't good people."

"Does this mean they're dead?"

"Yes."

"Oh. I'm sorry."

"You don't have to feel sorry, or even pity me. They're not worth either emotion."

"Do you ever miss them?" Robin stroked a finger across his chest.

"Do you really want to know?"

"We can't talk about our time together. Why not share your past with me? What will it hurt?"

"It's not a good past."

"Most life stories aren't easy. I can handle it if you're worried I can't."

"I'm not worried about that." He reached a finger down to the base of her back and he watched as she tensed up. "You've seen it?"

"I don't know what it means, but yeah, I've seen it. I know it exists. Does it bother you?"

"Truth?"

"Yeah."

"It does bother me, more than you could know, but that's because I know what it means."

"Does it bother you that you're having feelings for me? I know my dad's close with you."

"No, it doesn't."

"I keep digressing. Tell me about your parents. Your life. What brought you to here and to be the president of the Twisted Monsters MC?" She rested her chin on her hands, and he stared into her eyes, captured by her beauty. In the two years they'd been apart, she'd matured in ways he didn't think were possible. Staring at her now, she was a sight to behold. A rare kind of beauty.

He never spoke about his past with anyone. His past was his darkness, his pain, and no one would ever be able to share it with him, but he didn't want to keep anything from her.

"My mom and dad weren't good for each other. They were drunks, both of them. They liked to party and do their own thing. Having a kid was never high on their list of things to have and if it was, well, they should've found another hobby. From a young age, I was neglected. I believe I was left in random places, you know? Hoping someone would take me and keep me. It never happened. My father liked to use me to get people to feel sorry for him. They'd give him money and he'd spend it on drink or drugs. My mom would spend all her spare time sleeping around, trying to get her next hit."

"Wow," she said.

"The beatings started to happen when I was four. I wasn't earning either of them enough, and so I was an extra mouth to feed. I kept getting beat up for as long as I can remember. I grew, though. I came to realize, people can beat on kids all they want but they fail to see that kids grow up. We get stronger, and when we finally reach maturity, we like to hit back."

"Did you start hitting back?"

"Yes, and when I did, I didn't stop. I kept on hitting. I made sure both of them paid for the life they'd given me. They had made me strong. Turned me into the man I am today. I guess I blame them for all my mistakes. Even when I think about Bishop, I fucked up with him. I wasn't there enough."

"Thank you for telling me. I don't imagine it's easy to relive those kinds of memories."

"It's not easy at all. I don't like to remember. It's easier for me to forget. It's what I like to do, forget."

"I wish I'd been there. To take the pain away."

He laughed. "You weren't even a thought then. After I killed my parents, I left, jumping from town to town until I fell into the Twisted Monsters. From here, I took over, killed the guy in charge because I knew I could do a better job of it, and believe me when I say I did. This is all mine. I built everything around you." There was no point to go into further details. She didn't need to know the years of sexual, physical, and emotional abuse, or how he'd tried to end his own life when he was younger. There were some areas of his soul he never wanted to see again.

"How did I end up married to Bishop?"

"I'm not going to tell you those details. When you remember, you'll be ready to know the truth."

"That's so not fair."

"It's the best you're going to get." He lifted up,

smacked her on the ass, and climbed out of bed. "I'm going to feed you again."

"You are?"

"Yes. As much as I want to laze in bed without eating, it's not going to happen." He leaned down and bit her ass. She let out a squeal. "Come on, let's get you fed. I want you to keep your strength up."

****

The next couple of days went by on cloud nine for Robin. She didn't want her happiness to end, not even for a moment.

Not only were her feelings for Preacher growing, but she felt at peace. Even if her memories didn't return, she had this. Bear wasn't happy with her moving back in with Preacher, a decision she'd made quite quickly. He believed she was moving too fast, and in a way, she probably was, but she was chasing this feeling and wouldn't let it go again, not ever. Whenever she was with Preacher, she actually felt something, something real, and happy.

There was still no sign of Bishop and she hadn't seen him since the situation in the barn. Time was moving by and even though she was happy, there were moments. Fleeting moments when she'd start to feel a panic build within her for no reason at all.

She couldn't figure out why she was so afraid. Time was ticking against her, and she needed to get her shit together or lose, but what exactly, she didn't know. Only that she had a time limit on everything. It was hard to talk to anyone about a feeling though. They really didn't understand. Nothing in an emotion or feeling was tangible.

"You look happy," Bear said.

They were meeting up at the diner. They'd just put their order in and she turned to Bear, smiling.

"I feel happy."

"Any new memories?"

It was like a broken record with all of them. Any new memories, or triggers?

"Nothing new so far."

"Preacher told me about your panic attack. How are you feeling now?"

"I'm feeling good. I mean, I think I'm doing good. I don't know. I guess time will tell."

"What's bothering you?" Bear asked.

She sipped at her water and looked around the diner. She noticed people were watching them. Some whispered behind their hands. Not one person other than the Twisted Monsters had dared to come near her. They didn't offer her any solution or clue as to who she was. "I don't know. Bishop being away. I wanted to talk to him about something."

"What?"

"Why does everyone look tense when I say Bishop's name?" she asked. She'd been asking Preacher how his search was going. She didn't have the first clue as to why it was such a huge problem for everyone.

"It's nothing."

"And again with the lies. How can I help anyone out when you're all keeping secrets from me? This doesn't help me."

"We're not keeping secrets from you. Just know the club is doing whatever it can to protect you."

"I don't need protecting," she said.

Bear took her hands in his. "Sweetheart, you didn't see the way you looked when you were found. The car did a number on you, sure, but you were hurt before the car."

"So, I don't make the best of choices. That shouldn't be a reason for you to ... you know, keep me in the dark. Besides, what I wanted to talk to you about kind of concerns Bishop."

"Why would anything concern him?"

"I'm married to him and I'm sleeping with his dad."

Bear scrunched up his face. "No, no. I don't need to hear that shit. You're still my little girl. You don't even know what sex is all about."

She winced. "Sorry. I guess I wasn't delicate enough for you." She still had to feel that connection with Bear. The one that made her really believe he was her father.

"Delicate enough? Try not at all. Wow, you do know I need time and space to build into that kind of chaos. I'm now going to be thinking about killing Preacher. Not a thought I need when we've got church."

"You go to church? How come you didn't invite me?"

"It's special for the club. It doesn't concern you."

"Oh, how charming."

"I don't mean it like that."

"Exactly how do you mean it?" she asked.

"Can we move on?"

"Did you know about Preacher and me before I … you know, came back?"

"I knew about you on the night you were taken. Up until that point, I figured you'd both developed a friendship, which was expected. You were always close, especially with … you know."

"The baby?"

"Have you remembered this or is this Preacher trying to cut out the middleman?" he asked.

"I don't remember, but Preacher did tell me some things. Not a lot, but some."

"Can we move on? Preacher and I, we have an

agreement, and I don't want to go and kill him."

"What kind of agreement?"

"You want to cause a fight?"

"No, I'm just, me and my curious mind is all."

"If you must know, he's agreed to keep it clean. I don't have to witness you making out, or post-fucking or pre-fucking. It works for us. I don't want to think of the two of you together. Let's move on. What is all of this about Bishop?"

"I'm sure it doesn't come as a shock that I really don't want to be married to him anymore."

"Oh."

"And I don't know how to go about finding the right paperwork or anything, but I want to annul the marriage. Unless we did it before?" She was a little dark on all the details and no one was forthcoming with how she went about becoming her own person. It felt right to end things once and for all with Bishop. They didn't have anything real, so she didn't see a reason to prolong their relationship.

"I'm going to have to talk with Preacher about this," he said. "Why didn't you ask him?"

"It didn't come up and I figured if you were there to give me away, you would be able to help me along the way. Don't you think?" She didn't know what other options she had, only that these were the ones open to her.

"Are you sure you're ready for this?" he asked.

"Yes, I don't see any other reason why I'm married to one man but falling for another. It's time to end things and to move on as best as I can."

"You're falling for him?" Bear asked.

"I ... I ... is it too soon?"

"I know you and Preacher were close before you were taken. I mean, obviously I never saw you both kissing or doing anything like that, but when I did see you together as friends, it worked, for the both of you."

"Do you think I was in love with him?" she asked.

"You had feelings for him, deep feelings. It must have been to piss off Bishop."

"Does he hate being in Preacher's shadow?"

Bear sighed. "Sweetheart, believe it or not, you'd be the best person to know that information. You and Bishop were always tight."

"Do you think I can do this, though? Get my marriage annulled? I don't know if Bishop and I were ever together. It doesn't feel like we ever were, but again, I really don't know the answer to that. I'm babbling."

Bear rubbed the back of his head, turned away with a wince. "I know Bishop was with a lot of other women even when you were together. I guess you can end the marriage and if that doesn't work, divorce his cheating ass."

She smiled. "Has there been any sign of him?"

"No. He's not exactly welcome right now at the club."

"Why?"

"I can't tell you."

"Club stuff?"

"You got it."

"So, let's talk about something else. How about you? Have you met anyone yet?"

"You want to know if I'm dating someone? Me? At my age?"

"You're the same age as Preacher. Why not? Love doesn't stop."

"Honey, I don't believe in love."

"You never felt anything for my mom?"

"Nothing. Not even a shred of happiness with

her." He shrugged. "Again, let's move on from this as well."

"We keep bouncing around topics."

"It's easier this way."

She didn't know what else to say. It wasn't an awkward silence, but they didn't talk about anything important. They settled on easy conversation about their days and their plans. Nothing too taxing on the mind.

Chapter Ten

Her time with Reaper

"I can't believe you made me do that," Robin said. The pain in her back radiated, making the burn even more intense.

She lifted her shirt to try to keep it away from the tattoo on the base of her back. The ones around her wrists were as equally painful, but she didn't want to look at them. This one on her back was a brand, an ownership.

Reaper had taken all the decisions away from her. Being held down, it made her feel sick.

"It's going to look good. Trick is fucking hot and believe me, you're going to thank me one day." He put his hands on her hips.

She shook her head. "There's no way I'm going to thank you for this." She tried to pull out of his arms but he was determined to hold on to her. "Let me go."

"Not yet. I don't like you being pissed at me."

"Then maybe you shouldn't hold a woman down and permanently mark her body. That would be a good start in not getting me pissed off." She wanted some space. "I need some time alone." She pulled out of his arms and left the hotel room. This one had a pool and rather than go outside, she went to the pool. There was possibly a chance of her sneaking away, but right now, with the ink across the base of her back, she didn't want Preacher to see her like this.

When she got to the indoor pool, there were only a few people swimming around. Two sets of adults were making out, and another couple was swimming. She took her shoes off, sitting at the edge of the pool, staring into the bright depths below.

The pain was still there and she felt the tears

close to the surface. All she wanted to do was cry, but instead, she held her tears in and just stared ahead.

Within minutes, several of Reaper's men entered the pool room and moved all the people out.

"What's going on?" she asked.

Reaper entered the room and his men left.

She was alone with him. He removed his shirt.

"What are you doing?"

"I'm going to go for a swim."

She watched as he removed his boots, followed by his jeans, before he dived into the pool. He was all heavily inked muscles and strength.

Reaper came right toward her and she stayed perfectly still. He wrapped his fingers around her ankle, pressing a kiss to her flesh.

"You didn't have to remove all the people for a swim. Normal people share things."

"In case you didn't notice, I don't share well at all."

"You've taken me as some kind of revenge plot. I don't even know what you want with me, why you would even want me." She shook her head. "You know what, there is no point in even talking about this because the truth is you don't want me, do you?"

His hand moved up her leg, cupping her thighs and pulling her into the water.

She let out a scream but that didn't stop him as he began to remove her clothes. She couldn't get away from him. He captured her wrist above the ink and pulled her close. "I shouldn't be getting this wet!" She wanted to do anything to piss him off.

"It's all bandaged up and you'll be fine."

"You're a doctor now?"

"I'll talk to Trick. He handles everything."

"Even death. For all I know, that's what you

want. Ugh! I want to hit you right now."

"Then do it. Hit me. It will make you feel better to hit me."

"No. I'm not going to be angry at everything like you are. I'm not going to hit you." She tried to pull away again but he simply held her. "I don't like being used as revenge."

"Would you believe me if I told you I happened to like you?"

"You don't like me. You don't even know me."

"I know you were pregnant with Preacher's child. Bishop wanted you to get rid of it."

"Don't talk to me about him. He betrayed everyone, including his club."

"It's not on me, though. You have to understand that."

"I don't want to talk about this." She tried to pull away from him again, but like always, he controlled her. Gritting her teeth, she forced herself to look at him. "What do you want from me?"

"You can't tell me you're not having a good time."

"Because being taken against my will and raped is all about fun."

"I know how your body responds to me. You can't call the rape card, not anymore."

"Do you even care?" she asked. "You took what you wanted. I didn't have a choice in that. You forced me and I hated it."

He looked at her and she saw the frown on his face. It made her a little uncomfortable that he kept staring at her.

"Please, don't do what it is you're doing."

He chuckled. "I don't mean to freak you out."

"You're doing a pretty good job of it at the

moment." She wanted to look anywhere but at him.

"Okay, I know I've scared you, and I've crossed over the line of what you can deal with. How about I compromise?"

"You know the word of *compromise*? You understand it?"

He chuckled. "Believe it or not, yes, I do, and I'm going to be compromising right now. So, here is what I suggest. From now on, I won't touch you. You'll be free to say no to me. In fact, I won't have sex with you, touch you, fuck you, or have anything to do with you at all. You're free to make your own choices."

"What's the catch?" she asked.

"There's no catch. If you want to fuck me again, you tell me. You come to me."

"You're not going to let me go, are you?"

"No, I'm really not."

She nodded her head. "I guess I should accept that. Fine. Okay. Deal."

****

Present day

"I don't think I should be here," Robin said.

Preacher glanced over at her, seeing the nerves she tried to hide. "What are you afraid of?"

"Everyone. I mean, look at them. They're all scary and I've been away and all this time I haven't come back here. What if they do hate me?" she asked. "What if I don't live up to what they expect?" She nibbled her lip and he reached out, pulling her bottom lip from between her teeth.

"You're really cute when you're nervous." He looked out of his car window to see the club. It was already dark and it had been a long time since a party had happened. This one though, was special.

After nearly nine months of being at home, they

were finally celebrating her return. It felt good to be doing something positive.

He had feelers out for Reaper and now Bishop. Preacher knew his son was using Reaper to stay hidden, but it was fine. With Dog on his side, and several favors being called in, it was only a matter of time before he finally found the men responsible.

After Bishop's disappearing act, Preacher didn't doubt for even a second the little bastard had set Robin up, had taken her nearly three years ago.

"It doesn't stop the nerves. Look at everyone. They look like they're having fun. I'm going to spoil it."

"You're not going to spoil anything. Come on. This is all for you and you will see why the moment we get there."

He climbed out of the car and took her hand as she vacated the vehicle. Together, they walked hand-in-hand toward the clubhouse, only he didn't go around the back. He walked straight into the main room.

The lights were all turned off and as he cleared his voice, the lights came on and everyone screamed a *welcome home.*

Balloons, streamers, and confetti spewed forward.

"Oh, wow," she said.

Her hand gripped his tightly and for the first time since planning her coming-home party, he had to wonder if he'd made a mistake. Randall had advised him about crowds and he quickly recalled how he found her at the bar. This wasn't designed to be too much for her. He expected her to be able to handle it.

"We're so glad to see you," Joanne said, rushing forward.

"Great."

Men and women all came toward them, embracing her, and for the first time, Preacher knew it was a mistake.

Bear handed him a beer and he shook his head.

"Do you have any word on Bishop?" Bear asked.

Joanne and a couple of the women took Robin and he watched her go. She looked back toward him and he smiled at her, giving her a little wave.

If looks could kill, he'd be dead.

"Not yet but we're getting close."

"Have you spoken with Myers?" he asked.

Edward Myers was the one in charge of keeping them all out of prison. He was a grumpy guy and hated the job he'd been given, but they paid him very well to do his job. He also overlooked all the legal stuff with their clubs and businesses. Whenever they needed a lawyer, he was the one to call. So far, he'd never failed them.

"He's getting the necessary paperwork. However, he warned me Bishop needs to be alive to sign them."

"Oh, dear."

"Yeah."

"Then what are you going with? Making her a widow?" Bear asked.

Preacher didn't say anything. He looked over the party and it no longer felt right to him. He'd fucked up big and he was going to have to make it up to her.

"I hate to be the party pooper here," Bear said.

"You're going to, anyway. May as well get it done," Preacher said, drinking his beer.

"Fine. He's your son, Preacher. I know I've only had a girl and you and Bishop have had your difficulties. He's still your boy."

"Your point being?" He wasn't stupid. He simply didn't want to have to answer any more questions.

"Will you kill him?"

Preacher turned to his friend. He and Bear had

always been close.

"I love Robin, but I don't think even if she was to turn rat, I don't think I could kill her. She's my flesh and blood."

Preacher nodded. "I understand that, but that's why I'm president and you're VP. I can do what no one else does."

"You'd kill Bishop?" Bear asked.

"He's a rat. He turned Robin over to our enemies. That's the kind of shit you never forgive or forget. He'll pay for what he's done. Robin, if she wants an annulment, she'll get it. She's been through enough."

"What if she wants Bishop to live?"

"Then I'll make sure she gets something else. Bishop will die." He couldn't see Robin anymore and he didn't like it.

Bear grabbed his arm as he attempted to go find her, stopping him from moving. "You know, I'm really getting tempted to break your hand," he said.

"What would you do if Robin's a rat? Would you kill her?"

Preacher turned to look at Bear. "That would never happen."

He wasn't about to answer Bear. There was no reason for him to find an answer.

As he left his friend, he made his way through the main part of the club, but there was no sign of Robin. He spotted several of the club pussy. They were on the arms of his men but still nothing of his woman.

He left the clubhouse, looking outside and finding nothing. Next, he made his way back inside, stopping Grave. "You seen Robin?"

"She went to the bathroom."

He nodded his thanks and went toward the bathroom. There was no one outside and he walked in.

The bathroom was clean and he made a note to give the club cleaner a pay rise. He'd used the bathrooms a couple of times and his boys were not the cleanest.

He heard the unmistakable sound of sniffling.

"Robin, baby?" he asked.

"It's okay. I'll be right out." Her voice was croaky.

He leaned up against the sink, arms folded, waiting. Fuck, he had a bad feeling. Running a hand down his face, he tried to clear his thoughts.

"You're still here, aren't you?"

"I'm not leaving."

"I want you to leave."

"Are you pissed at me?"

"No. I don't even know if I can get pissed at you."

He laughed. "Of course, you can. It's a rite of passage. Every girlfriend has a right to be mad at their boyfriend."

"You're my boyfriend?"

Preacher hesitated. "I guess I am. You're mine and I'm yours. I've never had a girlfriend before."

"But, Bishop…?"

"I was never dating his mother. I never liked her. She was a fucking rat."

"I don't know what that means."

"It means something," he said. "You don't ever have to worry. Do you want to tell me why you've locked yourself in the bathroom, crying? I can't hold you. I can't help you."

"I don't need any help. I just need a few minutes."

"Okay."

He waited.

"You still haven't left, have you?"

"Sorry, baby girl. I'm not leaving."

"I don't know what to do," she said. "Everyone is so nice and they are all acting like they know me and I don't have a clue who they are." She sniffled. "I'm sorry. It's not worth crying over."

"It clearly is, otherwise, you wouldn't be."

"It's fine."

"No, it's not." He sighed. "Look, if it makes you feel any better, then it's all lies."

"What's all lies?"

"The way they're being. The only person you were ever really close to was Bishop." He wasn't about to tell her about Milly. There was no reason for her to remember a woman who wanted to destroy her. "You were rarely at the clubhouse, but this is your home. I want you to feel like you've got more than Bear and me."

The door unlocked and she pulled it open. "It's not just me then?"

"No. They're my club. They're doing what I asked them to and that is to help you feel part of us again."

"I really appreciate it but it's a little much. I ... I thought I didn't remember them. That I messed up."

He reached out, taking hold of her hands and pulling her close. "You don't have the power to mess up."

"Did they know we were together?" she asked.

"No. You were gone before we had a chance to announce it. Would you like to go out there, let them know who you belong to?"

She shook her head. "No. I think I'd like to go to bed. I feel really tired."

"Would you like me to join you?"

"Only if you're not busy? You know, this is your club. Do you have club stuff to do?"

"Nah, nothing is more important to me than you. Come on, I'll take you upstairs."

"We're not going home?"

"This is your home." He kissed her head. It didn't matter how many times he told her though, she would always feel like an outsider until she remembered. There were times he didn't know if he really wanted her to remember. Some of those memories were not ones he wanted her to have. Especially the one where she lost the baby as even now, it plagued him.

Without another word, he led her toward the staircase, taking her up to his room. As they passed Bishop's room, she paused.

He hadn't gotten around to giving the order for the room to be cleaned out so all of Bishop's things were still inside.

"What is it?" he asked.

"I don't know." She shook her head. "I guess I just … this room?"

"It's Bishop's. Would you like to go inside?" he asked.

"No, not tonight. I'm really tired. I'm sorry. You must think I'm being a huge drama queen."

"Not at all." He kissed her head. He didn't want her to feel worried or fearful. There were moments she would stop and look at something and he had to wonder if her mind was fighting to be free. If the Robin of two years ago was there beneath the surface, just waiting for the right trigger to come out.

Randall said it didn't always work like that. Robin could remain this way for the rest of her life.

Preacher loved her, but he also knew in his heart, something was missing. They had each shared a pain that only he remembered right now. If given the choice, he knew she would want to know what happened.

For now, he had to constantly wait, accept her for who she was now.

They entered his room and she paused. Her hand left his as she looked into his room.

"I just got a bit of a chill."

"Are you okay?"

"Yeah, of course. I'm fine. Can I take a shower?"

He wasn't about to tell her she had one before they left the house. He'd noticed she enjoyed taking long showers of late.

"Sure, go ahead."

He sat on the edge of his bed, removing his boots as she left to go into the shower. After running fingers through his hair, he shoved his jeans down his thighs and was about to remove his shirt when his cell phone rang.

His cell didn't recognize the number but seeing as he had a great deal of contacts running around, he accepted the call. "Preacher," he said.

"So, tell me, Preacher, what's it like fucking a woman with another man's name on her back? Have you taken her from behind yet?" Reaper asked.

Preacher gripped his cell phone tighter in his fist, anger and rage mingling together, dancing within him. "You know it's easier to call someone when it's safe for you."

"You think I'm doing this for me to be safe?" Reaper laughed. "You don't know me at all."

"Oh, I know a coward when I see one, believe me. I know what kind of game and bullshit you're playing, but it's not going to wash with me. Come out, let's end this bullshit now."

"And why the fuck would I even dream of doing that?" he asked. "It will be so much fun messing with your head. How about this? Have you asked her about her time with me yet?"

"You know she doesn't remember anything."

"Oh, that's right. Now you have to ask yourself this, Preacher, what are you going to do when she does remember?"

"I'm going to give her all the help she needs to deal with what you did to her."

Reaper laughed even harder and louder. "You really do assume the worst of me, don't you?"

"I know the kind of monster you are."

"And you're claiming not to be one?" Reaper asked.

"I know who you are because I'm exactly the same. There's no difference between the two of us."

"Ah, so pleased you agree with me. Preacher, you're so determined to think she ran *from* me. What will you do when you find out she was running *to* me?"

Before Preacher could ask him anymore, he hung up.

Reaper was messing with his head and he couldn't allow him to get there. Whatever happened between Reaper and Robin, it was in the past.

Pulling his shirt over his head, he entered his small en-suite bathroom. He'd made the decision early into acquiring this land and building to have his own bathroom. There was no way he was going to be sharing bathrooms with his men.

He had certain … standards.

Robin stood beneath the spray, her head bowed.

Opening the stall, he climbed inside.

She gasped, turning around. "Preacher."

He didn't say anything. Cupping the back of her neck, he pulled her close and slammed his lips down on hers. He felt her naked body pressed against his.

The ink on her back meant nothing. Whatever bullshit Reaper was trying to do, he wouldn't win. This woman was his.

She wrapped her arms around him, and he slid his hand down her back, cupping her ass, drawing her close. He wouldn't allow Reaper to get into his head, not now. Robin was with him, in his arms, and he wasn't going to allow anyone to take her from him.

"I love you, Robin."

She pulled away from him, but he wouldn't let her put too much distance.

"You love me?"

"Yes. I will never stop looking for you. I love you more than anything in the world. I never got a chance to tell you before, but I need you to know now. You own me. Body, heart, mind, and soul. I belong to you, forever, for all eternity."

He saw her eyes were red and he didn't know if that was from his confession or from her crying before.

"I don't expect you to tell me you feel the same. There's a lot you need to work out and to know. I get it, but know this. I love you more than anything in the world. You are my life and I will be with you always."

"I … I think I love you as well."

He took possession of her lips. The old Robin loved him. The new Robin would as well. He would show her.

Pushing her up against the shower, he lifted her, and she wrapped her legs around him, moaning his name. He teased her pussy, finding her already wet but not wet enough for him. Sliding his fingers through her wet slit, he stroked inside her, adding a second then a third finger, spreading her wide.

"Do you like that?" he asked.

"Yes, please. Don't stop."

"Seeing you all this time and not being able to have you, do you know how much it tortured me?"

"Please," she said.

He knew she didn't understand the feelings he had. They were currently not the same. Not even by a long shot. She only knew what she felt for him, and for now, he had to work with that, hoping the old Robin would remember.

Preacher continued to stroke her pussy, watching her slowly come apart. Seeing the pleasure in her eyes as she gave herself to him. This was how it was supposed to be between them.

He loved her more than anything in the world. He'd die for her. There was no woman he'd ever cared so much about, but Robin, she was different. She'd gotten beneath his skin and there was no way he could get rid of her. He never wanted to. There was nothing he wouldn't do for her.

She came, screaming his name, and even as the last remnants of her orgasm consumed her body, he stopped, gripping his cock, placing the tip against her entrance, and slowly pushing into her pulsing cunt.

He felt her continue to orgasm as he started to rock inside her.

Robin held on to him tighter and he gripped her ass, pushing inside, wishing and hoping for her to remember as he continued to fuck her, taking her harder than ever before.

Staring into her eyes, he felt her deep into his soul. There was nothing he wouldn't do for this woman. She owned him, and all he had to do was be patient for her to come back to him. It didn't matter that he didn't want her to remember everything. She had to remember everything, even if he didn't want her to.

When she came a second time, he held off his own release, watching her, waiting for the moment of truth to consume her.

Nothing happened. Nothing changed.

He spilled his release inside her, holding her close. "Fuck, I love you," he said.

She let out a little giggle. "I love you as well."

She kissed his neck, but deep down, Preacher knew it wasn't enough. Robin still belonged to him. She was still all his, but there was a part of her missing, and until he found that part, he would never be free.

Not ever.

****

The following morning, Robin left Preacher alone in bed. She pulled on a pair of jeans and one of his old shirts and went in search of the kitchen.

She had this overwhelming need for pancakes and coffee.

Closing the door, she made her way downstairs only to come to a stop outside of Bishop's room. There was something about the door and the feeling twisting in her gut that made her want to go through the door.

She stepped close but stopped, rubbing at her temple. The pressure intensified.

Would she remember anything if she went through there?

She put her hand on the door, about to press forward, but she held back. Her stomach growled and anything important like this had to be done on a full stomach. She didn't know if that was true, but at this time, she didn't care. She walked to the kitchen only to find her father already there.

A steaming cup of coffee was in front of him on the table but he had his head in his hands, looking all stressed.

"Rough night?" she asked.

"You could say that." He didn't look up and she walked over to the coffee maker and poured herself a cup.

It was strange to her to know how she liked her coffee and even what kind of food she preferred, but nothing else from her life.

The connections she'd made.

Strange.

With her coffee black and one sugar, she went to the table, taking a seat beside her dad. "Are you okay?"

"Yeah, I'm fine."

"Did you drink a whole lot?"

"I didn't touch a drop."

"Oh. Do you have a problem?"

"I thought I did, which is why I went through a quick program but no, I don't. I just don't want to drink. It's complicated."

"Okay. It's not like I don't understand complicated. I mean, look at me. I remember how I take my coffee but I don't remember my mom or Bishop. Getting married or being pregnant. There's a lot of complications in my life."

Bear sighed. "I'm not trying to keep you out or exclude you."

"I know. I get it, Dad. You've got … your reasons and I respect them." She reached out, taking his hand. "I just wanted you to know that I do understand."

"I drank when you were gone to numb the guilt I felt."

"Why did you feel guilty?"

"I didn't know a lot about what was happening in your life. You never got to tell me about Preacher and yourself. I had to hear about it after. I know you were sad about the loss of your baby but … again, I didn't know how much you wanted to be pregnant. I spent so much time wrapped up in my own shit, I didn't give a fuck about what was going on outside, and I should have."

"You can't hold yourself responsible for every little detail that goes on in my life."

He laughed. "Forgive me, sweetheart, for saying this, but you don't know what the hell went on."

"I know but I'm here now."

"You're only partly here. You're not completely here." Bear held her hand even tighter. This time, he tried to comfort her. "You think I don't see how nervous being here makes you? This is your home. You didn't spend a lot of time here growing up and if you did, you were always in Bishop's room, but you were safe here, for the most part. Fuck, I don't even know what I'm trying to say."

"You're trying to say that even though she belongs here and is safe, she doesn't know it. She's part of our life again, but the old Robin, she's not sitting here drinking her coffee with one sugar. She's gone," Preacher said.

She turned toward the door to find Preacher leaning against it. He wasn't wearing a shirt, just a pair of jeans.

"Watching you drool over my president is gross," Bear said.

She couldn't stop herself from laughing.

Preacher flexed his arm, showing off his muscles.

Bear made a gagging sound while Robin admired the man she'd left in bed.

"You should have woken me," Preacher said, coming toward her. He kissed the top of her head, and she closed her eyes, leaning back and basking in his love and touch.

"I was only coming down for some coffee. It's all good, I promise."

"Don't worry, Preach, I've been keeping my daughter company, telling her about all the things that are wrong with me."

"That's what I worry about."

She smiled. Sipping at her coffee, she didn't mind the heat as it slid down her throat.

"So, what's happening today?" she asked.

"You want some pancakes?" Preacher asked.

"I'd love some."

"I'll take some with chocolate chips and syrup," Bear said. "Damn, I haven't had your cooking in so long. You need to bring my daughter around more often."

"Yeah, because that is so not weird," she said.

"It's not. Believe me," Bear said.

She finished her coffee, getting up to pour herself a second cup as Bear excused himself to go to the bathroom. When they were alone, Preacher pulled her close. He stopped mixing up the batter to talk to her. "Are you okay?"

"Yeah, I'm fine."

"I don't like you leaving me alone in bed."

"Sorry, I didn't mean anything by it. I promise. I was just coming down to have a drink. That's all."

He tilted her head back. "You're sure?"

"Yeah, of course. Why would I lie?" she asked.

"I ... I want to make sure you're feeling okay. If you're ever worried or sad, I need you to tell me. To talk to me."

"I will. I promise."

"Did you go into Bishop's room?" he asked.

"That's a subject change. No, I didn't."

"Why not?"

"I don't know. What does it matter?"

"Because I'm curious about, you know, you, everything. All of it." He stroked her cheek. "I know you and Bishop were close once. I don't know what could trigger your memory."

She thought about what her father had said. "Does it bother you?"

"Does what bother me?"

"Me not having my memory back. Do you wish I was the old Robin? Does it bother you that I don't remember us, the baby, anything?"

He sighed but didn't answer right away. It scared her a little.

What if he really loved the old Robin and she could never remember the past? Would he hate her? Would he want her to change?

There were so many questions and fears rushing through her, she didn't know who to trust.

"Don't freak out."

"I'm not freaking out."

He raised a brow. "I can tell you are."

"Okay, a little, but you tell me you wouldn't freak out a little in my situation. I'm struggling. There's a part of me I don't know. I don't know if I'm ever going to remember anything and it scares me, a lot. It freaks me out." She shook her head. "I'm sorry, I really shouldn't say anything."

"It's fine."

"No, it's not." She blew out a breath. "I honestly don't know how to feel right now."

"I love you, Robin. Yes, at times, I wish you could remember me. I know there's a lot we've been through together but then I think about the two years you were gone from my life. I don't know if they were good or bad years, and if they were bad, I don't think I want you to remember them. They were part of your life, but I don't know how you're going to react to them. I'm going to be by your side, regardless. If you remember, great, if not, I'm just pleased to have you in my world. I didn't stop looking for you, and I will never stop looking.

You're my life, my love, and I vow to protect you."

She smiled. "Thank you."

"Does this mean once the annulment comes in you're going to make an honest woman out of my daughter?" Bear asked, coming back in.

She groaned. "Seriously?"

"Yes," Preacher said, startling her. "I'll make an honest woman out of her."

As far as marriage proposals went, she didn't have any comparison, and she found it rather sweet.

****

"I can't go back there," Bishop said.

His hands shook and fear gripped him. In all his twenty years, he'd never been afraid of his father.

Preacher hadn't been the best kind of dad, but he'd never been mean. Sure, there had been a couple of beatings through the years when he'd done something wrong, and even he knew he deserved some of the punishments. He'd never been a good kid.

Robin was always the good one.

He'd been the one who liked to find danger and play with it. It often meant Robin ended up hurt, but he hadn't cared enough to stop. All he ever wanted to do was have some fun, no matter the cost.

"You're not staying with me," Reaper said.

His men were all sitting around the room, waiting, each of them prepared to do what their leader said.

"Please," Bishop said. "I don't know how he knows, but he does. I don't…"

"Have you spoken to Robin?"

"No. Not since I took her out to the bar. You wanted to see her, and you saw her, didn't you?" Bishop asked.

"In case you didn't fucking know, I wasn't there

when she had her little panic attack. What I did hear was how you were mean to her," Reaper said. "You were yelling at her."

"No, I just wanted her to get inside so you'd be able to see her. I followed your rules. I've helped you every single step of the way and now you're telling me you're done with me?" Bishop glared at the man before him. There was no way for him to take him out without getting caught in the crossfire. "Do you have any idea what kind of men my dad has tracking me down?"

Reaper burst out laughing. "You think I don't know? I've been dealing with his men for over two years. I still avoid them. Believe me, they're not worth worrying about."

"For you, but I need help."

"No, you need to go back to town."

"Don't you fucking listen? Preacher knows I gave you Robin two years ago. He knows I've been helping you. I can't go back there. I'm his son, but he loves her."

"Does it bother you to know he does? To know even now without her memory she still can't stand for you to touch her?"

Bishop swung without even thinking. Reaper grabbed his arm, twisting it. With a single tug, it would snap in two. "Now, now, why do you have to go with all the violence?" Reaper asked. "I don't recall hurting you. I've accepted you into my home, I've listened to your concerns, and now you're going to try to piss me off. Do you have a death wish, boy? Is that what you're trying to ask me for? You want me to kill you? Is that it?"

"No!" He cried out as Reaper grabbed his hair.

"I didn't hear you."

"No, I don't want you to kill me. Please, don't hurt me."

Reaper sighed. "I do love the sound of begging. It

has a certain level of … enjoyment. I've helped you as much as I'm willing. I suggest you learn how to deal with your father on your own."

"I could give up your location," Bishop said.

He didn't know why he didn't just keep his big mouth shut, especially as Reaper simply laughed.

"Sure. Tell Preacher where I'm hanging out. You think we're going to be here long once you're gone? I can make it so you're leading him on a merry dance, and believe me, it will be a lot of fun. Just remember, one day soon, Robin will remember everything and when she does, you're going to have to look that girl in the eye. I never did allow her to hurt you. I do wonder, will she still fight for her friend, or will you be first on her kill list?"

Reaper let him go, throwing him to the ground. "Get out before I throw you out."

Bishop got to his feet, wanting to argue, to do anything that would make Reaper see reason, but there was nothing. He was alone. No one willing to help him. It was all his fault.

Turning on his heel, he fled, hoping no one was watching him.

There was no way he'd be able to hide from his father. Preacher was a hunter, and right now, he was his target, unless he was somehow able to get to Robin, to convince her to keep him alive.

****

"You're going to keep him alive?" one of his men asked.

Reaper didn't respond. He stared down at the last picture he had of her. One Bishop had been able to take, but it was blurred.

Robin was on the back of Preacher's bike. She wasn't supposed to be there, but right now, there was no way for him to stop it.

Tearing up the image, which he'd printed out a few weeks ago, he turned toward the fire and let the flames lick up the picture. "I don't need to kill him. Besides, when Robin remembers, I'm going to allow him to be her first kill."

After all, he'd been the one to promise her Bishop's head, and all she had to do was make the final decision on if he lived or died.

Chapter Eleven

Her time with Reaper

Robin expected Reaper to have lied.

For the next month, she kept on waiting for him to either break his promise or to do something scary like rape her again. Only, he didn't do anything. He made sure she was safe from his men. Not once did they make inappropriate comments her way or try to grab her. Reaper had put the fear into them, and they kept their distance, for which she was thankful.

Each night, she'd sit with Reaper around the fire he'd built, or in a hotel room, wherever they stayed, depending on what they did. Rarely did they enjoy a quiet night in front of the television. She didn't know what was worse. Sitting near the fire while he was laughing and joking with his friends, or sitting together watching movies.

Of course, she never went to him for sex or for anything. There was no reason to. She heard the women they brought back with them.

One night, she heard a lot of laughing and partying after she had gone to bed. Reaper had yet to return and as she pulled back the curtain to look outside, she saw the men having sex with the woman.

The woman in question was loving it. She was smiling, riding one man, as she worked two others with her hands.

She looked, trying to catch sight of Reaper but not seeing him.

Where could he be?

She … didn't like waiting around for him to come to bed, especially if he'd been drinking. It often made her worried he'd attack her, like some men could do.

She wasn't going to think of Preacher because he

didn't attack her, not really. He'd been drunk that first time they were together.

Shaking the doubt from her mind, she sat down on the edge of the bed. The knot in her stomach tightened even more. She couldn't handle the thought of not knowing where he was, and so, she quickly pulled up a pair of jeans and a shirt. She left her hotel room and looked out toward the crowd. No one paid her any special attention.

Ignoring them, she quickly walked around toward the back of the hotel.

This hotel didn't have a lot of clientele and so the owner had given them the reins of the place. Reaper had paid him a great deal of money to leave for the next couple of days. She wouldn't give herself the luxury of thinking they were sticking around for longer than that.

Tucking her hair behind her ear, she saw Reaper sitting beside an empty pool. The owner had said they didn't fill it because it cost too much to keep clean.

What made her pause wasn't that Reaper on his own, but he was alone, with a book. A small light was perched on the table beside him, and she saw he'd pulled it from one of the hotel rooms with an extension cord.

She smiled.

"You do realize you could have run and no one would have been the wiser until morning," Reaper said, startling her. He hadn't even looked up.

"How did you know it was me?"

"I've got a sixth sense for these kinds of things." He pressed down the corner page of the book, and she winced.

"You could get a bookmark."

"Bookmarks fall out."

"Yeah, well, that's not exactly a good way of treating a book."

"Are we really going to talk about how I treat a book to know where I last read, or are we going to talk about why you're standing here talking to me and not running?" he asked.

"I don't want to talk about any of that."

"Right," he said. He put the book down, leaning back in his sun lounger and watching at her. He looked so calm and relaxed.

"How come you're not enjoying the party?" she asked. "All of the guys are, and the women."

Reaper smiled. "Do I detect a hint of jealousy?"

"Why would I be jealous? I've got nothing to be jealous about." She gritted her teeth, hating how she sounded.

Was she lying?

Even to herself?

Was she jealous?

It made no sense.

What did she have to be jealous about?

Reaper breathed in. "I don't know. You're a smart woman, Robin. I'll let you figure it out."

"You're talking in riddles, and you're doing it on purpose. Stop it."

His smile widened. "You want me to be blunt, I can be blunt. You have the perfect opportunity to run. You know from past experiences, I don't hurt you, not anymore. I simply bring you back and chain you up until you know the score. Tonight, you had the opportunity to run. I even gave you a chance to. Instead, my men are partying. Fucking that woman from one orgasm into another. She's probably lapping up the attention and is loving having each of those men. You come here. You come to find me, and you can't even accept the reason why."

"It doesn't matter," she said. She went to turn

away from him and to go back to the hotel room.

"You were jealous because you thought I was enjoying her."

She heard the lounger move and she turned to look at him. He'd gotten to his feet, and her heart started to race as he advanced toward her.

"You thought because I'm no longer taking you, against your will, I'll add that little detail so you don't feel so bad. You thought I'd be with this woman."

"I should go."

"Scared, Robin?" he asked.

"I don't know what it is you want from me."

"I want you to acknowledge that you may hate me, but a part of you, a part of you wants my touch."

She shook her head. "You took me, remember? You forced me here."

"That's right. I did. But tell me now, Robin, why aren't you running?"

She took a step back, hating how … right he seemed to be. "I can't leave."

"Not now. Not with me here and knowing I could have given you the idea." Reaper sighed. "It's okay."

"Did you want to?"

"What?"

"Be with that woman? Did you want to be with her?"

Reaper didn't answer right away.

"You know what, I don't want to know." She held her hands up and took a couple of steps back. She hadn't been watching where she was going, and she was near the edge of the open pool.

She let out a cry as the ground suddenly left her. She expected the pain of hitting the bottom of the deep, empty pool, only the pain never came. Reaper had grabbed her and pulled her close.

"No," he said.

"What?"

"No, I didn't want to be with that woman. Why would I want to be with her when I had a perfectly good woman waiting for me back in my room?"

She frowned. Her heart raced. She could have seriously injured herself, or worse, died.

"I don't know what you're saying. We don't do anything. I'm not giving you sex. How could you want to come back to the room with me?"

"Have you ever thought that there are times I just want to hold you?" he asked.

"You're a monster." She was more confused now than ever before.

"Am I? Well, I wonder how much of a monster you think I am when you wake up in my arms each morning. All these people, they want one thing. You're kidding yourself if you don't see the lust in their eyes, burning for each other. It doesn't make them monsters, Robin. It makes them people. Fucking, taking, begging for it. It's not wrong to want it. It's not wrong to want me, and I know you do. You don't think I feel a difference within you?"

He pressed a kiss to her head. "You're tired. Come on."

She didn't put up a fight as he walked her back to their hotel room.

Why hadn't she run?

It had been a long time since she'd even given running a thought. What was happening to her?

Preacher, she had to remember who she was trying to return for.

She took off her clothes and climbed into bed. Reaper did the same, and even though the room was in a blanket of darkness, she saw him. The outline of his body as he walked around the room.

The party was still going strong.

The bed dipped as Reaper joined her.

In her head, she counted.

One.

Two.

Three.

Four.

Five.

His arms wrapped around her.

She didn't try to fight him. Closing her eyes, she felt his warmth seep into her flesh, and a deep calm settled over her. There was no way she could believe for even a second that she missed him. That she couldn't sleep without him.

It wasn't possible.

Falling for her captor wasn't going to happen. There was only one man she wanted, and it was Preacher. She would return to him one day.

Until then, she had to remind herself that Reaper was a monster. He didn't get to take her heart, and he certainly wouldn't ever get her acceptance or her begging for him.

****

Present day

"No!"

"No?"

"You heard me. No."

"Are you kidding me right now?" Robin asked.

Preacher sipped at his scolding coffee, counting to ten in his head as he looked across the kitchen at his woman.

"Am I kidding you? Let's see … no."

"You can't be the boss of me."

"I know what's good for you. I can do whatever

the hell I want."

"You're so frustrating." Robin threw her hands up in the air.

She looked cute when she was annoyed. "Frustrating or not, it's not going to happen."

"Why not?" She put her cup in the sink. "I mean, what exactly am I doing all day? I can't go to high school because I'm twenty years old and that is so not happening. I sit around all day, going crazy. I've got to do something."

"Then go shopping? Go to the spa. Or whatever it is you women do."

"Do I look like a spa girl?"

"You wouldn't even know what kind of girl you used to be."

She glared at him, and he liked to see the fire in her eyes. Randall had told him anything could trigger her memory, and right now, he hoped something sparked. He loved Robin more than anything, but the more time he spent with her, the more he missed the woman who knew him.

He shared a great deal of his life with her, his art, his family. He'd given a part of himself to this Robin. He wouldn't have even dreamed of telling her past self. The problem was her past self knew a great deal of loss and pain, and they shared in that.

It was one of the many reasons that drew them together, and why his son got so pissed because of how close they had become.

"You know that's not fair."

Preacher cursed as he saw the tears in Robin's eyes. She looked away from him, storming out of the kitchen.

Of course, him trying to trigger her memory could also result in her hating him, which he hoped to avoid, but it seemed he had a knack for doing it anyway. Preacher followed her out of the kitchen. She was making her way toward the stairs and he caught her arm.

She pulled out of his touch, folding her arms across her chest and closing him off. "Okay, I know I was an asshole and I can see that now."

"You only know it now?" she asked.

"That was … insensitive. I'm sorry."

She pressed her lips together and wouldn't look at him. He hated this silence more than anything else. "Robin?"

"It's fine. It's what you feel, and I've got to learn to respect what you feel, right? No matter how I feel about it."

This wasn't what he expected and now, he felt like a fucking asshole even more. He knew he could be one, but when it came to Robin, he'd always been more than patient. She'd been through a lot. "I just don't believe you need to go out and get any kind of work."

She shook her head. "I'm not asking your permission."

"Yeah, you are, and I'm not granting it."

"Preacher, I'm not a child. You can't keep treating me like one. I'm certainly not your child."

She ran fingers through her hair and he watched her pull away from him and start to pace up and down the kitchen.

This wasn't the topic of conversation.

"It's only for a couple of hours a day at the library. I need something to fill my day."

"What about shopping?"

"Seriously?"

"Women like to shop."

"And was this something I did prior to being lost?"

"I … no…"

"Then what makes you think I want to shop now?"

"I don't know. You'll be free to do it."

"Why are you so against me having a job?" she asked. "I thought about this long and hard. I would be surrounded by books all day long. I won't have to worry about many fights. It means I can do something about my day, which means I'm not sitting around thinking about everything I haven't done and can't remember. Do you know how hard it is to know there are eighteen years of my life I don't remember? I can spell, count, and remember everything else but any personal little details, it's all gone."

"I know."

"I want to do something with my day besides sitting around. Is that too much to ask? You know what, I'm not asking you, Preacher. I'm telling you. I've already taken the job at the library, and you're not going to stop me."

She took a step toward him, the steel in her gaze clear. She wouldn't budge on this, and he didn't want to force her to give up something she loved. "Is it really that important to you?"

"Yes."

"Then consider me giving you permission."

She chuckled. "I told you I wasn't taking your permission."

"It has been given regardless." He pushed some of her hair off her shoulder. He was already thinking of the men he could put on her protection detail without her even knowing it was happening. "I've never dated a librarian."

"According to you, you've never dated. Unless you count me, of course?"

"Yeah, this is you." He leaned down, brushing his lips across hers. "You gave me this information because you've got to work today, when you know I'm heading out of town."

"Maybe. I'm heading over to see my dad later tonight. We're going to have dinner. Did we always have dinner?"

"You were close with Bear, but not this close. Not dinner close. He spent a lot of time at the club."

"Ah, I see." She ran her hands down his leather cut. "I'm going to miss you."

"I'm going to miss you too. In fact, I'm missing you already." He tilted her chin back and stared into her eyes. "You don't have to work, you know that?"

"I can't go to school."

"You still need to graduate."

She shrugged. "I don't know if I want to."

"This is confusing. Graduating is part of who you are."

"And ... I don't know."

"What's really bothering you when it comes to graduating?" he asked. "I know that look. There's something else on your mind."

"There's a lot I can't remember and I guess I'm worried that I won't remember everything from before." She stepped back. "If graduating is really important to me, I want to have the best kind of chance and the only way to do that is to, you know, remember everything."

"What if you don't?"

"Then I guess I'll never graduate. Is that a problem?"

"You're an intelligent woman. You could pass anything."

"Thank you for your vote of confidence. It means a lot, but I won't budge on this. I'm going to be stubborn." She nodded her head. "Now, shouldn't you be leaving?"

"I'm heading out, but how about I drop you off at the library?"

"Only if you promise not to go inside and threaten everyone with my safety. I want people to like me while I work, not be afraid of my boyfriend."

"It still feels weird, you calling me that."

"You're my boyfriend?"

"Pretty much."

"I don't know. I kind of like it. You're much older than me." She ran her hands back up his chest.

It was these little moments that caught him off guard. The old Robin wouldn't have been so forward with him. He liked it, but when she got her memory back, would these moments be gone?

Pushing those thoughts to the back of his mind, he grabbed her bag and left his home. He locked the door, pocketing the keys.

She wasn't coming back here until he returned and even though Bear was his VP, he was staying home to keep her in check, which was more than fine with him. The last thing he needed right now was to be worrying about where she was staying or who was seeing her.

Climbing onto his bike, he waited for her to straddle the machine. He revved the engine and took off, gunning toward the library. She wrapped her arms around him and held on tightly.

Fuck, he missed this.

He'd never gotten much of a chance to show her how much fun riding could be, but having her now, he didn't want to stop.

At the sign for town, he was tempted to veer off, to take her for a long, hard ride. She wouldn't see it as him wanting to spend time with her though, which was all he wanted to do. If work was what she needed, he'd gladly give it to her. Okay, not gladly, but reluctantly. He didn't want her stressing out or worrying about anything unnecessarily. If she wanted a job, he'd make sure one of his men gave the library a message to keep her happy. He'd even pay for her to work there if he had to. He'd do whatever it took to make her life easier.

Arriving outside of the library, Robin climbed off the bike and held her hand out for her bag. "Thank you," she said.

He caught her hand before she could leave. "If you are worried about anything—"

"I know. Call you or one of the guys. I got it. Please, stop worrying. I'm the one who should be warning you. You're the one heading out into the great unknown."

He laughed. "I'm going to do some business, hardly the same thing."

"The secret kind of business."

"Club business."

"Still secret." She stroked his cheek. "I'll miss you."

"I'll be back before you know it." He pulled her close, gripping her ass and not wanting to let her go. Riding away from her was always the hardest part, but he and Dog had some business down at one of the docks, and he was bringing the strength while Dog came with the savage.

She pulled away and he watched her walk into the library.

Taking out his cell phone, he arranged for Cheeky and Grind to keep an eye on her. Next, he also gave an order for Billy to also keep an ear out. With Bishop around, he had no doubt his traitorous son would try to pay her a visit. All he needed to do was make sure she was safe, and that one of his men was available to keep an eye on her.

With the instructions complete, he took off, wanting more than anything to stay close.

He joined the rest of his crew. Frost, Grave, Simple, Rider, and a few others were in the back waiting for him. Bear was staying behind as were a couple more to keep an eye on club business.

The prospects were never allowed to join in on the fun.

Taking the lead, he headed toward the location where Dog said he and his crew would be waiting to go to the docks. They arrived an hour later at an abandoned hotel. Dog was waiting with six large vans. He was pacing as Preacher approached.

"I didn't think you were coming," Dog said, holding out his hand.

He shook the offered hand and nodded. "Just had to take care of some business."

"Anything you need help with?"

"Nothing important." He wasn't going to talk about his woman with Dog. This was private and not business. "What's the deal?"

"The last shipment of product has been down. I spoke to my suppliers and they have all the documentation to state they packed everything."

"They could be lying," Preacher said. "It's not the first time."

"Yeah, and I've heard the crew at the docks have sticky fingers. They're taking my coke before I can distribute it. They're mixing it with some toxic shit and it's killing kids," Dog said. "I got contacts to say they're also selling it for double the price and all of this bullshit will come down on me."

"That's a lot of information."

"I've got a lot of nice friends who are willing to give me their information," Dog said. "The deal is we go down in force. These are your docks as well. United, we'll deal with this problem. If someone is stealing from us, then my gut is telling me whoever wants it is willing to pay a decent price. They're doing it on purpose."

"Then lead the way. I'll follow," Preacher said. He walked back to his bike.

"When did you become good pals with Dog?" Grave asked.

"Is that any of your business?"

"Men talk, Preacher. We've all accepted your obsession when it comes to Robin, but there's a whole lot of us pissed off with how you handle business with Dog. From the fights and now this."

"And who exactly has an issue?" Preacher asked. He stepped up to Grave.

"I guess we'll find out come church time." Grave stepped away.

Preacher was aware of his men's lack of encouragement when it came to his dealings, but with what they were about to face, his men would understand why he was keeping Dog as an ally and not as an enemy.

He wasn't afraid of Dog. The man was as vicious as they came, but what benefitted him with this friendship was having him on his side. They all had enemies and Preacher wasn't a fool to think he could take them all on. Look what happened with Bishop. He'd been so concerned with finding Robin, he hadn't given himself time to think of his son's betrayal.

It had been obvious, though. He simply hadn't seen it. There were a lot of mistakes he'd made with his son and with Robin. He wouldn't repeat them, and he certainly wouldn't make himself weak, even if it meant forming an alliance with Dog.

TAKEN BY A MONSTER

****

Working at the library was fun. Robin enjoyed it.

First, for the most part, it was quiet, which she liked. The quiet always made her feel at peace. Then of course there was being surrounded by books. She didn't need a rocket scientist to tell her she felt at one with all the books. They were everywhere and helped her to feel calm and ready to face anything and everything.

Her first day went by way too fast, and by four o'clock, it was time for her to leave. She knew she would be asking for more hours, as the thought of spending the next two hours by herself didn't appeal right now.

She'd told her father she was finishing at six.

Yes, a small lie, but she needed the peace, wanted it even. Only now, being on her own, she had to wonder how wise it actually was. Not because she was afraid or anything. Being alone wasn't a problem. She didn't mind it, in fact.

No, it was the complete lack of memories. The knowledge people were waiting for her to figure out the life she once had. A life she could no longer remember.

Grabbing her bag, she made her way out of the library and went straight toward the diner where she'd ordered herself a burrito to go. She was hungry and it was the first thing that came to mind. She paid for the food and headed out to walk down the long stretch of the street. There were several shops. One for clothing, another offering fabric, each one seeming to offer a special something or a trinket. None of the shops sparked anything within her.

She came to a stop near a park. It was quite busy and she watched the children playing, feeling a yearning within her, but again, she didn't know why. Everything was always a little unclear to her.

Shaking her head, she finished her burrito and

came to a stop near a church.

There was a cemetery off to the side.

Did she like going to church?

Staring up at the large, imposing building, again, she felt nothing. Rather than head back to the library, she walked into the cemetery. Some of the dates on the stones were old, and as she moved around, she saw some with recent dates.

Walking up and down the paths, she tried to find her mother's, only she came to the end without finding her. She returned and followed the same path.

Nothing. No sign of her parent.

She hadn't seen a picture of Rebecca. Only the name of her mother, but there was no marker on any of the stones to say where her mother's final resting place was.

This … unsettled her.

Checking the time, she saw she only had twenty minutes to head back to the library. Picking up her pace, she ran back to the library and was relieved to see no sign of her father. He hadn't arrived yet.

There were three benches nearby, two of which already had people waiting. The third was empty and she took a seat to wait. It was here Randall found her.

"I didn't expect to see you here," Randall said.

"I'm waiting for my dad." She checked the time. "Who is ten minutes late."

"I'd give him a call. If I know your dad, then I know he's forgotten or hasn't looked at the time recently."

"Oh, right." She searched in her bag for her cell phone. When she found it, she quickly sent her dad a text. Preacher had given her the phone in case of emergencies, but she didn't use it, not all the time. In fact, that was her very first text message.

"You can call him."

"It's okay." She tucked some hair behind her ear.

"How have you been?"

"I've been good."

"The foot?"

"It's doing okay. I mean, every now and then I'm in pain and I can't wear heels yet." She had tried, but to no avail. The pain wasn't worth wearing them.

"And your hand?"

She held her hand out and gave it a stretch. "It's still attached."

Randall laughed. "Yes, it's looking good. What brings you out here?"

"I'm working." She told him about the job at the library.

"Preacher allowed that?"

"As I told him, I wasn't asking for permission. He wanted me to take up shopping. I don't even know if I like shopping."

"That sounds like him. All he wants is for you to do something to make you happy."

"I don't know what makes me happy anymore. I'm sorry, I shouldn't unload on you like this."

"It's fine."

"Is it, really? I don't think it is. Forget about it."

"Robin, you've had a lot going on in your life. No one will blame you for trying to make the best kind of go of it as possible. Even I wouldn't."

"Half of the time, I don't know what I'm doing," she said. "Then of course I think I'm going crazy."

"Talk to me about these moments."

She chuckled. "Are you a shrink now as well?"

"No, I'm your doctor and you haven't been by to see me in some time. I know this can be quite difficult for you."

"I don't know. I think it's easier if I just try to forget about them."

"Try me. There can't be anything wrong with sharing your worries and concerns now, can there?"

"I don't know, it seems kind of pointless to me."

"The only pointlessness about all of this is if you're not willing to give it a try," he said. "I may not be able to help you, but what's the harm in finding out?"

She released a breath, running her fingers through her hair. "Okay, you're right. You're totally right. I can't say specifically when it happens, but it's like I hear a voice. A man's voice. Someone I know. It's not Preacher or my dad, or even Bishop's. It's another man's voice."

"Does it make you afraid?"

"No. In fact, it makes me feel like I've got to remember. Like there's something I'm missing and it's really important for me to know what it is and why."

"And if you don't remember?" Randall asked.

"Then I'm missing something vital. I don't know. It doesn't make any sense." She put a hand to her stomach. "I get a twisting in my gut and this need to know my past. All of it. At the same time, I don't know if I can even handle whatever it is that's out there, you know?" She nibbled her lip. "I'm so confused about everything, and none of it makes any sense."

"I don't know what kind of life you had while you were gone, but it sounds like your past life is trying to make you remember."

"How do I speed it up?" she asked.

"These things you can't speed up. All you can hope to do is wait."

This didn't help. "I don't think I have much time."

"Robin, what do you think will happen if you don't remember soon?" Randall asked.

She opened her mouth and closed it. "I don't know." She looked past Randall's shoulder to see her father running toward them. She had never been so thankful to see him before. "That's my dad. I better go to him."

"Robin, it's going to be okay."

"I wish I believed you." She also wished she hadn't told him. "Please, don't say anything to Preacher. I don't want him to worry. He's got enough on his plate without throwing my troubles his way."

"He cares about you."

"I know and I care about him, but there are some things he doesn't need to know. This is one of them." She left Randall and met her father.

"I'm so sorry. I was in the garage working on my bike. I had the music on loud and I lost track of time."

"It's all good."

"You're sure? I saw Randall. Do you still go to see him?"

"He was passing by. We talked. It's all fine." She didn't want to talk anymore. She'd spoken enough.

"How about I order us some pizza?" he asked.

"I'd like that."

They walked to the pizza place. She let her father order her some food, and once they had their order, they walked back to his truck. She rested the boxed pizzas on her lap and waited.

They rode in silence and she thought about what Randall said. Would he tell Preacher about her conversation with him?

She honestly didn't know. She knew he was good friends with Preacher as well. They had a trust.

"You're quiet," Bear said.

"It's nothing."

"How was work?"

"Fine. I enjoyed it. I want to do more."

"I was thinking I could get in touch with the principal if you'd like. Find your old records and you could finish off your exams. You know, graduate."

"I told Preacher I would wait until all my memories returned. I don't know how much I remember from my high school days." She seemed to be repeating herself today. "I went to the cemetery today," she said.

"You did?"

"I was waiting for you. I got a little bored and so I went for a walk. There's no stone with mom's name on it. Where did you bury her?" she asked.

"You sure had a lot of spare time on your hands to go to the cemetery."

"I finished early. I was wondering why Mom wasn't there."

She stared at her dad and he didn't answer right away.

They arrived at home, and she went straight to the dining room. Opening up the pizza box, she grabbed a large slice and took a bite.

"I can't tell you what happened to your mom," Bear said.

"Why not?"

"There's a lot you don't know."

She frowned. "You're not making any sense."

"Your mother ... she's gone and she's not coming back. You'll never find her body, and there's no way of you ever ... knowing where she is. Ever."

"But if she's dead then that means there's a body somewhere."

Bear sat down and took a slice of pizza.

"This is club business, Robin. When Preacher's ready for you to know, you'll know. Don't ask anyone about your mother. As far as anyone is concerned, she skipped town and never returned."

The knot tightened in her stomach as she stared at her father. A part of her wanted to be horrified by what she knew he wasn't saying, but another part, she knew, she got it. She accepted it. That wasn't normal.

Gritting her teeth, she tried not to think about everything she didn't know. "So ... what you're saying is, I can't talk about it, not to anyone?" she asked.

"No."

"That doesn't exactly seem fair."

"I know it's not fair, but that's just the way it is. There's nothing we can do. You're going to have to accept it."

She nodded. "Have you heard from Preacher?" she asked, wanting to change the subject.

"Yes. He was the one who called me and I saw the message on my phone to come and pick you up."

Silence fell between them.

She finished a second slice but now she'd lost her appetite and just wanted to go to bed, to do something other than sit with her father.

"I really need to have a shower. I'm kind of tired."

"Robin," Bear said. "I'm sorry."

"It's fine."

"No, I need ... I'm sorry," he said again.

"I know. I'm going to go and have a shower." She gripped his shoulder, trying to offer him comfort.

Leaving him alone, she headed up to her room, removing her clothes after she closed the door. The silence was peaceful.

Once she was naked, she walked into the bathroom and stared at her reflection. The ink on her body was another mystery. Turning to the side, she tried to look at the possessive ink across the base of her back.

What did it mean?

Shaking her head, she tried to clear the fog from her mind, but no matter what she did, it didn't work. There was nothing there. Her mind was a constant blank. Turning on the shower, she let out a little gasp as the cold seeped into her skin. She closed her eyes, tilting her head back and letting the water run across her body.

In the back of her mind, she felt another time. Another body. A man? He was larger than her.

His arms coming around her.

When she opened her eyes, the sensation was gone. There was no fear and she quickly closed them again, wanting the memory to stick.

The arms, they didn't feel scary.

Were they Preacher's?

She couldn't see clearly. There were no distinguishing marks. Just the feeling.

She wasn't afraid, but … content. Those arms, they didn't do any harm. When his lips brushed across her neck, it felt right.

Pressing her palm against the tile, she opened her eyes. Her body was on fire with need, but the image in her head didn't disappear. The man, whoever he was, he had to be real.

None of it made any sense to her. She was slowly and surely losing her mind.

Chapter Twelve

Her time with Reaper

Jealousy?

There was no way she could be jealous.

Robin took a bite of her pancake and stared across the table. All the men were gathered around several tables. Reaper was beside her, his large, muscular body imposing. She couldn't not look at him. Out of the corner of her eye, she watched him, waiting for him to lose control or to do something that scared the crap out of her.

He lifted his coffee cup and took a large sip.

Not scary.

She finished off her pancakes and then drank her tea. The food settled heavy in her stomach and she didn't want to think about what his words meant.

"Damn, you should have seen the way she was riding my cock. She was a pro. I wanted to keep her but let's face it, bitches like that, they don't exactly stick around for long," one of the men said.

She hadn't learned any of their names. Other than Reaper, she wasn't allowed to stay near any of the men. They were always there, guarding, watching, but never getting too close.

"Enough," Reaper said.

The men looked toward Reaper and she saw the tensions rising. No one spoke.

"Can I use the bathroom?" she asked.

"Yes."

She pushed her chair away and went toward one of the bathrooms. She didn't need to use it but there was no way she could sit around the table. Running the water, she splashed some on her face, trying to cool herself down.

"I'm not jealous." She looked at her reflection and came to a stop when she saw the window over one of the toilets.

It couldn't be that easy.

None of the men had gone to see the bathrooms. It was also a busy little diner. So many faces had come and gone in the short space of time she'd been eating. Would it be so hard to … escape?

Jealous.

No, she wasn't jealous of Reaper. He had gotten it all wrong. The only reason she hadn't tried to escape before was because of how pointless it was. There was nothing keeping her with Reaper.

She wanted to get home to Preacher. She loved him, missed him. She had a great many dreams about him, and he was the only person she cared about. The only person she wanted to be with.

After opening the stall, she put the lid down on the toilet and lifted herself up. She shimmied out of the window. The drop to the ground wasn't too steep and before she could question herself, she dropped right out, wincing as her body hit the ground.

"Ouch! Bad move, Robin. Really bad move." She would totally be feeling that all day long.

Getting to her feet, she didn't know what the hell to do now. If she ran, it wouldn't take Reaper long to realize she was gone. Without even thinking, she took off, heading in the direction they'd come. Reaper wouldn't think to go back, would he?

She had no way of contacting Preacher. If she could find a phone and remember his number, or even the station's number, it would all work, right?

What if O'Klaren was still there?

She didn't stop to think. She kept on going. Running.

In the distance, she heard the bikes and freaked out, heading into the thick forest, knowing she couldn't stay there.

Bears or coyotes could be lurking.

She heard a bike pass and she leaned up against a tree, closing her eyes as the bike came to a stop.

"Robin, I know you're out there," Reaper said. "I gave you just enough time to make a run for it, but you and I both know spending the night in the woods isn't on your to-do list."

She cringed as she heard a twig snap.

This was the first time she had run in so long. The last time, he'd hurt her badly.

Suddenly, running didn't seem like such a good idea.

Tears filled her eyes, and she wanted the ground to open up and swallow her whole. This couldn't be happening.

"I won't hurt you," Reaper said.

"You're lying." She slapped a hand over her mouth. Why did she have to talk? She had just given away her fucking position. She didn't hear Reaper stepping forward though. "It's what you do. You hurt me."

"Is that what you want me to do? Hurt you?"

"I don't like pain. I want to go home."

"You're not going home. It's the one thing I won't be giving you and you know that. You've got to learn to accept it."

Silence.

She didn't trust him.

"You will have to hurt me because of your men."

"I've told them to carry on to our next stop. They don't know you ran."

"I went to the bathroom and didn't come out."

"You think I don't know what you were going to try to do? I'd already spotted the open window in the bathroom."

This made her frown. "How?"

"I check every stop we make. I always look for an escape route for you. After the other night, you don't think I knew you were going to try to run?" Reaper asked. "You're quite predictable."

She didn't respond, resting her head against the tree. His voice gave away the fact he was getting closer and because of that, there was no point in running.

Opening her eyes, she watched as he rounded the tree. She didn't know what she was expecting, maybe his anger or rage, but instead, she got a nice smile.

"Hello, beautiful," he said.

"You're not angry."

"Why would I be angry? Oh, you think I'm pissed because you tried to run?"

"This wasn't a try. I did run."

"There was a pay phone across the street, Robin. You could have called for help."

She hadn't seen the pay phone. "I didn't have any money."

Reaper laughed. "You're still going to keep on dodging the truth, I see. Okay, fine, I can handle it."

"I don't want to talk about this anymore," she said. "Whatever you think is happening here, you're mistaken."

"We'll see." He reached out, taking a strand of her hair.

She held her breath as he circled the curl around his finger. He didn't hurt her. There was no tugging or fighting. He twirled her hair around and then let it go. "I wonder what Preacher will think of our new ink."

"You forced me. He won't think anything of it."

"You play the hard and tough woman, but we both know that's not the case."

"You seem to think entirely differently to everyone else," she said. "There's no way I will ever have feelings for you, Reaper. What you're doing isn't going to make me fall in love with you. You're delusional. You think I'm just going to forget the way you've treated me?"

Why don't you shut up before he hurts you? Do you want another black eye? Broken bones? Bruises?

"I want you to think about the woman last night."

"Why?"

"I was the one who brought her to the club. I make sure all my men are taken care of. I approached her, asked her if she wanted a good time. I know I'm a pretty face and it didn't take a lot to convince her to come back and play. Even while we were driving back, she was coming onto me. Wanting to suck my dick in the car."

"Why are you telling me this?" she asked.

"The woman was like a bitch in heat. I could have asked her for anything. Her mouth, her ass, her pussy. She would've given it to me, but I didn't touch her. I had no reason to. The men took one look at her and they wanted her."

"But you didn't."

"Nope. Now tell me what it feels like to know there was a woman who wanted me. Who craved my touch more than anything."

"I don't want to do this."

Reaper laughed. "You know, I used to think you were a strong woman, but now I see you're weak."

"I'm not weak. I'm still standing here, aren't I? I tried to get away from you. I wanted to be free."

"And you could have been, but you took the hard

way out. Come on, Robin, admit it. You were jealous of the thought of me taking comfort in that woman. You like me and you hate yourself for it."

"I don't know what it is you think you know, but believe me, it has nothing to do with me." She glared at him. "Do your worst."

He sighed. "You still think I'm going to hit you."

"Why not? You've done it before." Part of her wanted him to hit her. If he raised his fist at her, she could be free of any possible feeling. He was merely a monster.

She stared at him, waiting.

He didn't raise his fist.

Gritting her teeth, she waited.

His hand came up but there was no pain. He stroked her cheek with the back of his fingers and smiled at her.

"There's nothing I would ever do to hurt you, Robin. I made my mistakes with you and I won't make them again." He leaned down and brushed his lips across hers. "I can't tell you how sorry I am for being an asshole to you. I can only promise you from now and for the rest of my life that I will never hurt you."

The tears she'd tried to keep at bay fell. "Why are you doing this to me?"

"I'm not doing anything."

"You know you're doing this on purpose. You're making it hard for me to hate you."

"I made a lot of mistakes."

"This is all lies." She sniffled.

Reaper pulled her into his arms and she squeezed her eyes closed, not wanting to believe him.

There was no way he cared about her. He'd taken her. No matter what words he said, they were lies. This was all part of his revenge plot, and she was merely a bargaining chip. There was nothing else she could do to make him see reason. She was his prisoner.

Reaper didn't let her go. He held her until the tears subsided, and together they walked back to his bike. She didn't talk to him. Words weren't important to her right now. Nor would they ever be.

He's a monster.

He took me against my will, forced me, hurt me, and even though he's acting all changed, he's not.

Remember the monster.

Don't forget Preacher.

There is a life you want.

Never ... ever ... forget.

****

Present day

Preacher jerked awake at the sound of Robin's gasp. He didn't have time to stop her as she hurtled out of bed and ran.

He quickly followed her, not caring about his naked state. The pain in his ribs took a direct hit but he ignored it. The raid the other night with Dog didn't go according to plan. The men at the docks were stealing from them, but they'd also been made aware of exactly what was going on. They were expecting them.

Rather than a nice quick capture and torture, it had ended in a gunfight, and a lot of punches were thrown. For his troubles, he got a nice direct hit to his ribs. Nothing was broken and according to Randall, he'd be feeling better in no time. So far, he called bullshit, but then it had only been a couple of days.

Reaper was the one responsible for the docks, he just knew it. The men who had taken his dope didn't have a name for the man who paid them, but in his gut, he knew Reaper was close.

What he didn't know was why his enemy was

lurking in the background but refusing to come out and play. Instead, he was making bad deals. The kind to draw attention to himself, but why?

From his experience with Reaper, the man had a reason for everything. What Preacher needed to do was be one step ahead of the game. So far, he'd been too distracted by Robin. If he didn't get inside Reaper's head soon, he had a horrible feeling it was going to come and bite him in the ass.

Rushing downstairs, he found Robin, completely naked, trying to get out the door. Wrapping his arms around her waist, he tried to pull her back.

"Get off me. I have to go. I have … I have to … I'm needed … she needs me."

"Who needs you?" he asked.

She didn't answer. Her heart raced.

She pushed him away but he was by far stronger than her. Anything she tried to do to get away from him, he was easily able to stop.

She growled at him, begging for him to let her go.

He refused.

She didn't like him holding her, and she kept mumbling about being needed. It was like she was caught up in a nightmare. One that only she could see.

Finally, when she gave up and collapsed to the ground, he still held her. She panted and sobbed but didn't try to fight him.

"I've got you," he said.

He'd repeat the words over and over until she realized she was safe. He was with her and he wasn't going to let her go. Kissing her temple, he continued to hold her, not letting go.

"What is happening to me?" she asked.

"I don't know. Do you know what set this off?"

"A dream. I think it was a dream, but it felt so

real."

"You kept mentioning *she*. What she? Your mom? Someone you remember?"

"I don't know." She curled up in a ball. "Please, Preacher, hold me."

He held her even tighter. "Don't worry. I've got you. You're safe now."

"What if someone's still out there? What if another woman was taken? Do you think that's who I'm remembering?"

"I honestly don't know." He kissed the top of her head. "Talk to me. Tell me how you're feeling."

He needed to know what he was up against. Her past was a complete mystery to the both of them, and there was no getting away from it, no matter how much she tried to fight it. "Can we move?" she asked.

"Sure." He lifted her off the floor and carried her through to the living room. After placing her on the sofa, he wrapped a blanket around her. "I'm going to go make us some hot chocolate."

"Okay."

"You're fine if I leave you alone?"

"Yeah, I'll be fine. I promise."

She offered him a smile but he wasn't convinced.

"I'll be back." Once he was in the kitchen, he heated up some milk. His hands were shaking. Nerves were getting to him.

He'd never seen her like this and it scared him. When the milk was hot, he added in the melted chocolate, which he'd poured out from a bag of chocolate chips. Giving them a stir, he added some sugar before pouring out the mugs.

Walking back into the living room, he found her huddled under the blanket.

"You're naked."

"So are you." He handed her the chocolate and took the seat beside her. Sipping at the scolding liquid, he waited.

"I'm so sorry."

"You don't need to apologize. Honestly, I'm fine."

"It's late and I woke you up acting like a crazy person. I don't even know what went wrong." She sipped at her drink. "This is nice."

"I'd rather be with you than have you suffer alone. Do you know what you were thinking? Feeling?"

"I … it's like I'm missing something or someone. Like I'm needed. It's important for me to remember. I … I wasn't afraid. I wanted to go back." She shook her head. "It makes absolutely no sense at all."

He heard her sniffle. "What's wrong?" he asked.

"I want to remember, Preacher. I'm tired of being this no one." She swiped at the tears. "Do you have any idea what it's like? I'm nothing." She laughed. "Did my dad tell you I went to the cemetery while you were gone?"

"Why?"

"To see my mom."

"Oh," he said. Bear hadn't gotten around to telling him that little detail.

"Yeah, I know. There's so much I don't know. I feel like I'm lost all the time. People smile or avoid me. It's like there's this black cloud everyone else knows and I don't get to have access to it. It sucks, big time." She rubbed at her temple. "I'm sorry."

"Stop apologizing."

"I can't help it. You deserve someone who isn't broken."

He took the cup from her hands and held them, forcing her to look at him. "You're not broken."

"Preacher, I don't even remember our first time. That nursery upstairs means nothing to me. I walk around lost. You look at me and you know me. I don't know you. There's so much I don't understand."

"I love you," he said. "That's all I know. Our life wasn't simple and easy. There are moments I wish I could join you in not knowing. You want to remember. I can tell you there's no peace in knowing what I do." He stroked her cheek. "I'm so glad you're here with me. Knowing or not, I wouldn't trade you for the world. You're everything."

"Really?"

"Yes, and you can't doubt me, not ever. I know what I'm talking about."

She laughed, wrapping her arms around him. "I love you too."

He held on to her words. They weren't heartfelt, but he hoped one day, they would be.

"When it comes to your mother, forget about her, okay? Trust in me and your father to know we're doing the right thing."

She held on to him tightly as he pulled her in for a hug. "Thank you. Please, Preacher, don't ever let me go."

"Not a chance." He'd waited far too long for her. There was nothing that would make him leave.

****

Robin placed the latest science book on the shelf. She looked at her cart and saw next was space.

Putting books back in place at the library was a calming process. Right now, she needed calm in her life. Between the bad dreams and her upcoming birthday, her nerves were shot.

Her hands shook without any reason at all. She didn't know what was going on with her. Every little detail of her life seemed to make her crack.

With the cart empty, she walked back to the front desk and served two children who were patiently waiting.

Once their books were scanned, she watched them leave. A yearning twisted inside her. Kids and babies seemed to do that to her, and she couldn't help but wonder if it had something to do with the nursery. Whenever Preacher left, and she had a short time to herself, which wasn't often, she'd go and sit in the nursery, staring at his artwork.

The chair was unfamiliar. The room itself didn't speak to her in any way.

One of the stuffed unicorn toys still had the tags on, and she'd sit in the chair, holding the unicorn, begging to know what was going to happen.

"You seem quieter than usual," Anne said.

Anne was a middle-aged woman with three kids in school. She worked full-time at the library. From the rumors Robin had been hearing, her husband was having an affair with one of the other parents, but no one told Anne that.

"Sorry, just got a lot on my mind."

"Anything you wish to share?" Anne asked. "You know, the whole a problem shared."

Robin chuckled. "Yeah, I remember that." She was starting to feel increasingly bitter about what she did know. She released a breath.

Anne held her hands up. "Sorry, I didn't mean to pry."

"It's fine. You know, just … trying to figure everything out."

"You're way too young to attempt to figure anything out."

"Do … never mind."

"What is it?" Anne asked. "We're having a bit of

a lull in here and I could use the distraction from them over there who think it's okay to talk about my husband's affair."

Robin's mouth dropped open. She looked from Anne to the women who spent a great deal of time gossiping.

"You think I didn't know?"

"I don't know what to think."

Anne shrugged. "My and my husband's life is private. I don't need people poking fun at my expense. Let me see if I can help you."

"It's not a lot. I was wondering if you knew me … before."

"If I knew you before you were kidnapped?"

"Yes, if that is what I was."

"Rumor has it you were taken against your will. So I guess, kidnapped."

"Right, of course." She was starting to get a headache.

"I'm older than you, so we weren't exactly friends or anything. You were a good kid, considering your parents, or should I say your mother."

"You knew my mother?"

"I knew a great deal of your mother. Rebecca wasn't a nice woman. She certainly wasn't the mothering kind. The fact you turned out nice was a miracle. I never thought you should have spent all that time hanging out with the Bishop kid. He was always bad news, and you could have done so much better."

"Bishop, right?"

"You and Bishop never seemed together. I mean, you must have been for you to be pregnant with his kid and married."

This was certainly an information overload.

"When I heard you lost the baby, I wanted to

come and visit you, but it didn't seem right. We were never close."

"Thank you, anyway."

"You don't remember any of this?"

"A complete blank. It's nice to know I was a good person at least."

"You really were."

Robin tucked her hair behind her ear, feeling a little uncomfortable. "Can I ask you something?"

"Sure."

"Why do you stay with him?" Robin asked. "I know it's completely impolite, me saying anything but, I just had to wonder why you put up with him if he cheats on you."

Anne nibbled her lip. "It makes no sense, does it?"

"I don't mean to upset you."

"I'm not upset. My husband … what can I say? I haven't loved him in so long." She shrugged. "There's not a whole lot of reasons I can give, really. This isn't the first time he's cheated, and it won't be the last. I no longer even care for his excuses."

"But you're still with him. Do you love him?"

"When I married him, I did, not anymore. I stay with him for the kids. We're a family and it's tough." Anne held her hands up. "What can I do?"

"Do you … see other people?"

"Me? No."

"Why not?" Robin asked. "Ugh, forget I asked anything. It doesn't matter. It's your life and I shouldn't be talking like that."

Anne laughed. "It hasn't come up. No one has asked me and I guess I don't like the idea of stepping out on my husband. It's complicated."

Robin was going to ask her another question but

they were both pulled away as the gossiping women wanted attention, as did a couple of kids.

With new returns being added to the cart, Robin was on return duty. She had no problem walking all around the library, returning books. It meant she didn't have to talk.

Hearing Anne's story, it did make her wonder though.

Bear had been lonely and he was only a few years older than Anne. Maybe it wouldn't be so bad to bring the two people together. There was no opportunity to ask for the rest of the day, but she made a note to talk to her father.

By the end of the day, she was tried and there was no sign of Bear or her father, so she started to walk through town, toward her home. She came to the park and stopped again to watch the kids. They were all having fun, playing on swings.

"You know, that used to be us," Bishop said, coming to her side.

"Bishop," she said.

She hadn't seen him since the disaster at the bar. Preacher wanted him, she didn't know for what, but seeing him now, a part of her knew it wasn't good.

"Hello, Robin," Bishop said.

He looked a mess. Pale, gaunt, dirty.

"What are you doing here?"

He laughed. "Because my dad is after me, you mean? I'm sure he's been alerted to my presence. To be honest, I don't even know why he hasn't caught me. Clearly, I'm not that important."

"Don't say stuff like that."

"Why not? It's the truth. When it comes to my dad, I've never been important. I've always been Preacher's boy. I'm not a problem for him. I'm not a huge priority. Not like Reaper."

"Reaper?"

"Ah, you know him? Has your memory come back? It seems only assholes and monsters get a taste of you, isn't it, Robin? I wasn't mean enough to you, was I?" he asked.

"I don't know what you're talking about."

"I could have been good to you. One day, you're going to remember and you're going to regret everything." He glared at her. "See you around."

He spoke in riddles but before she could say anything, Bishop took off at the unmistakable sound of a bike heading in their direction.

What the hell was that about?

****

"I've told you everything. He was speaking in riddles."

Preacher watched Robin. She looked nervous, but he didn't think she was lying.

Bear sat beside her.

He'd gotten the call from Cheeky about sighting Bishop. Preacher had told him not to let him out of his sight, but his son was long gone by the time he got there. He should've let Cheeky grab him, but he'd been dealing with issues forming within the club.

Grave had decided he was abusing his power as the president of the club and wanted to vote on his ability to continue to lead.

In all the years he'd been president of the Twisted Monsters MC, he'd never had a member believe he wasn't capable. Knowing the doubt was there pissed him off, and his anger consumed every single part of his body.

"Why are you treating me like I've done something wrong?" Robin asked.

"You were at the park?"

"Yes. I'd finished work and went to the park because no one was there to pick me up. Why is that such a shock to everyone? I don't know what the hell is going on with any of this." She got to her feet. "Can I go for a shower now?"

"Go," Preacher said.

"Her attitude is getting worse."

"She's angry. She's confused. We're pushing her too hard."

"What do you think Bishop's playing?" Bear asked. "He's your son. You know him better than me."

Preacher laughed. "Yeah, the irony is, Robin knows him better than anyone. She would always be able to get inside his head and know what he'd do. I only know he fucked around, lacked responsibility, and was pissed at me for taking his girl." He sat down at the table. "I don't have time for this shit."

"You're going to fight Grave?"

"I'm going to put him in the ground if I have to."

"Do you think he has a point?"

"Are you taking Grave's side now?" Preacher asked.

Bear ran a hand over his face. "You're distracted. All you can think about is Robin and Reaper, and I don't blame you. I've seen the ink at the base of her back. I've heard everything you've told me. I get the fear you don't want to talk about. Between Dog, Reaper, Bishop, and favors, you've been spreading the boys thin. You're not being Preacher. You're not balancing shit out. The boys have a right to be concerned."

"Are you?"

"No, I know when you need to make the tough decisions, you'll do exactly that. You kill, you fuck, and you make things good again. It's what you do. Right now, they only see you getting screwed and in doing so, they're being screwed. I've got to see it from their side as well."

Preacher looked at one of his oldest friends. There was a time he'd have put Grave in the ground for even hinting at a vote to overthrow him. The club belonged to him.

The only way they were ever going to get rid of him was to put him in the ground.

He didn't fucking want that.

Bear looked toward the door. "The club is your life, Preacher. I get it. I even understand it. You think I don't know that myself? But … I've got to consider my girl. I can't have you dying on me. Not yet."

Preacher laughed. "You want me to schedule my death for you? Would it make you feel better?"

"Don't be a dick."

"She needs you, Preacher. Regardless of what the ink and all of your feelings are saying."

"Oh, you think because I have a hunch she fell in love with Reaper, I shouldn't be pissed?" Preacher said, finally voicing one of his concerns.

Bear winced. "You're going to have to work on your tact. Right now, you sound pissed."

"I am pissed. Reaper's winning and there's no way in hell that son of a bitch gets one over on me. Not now. Not ever. Twisted Monsters is mine. Grave wants to try and take that from me, he can be my guest, but believe me, I won't go without a fight." Preacher got to his feet. "You good to keep an eye on her?"

"She's my kid. Of course I am."

"Good."

"What are you going to do?"

"I'm going to go and pay a man a visit."

Preacher left his home. He got on his bike and

took off, heading toward his clubhouse. The ride didn't appease the monster in his bones. He knew he'd been a bad president to the boys.

Shit needed to be done and rather than consider them, he'd just done what he felt was necessary, without a single care to anyone else. He acted selfishly, and that was just the way he'd always been.

Parking his bike, he saw several of the club men standing around a fire burning inside a metal bin.

"Yo, Preach, what are you doing here, man?" Rider asked.

He ignored them and went straight inside.

The moment he stood in the main clubroom, he saw Grave getting his dick sucked. Stepping up to the man who would dare to question his authority, he grabbed Grave's head and slammed it against the table.

"What the fuck!"

Screams filled the air.

Music was turned off, but Preacher didn't stop in his attack.

He grabbed Grave and dragged him out of the club. The man was big but Preacher hadn't gotten where he was by being lazy.

Hell no.

Preacher always made sure he was the biggest, strongest, meanest motherfucker in the club. He wasn't the kind of guy to get lazy.

When they were outside, he let him go.

"Preacher, what the fuck?" Grave asked.

His men started to approach, but Preacher ignored it all.

"You think to have a vote to overthrow me? I don't wait for that shit. You got a problem, you deal with me now. You don't want to start squealing shit behind my back. You do it now, right here. Right now."

"You're fucking crazy."

Preacher hit him, three times.

Grave shoved him hard, but Preacher didn't move.

"You have no right to the club. You've got us playing babysitter to your little slut."

The moment Grave called Robin a slut, Preacher lost it. He grabbed the man around the throat, slamming him to the ground, choking him.

"You think you can do better than me? You can't even keep your wits about you when your dick is getting sucked. The first thing you need to know is that as president, always be prepared. No matter where your dick is, you got to be able to kill. To hunt." He didn't let him go, relishing the sounds of Grave fighting him.

Finally, he let him go, and Grave collapsed to the ground, gasping.

Drawing his foot up, he slammed it on the man's back and then took a step back. He turned, looking at all the men.

"You're right, I've been using the club to get back at Reaper. Robin is mine. She will always belong to me, but I've also been working to save our reputation. A piece of shit like Reaper took one of our kids. Don't look at this as her being my woman, or just another piece of pussy. Robin Rose Riley, that was her name. She's Bear's little girl and was taken right out from under our fucking noses. For two years she was gone. We couldn't get her, and on top of that, when she does finally come to us, she's inked and without her memory. We didn't even fucking find her. She was taken to one of the hospitals where Randall worked."

He looked at all of his men. "If you want to think this is about me being pissed because of my little girlfriend being used as a pawn, you're fucking wrong.

I'm working to repair the damage Reaper has placed on us. You think the docks is the only concern we've got?"

He waited, allowing his words to sink in. "The clubs, our businesses, everything with our patch and our mark could become a target because we look weak. You want to take me on, be my guest. Let me warn you, when I took this club on, I was all in. This club is my fucking life and I'm not going to be overthrown. You're going to have to kill me. I will be six feet under. But before you make that final decision, let me ask you…"

He gave them time, looking at each man in turn. "Can you handle what will come after me? You think you know everything this club faces, you know nothing. Take me on, and let me show you just how fucking cruel this world really is."

He knelt down toward Grave. "If you want the patch, earn it."

With that, he got to his feet and walked away.

No one followed him. No one attacked.

Grave would make his decision, and when it was done, Preacher would have a public apology from the asshole.

****

"I heard through the grapevine Bishop approached Robin," Trick said.

Reaper turned to Trick and waited for more. The ink on his chest was getting a touch-up, and a name was being added. "Bishop still lives?"

"Yes. He was gone before Preacher could get to him."

"Not like my friend to let his son slip through his fingers. He must be getting sloppy in his older years."

"Have you seen Robin? It's her birthday soon, right?" Trick asked.

Reaper looked toward his friend. He wanted to

hurt someone, but instead, he sat there as Trick did his work. "Yes, it is her birthday soon."

"Why haven't you taken her back yet?"

"None of your business. Robin will come to me when the time is right." He looked down at the ink as Trick finished up. "Perfect." Beneath Robin's name, he'd added another, Bethany.

Robin would come back to him because he held someone precious and there was no way she'd ever walk away from him. Preacher could fuck up his own messes. At the end of the day, he'd won.

Chapter Thirteen

Her time with Reaper

Robin didn't get a beating.

Much to her surprise.

No pain.

Nothing.

Just … a sense of guilt.

A month after her last attempt to run, she sat in a shopping mall surrounded by his club, waiting for Reaper to return to her.

The malls were all the same to her. The way people responded to the club's leather cuts was nothing new. Some looked on with disgust and walked in the opposite direction. Others were more intrigued and loved the sense of adventure. Whatever their poison, Robin wanted none of it.

She dropped the burger onto the paper wrapping. She felt a little sick. The constant moving around had really worn thin. She ran the back of her hand over her brow, wiping the sweat off. With every passing second, a wave of sickness kept on washing over her. Looking around the food court wasn't helping either.

Finally, after what felt like an eternity, Reaper arrived.

"Your food is cold," she said.

He sat down beside her, taking a huge bite out of his burger.

The world had started to spin. Shaking the fog from her thoughts, she looked toward Reaper, but with him eating, it wasn't helping the sickness twisting inside her gut.

"What did you do?" she asked.

"I went to get you a present."

"A present?"

"It's not my birthday."

"I can only get you a gift for your birthday? I can't treat you any other time of the year?"

"Why would you get me any other present?" The conversation made no sense.

She leaned forward, rubbing at her temples. She was going to be sick.

"You okay?"

She got to her feet. "I don't feel so good."

The world was spinning, and before she knew what was happening, the world had gone black.

****

Reaper didn't wait for one of his men to catch her.

He was on his feet, sweeping her up in his arms, and he felt how hot she was. "She's burning up. We've got to go. Pay the bill. Meet me outside." He picked Robin's dead weight up in his arms, carrying her out of the shopping mall. That very morning, she'd looked awful, but he'd put it down to her not sleeping well.

One of his men had run on ahead to get the truck. He'd ridden his bike here, but one of the guys would bring it back with them. For now, he had to get Robin back to the hotel.

Climbing into the back of the truck, he signaled for them to get him to the hotel. She was still out cold as he held her. He put his hand to her head, and it felt like it was getting hotter.

"What do you think's going on?" Pete, one of his closest men asked.

"She's sick. I don't know when she could have picked anything up."

"You don't need to be near people to pick shit up," Pete said. "This could draw attention to us."

"It's not going to do anything. Just make sure the

bikes are all back in the lot by the end of the day."

They arrived back at the hotel and he'd paid a great deal of money for the reception guy to turn the other way. He knew a lot about lying low, and there was no chance of Preacher ever fucking finding him, not unless Reaper wanted to be found.

After carrying her up to their hotel room, he kicked the door open, and Pete followed him inside.

Robin came to, mumbling about being too hot.

He had to cool her down. After carrying her through to the en-suite bathroom, he climbed into the shower. Then he turned the spray to cold, holding her close as he got into the shower with her.

"What are you doing?" Pete asked.

"I need you to go and get me a doctor. Call Trick, ask him if he knows a guy. I need someone who'll keep their mouth shut. One that isn't associated with the Twisted Monsters."

Robin couldn't keep herself upright. They both collapsed into the bath and he didn't care about the cold. He held on to her as he felt her head. In one moment, she went from boiling hot to cold.

"Fuck! Shit!" He got out of the bath and removed her clothes before carrying her through to the bedroom, trying to warm her up.

She was shivering.

Climbing into bed with her, he removed his clothes, dried his body, and tried to warm her up, but she was shaking too much.

Pete came in. "Trick is on his way with a guy he knows. Someone he says we can trust."

"Good. Get the fuck out until he arrives. Find some way to get some fucking soup up here."

"Soup?"

"Yeah, soup is supposed to be good for illness,

right?"

"How the fuck should I know?"

"Just fucking do it. Don't make me shoot you," he said. Reaper didn't know what the fuck to do and he was panicking. He'd never been sick, at least not like this.

What was he supposed to do to keep Robin warm? What was this illness? Why the fuck did he really care?

If she died, it wouldn't matter.

Would it?

She wasn't that important to him. This meant nothing.

Pete left and Reaper held a shivering Robin. She came around. "So cold."

"I've got you."

"I'm going to die."

"You're not going to die. I've got you." He wasn't ever going to let her go. She would be fine so long as he held her through the pain. The doctor, whoever he was, had better be a fucking good one. Reaper didn't know if he could handle bullshit right now.

"Isn't this what you wanted?" Her speech was slow, filled with chattering lips.

"This isn't what I wanted."

She chuckled. "We never get what we really want. You took me and now I'm going to die."

"You're not going to die."

"You don't know how I feel, and I'm going to die," she said. "It is probably best. With all the ink, Preacher wouldn't want me now anyway."

"Then he doesn't deserve you."

"You only want me because of him."

He held her even tighter. Before he could respond, she passed out again, and he cursed. "Fuck!"

It felt like hours before the doctor finally arrived and when he did, Reaper was pissed for waiting so fucking long. "Fix her."

He didn't want her to die, and he also didn't want to think about the reason why he didn't want her to die. All he wanted was for the doctor to fix her.

Climbing out of bed, he pulled on a pair of jeans and waited.

The doctor made some assessments. "She needs to go to the hospital."

"No," Reaper said. "You need to keep her alive here. Whatever life you think you have waiting for you back at home, I will take all of that away if you don't heal her."

"She's very sick. I'm suspecting hypothermia."

"Then do what you need to do. My boys and I will get what you need, but do everything you can to make her well, otherwise, I'm going to use you to practice all of my painful torture methods." Reaper stepped away and watched the man work.

He hated to see Robin so ill.

Running a hand down his face, he thought she looked close to death.

What would he do if she did die?

When he first took her, he'd intended to cut pieces off her and send them to Preacher to taunt him. He'd given up the very idea of that. Now, he ... he enjoyed her company. What the fuck was wrong with him? All of this started purely for his hatred of Preacher, and now, well, he didn't even know what to do with his feelings.

Preacher had always had a superiority complex and as the years went on, it had only gotten worse. He believed he was better than anyone else, harder, stronger, fiercer, but he wasn't anything, not to Reaper.

Look at the way he was running around like a fucking loser trying to catch him. The prick couldn't find him, and why would he? Preacher thought his reach and fear were so great but they weren't even close. He would make sure Preacher knew real pain in this life, but he was starting to believe Robin wasn't the key to do it. Not anymore.

The doctor finished his assessment. "I need these supplies," he said, handing him over a list.

Reaper looked over them and didn't understand what they were, but he knew he could read. "Keep her alive."

****

Robin opened her eyes. Everything seemed a little … slow. She lifted her hand to touch her head and even her arm ached. What was wrong with her?

"You're awake," Reaper said.

She turned her head. Reaper sat in a chair beside the bed. He got up and stepped closer to the bed.

"What happened?"

"You were sick. The doctor suspected hypothermia and there's been a bug going around. A strong one."

She closed her eyes, wincing at his talking.

"Am I speaking too loud?"

"Yeah, sorry, and a little too fast."

"I'll slow it down."

"I'm sorry," she said.

"You've got nothing to apologize for."

"For being sick. I don't remember anything." She frowned. "We were at a mall, right?"

"Yes."

"That makes some kind of sense. Who am I kidding? It makes no sense."

He chuckled. "How are you feeling?"

"Like I've been run over by a truck. I think I'll live though, right?"

"Yeah. Let me go and get the doctor." He looked reluctant to leave.

When he did, she sat up, trying to clear the fog from her brain. It didn't take long for him to return. The doctor asked her a bunch of questions and checked her pulse and blood pressure.

"You're over the worst. I recommend resting for a few more days. No strenuous activity and continue taking the course of treatment I've set until it's all gone. You were lucky. This could have taken your life."

"I'm a strong woman, Doc. It's going to take a lot to get rid of me, or for me to give up that easily," she said. Her voice sounded croaky even to herself.

Reaper saw the doctor out, and she pushed the blankets off her. She was wearing a long shirt.

"What are you trying to do?" Reaper asked, coming to her side.

"Go to the bathroom. How long was I out? Do I need to shower?"

"You've been out of it for a week and a half. Let's not worry too much about showers and all of that."

"I really need to use the bathroom." She lifted her arm and sniffed. "I don't stink. Did you shower me?"

"I've been taking care of you." He helped her to her feet.

"You have?"

"Who else do you think I'd trust with your care?"

"One of the women you steal from the streets? One of your men? I don't know. Anyone who will get the job done."

"I don't trust anyone else with your care apart from myself. This is how I make sure you're okay." He helped her into the bathroom.

"Isn't this job beneath you or something?"

Reaper laughed. "You think caring is beneath me?"

"I don't know. I don't really know you. You've taken me to hurt Preacher. What more could I expect?"

"Tell me, Robin, did you ever suspect Bishop's hatred ran so deep?"

She clenched her hands into fists at the mere mention of his name. "I don't want to talk about him."

"You know he picked the easy route, right? He picked the one he wanted."

"I know Bishop always had an issue with his dad. He hated being referred to as Preacher's son. He always wanted to be his own man."

"He was in love with you," Reaper said.

"No, Bishop was in love with himself. He believed he was entitled to me, and he didn't like it when I didn't fall completely in line with whatever it was he wanted." She sat on the toilet, looking up at Reaper. "Privacy?"

He surprised her by stepping out. "You think he was entitled to you?"

"Hell no. Not me. No, I think he believed he was entitled. I had nothing to do with that. He was always only my best friend. I ... everything we did, it wasn't what I wanted." She finished on the toilet, flushing.

She went to the sink to wash her hands as Reaper entered. "What you two did?"

"You know, sex and stuff."

"You fucked Bishop?"

"No." She cringed.

"You may as well talk. I'm not going anywhere."

"And neither am I?"

"You can do what you like so long as you know you can't leave. You're staying here."

"Wow, okay then." She picked up a toothbrush and quickly brushed her teeth. After that, she washed her face, and there was a knock at the door.

Reaper helped her return to bed before answering it.

"The food you ordered, boss."

"Thanks, Pete."

"Look, the guys are wondering when you're going to want to be heading out."

She watched Reaper. His jaw clenched.

"We'll move out when I say we're ready to."

"It's just, the guys have been worried."

"If they can't handle us staying in one place, then they should move out and not come fucking back. It's not up to me to babysit."

"What about Preacher?"

"What about him? He's not going to find us. Stop fucking talking." Reaper slammed the door closed.

She flinched at his anger but when he turned toward her, there was no anger or aggression. He looked calm and relaxed. "How about some breakfast?"

"Preacher is getting close?"

"He's nowhere near finding us."

"You haven't moved?"

"The doctor believed you wouldn't make any kind of trip. He didn't know how strong you were and so we stayed here."

"But Preacher could find us."

"There's always a risk. Tell me more about Bishop." He placed a tray in front of her, and when she lifted the lid, she found a bunch of pancakes waiting for her.

She licked her lips and breathed in the scent. They were ... amazing. "I think I'm starting to become addicted to these."

"They're one of the better addictions to have. Why don't you tell me all about Bishop?"

"You want to know every sordid little detail?"

"Why not? It'll pass the time."

"Because it's boring. Look, I don't even want to talk about Bishop, okay? I find the whole thing with him boring and tiring. I don't even want to remember him." She cringed. "Wow, even after all this time, it still shocks me the way he makes me feel."

"It does?"

"You sound surprised," she said.

"Wouldn't you be? I figured you and your little boyfriend were always so tight."

She took a bite of her pancake, feeling a little sick. "We were. We were the best of friends, but with Bishop, it was always about sex. I never slept with him and it pissed him off."

"Why didn't you sleep with him?"

"Because sex is just part and parcel of everyday life, right?" she asked.

He held his hands up. "I didn't say that."

"No, but you implied it. Sex ... I wasn't ready. I don't know why I wasn't ready. Not that it made much of a difference. I lost it when I wasn't ready."

"Preacher?"

"I'm not telling you about what went on between Preacher and me."

"But you love him?"

"Why do you want to know so badly?"

"Call me curious."

"When it comes to Preacher..." She paused, thinking of the right words to say. "I don't ... I can't ... yes, I love him. I still love him. He's always been there. With Bishop, he was always fighting his father's name, and trying to make a name for himself, but it didn't matter what he did, or how hard he worked, he would always be Preacher's son. It's how he was seen. Nothing I did or said would change that."

"Do you love Bishop?"

"You're really determined to find out who I love, don't you?" she asked.

"I'm curious."

"I love Bishop as a friend. Not as anything else. He hated me for it. When I was pregnant, he couldn't stand to know his father had what I wouldn't give him. I didn't always have feelings for Preacher, they developed."

"How did they develop?" He held his hands up. "I'm asking as a friend."

"Do you really think you can just be a friend?" she asked.

"I can be whatever you need me to be."

"Apart from taking me home, you mean?" she asked.

"Anything but that." He winked at her. "Besides, what is there not to love? You've brushed death and had some kickass fun, right?"

She rolled her eyes.

"So, tell me. How did your feelings for Preacher develop?"

"If I tell you this, you cannot use my feelings or what I share with you against Preacher."

"I won't."

She didn't know if she believed him, but seeing no other reason to argue with him, she tucked her hair behind her ear and stared down at her nearly empty plate of pancakes. "He was the only one who wasn't going to force me to give up my baby. He simply wanted me to be happy and comfortable and the only way to do that was to, you know, get to know each other. He was there at every single scan without fail. Bishop was supposed to be there, but he would always leave me. I hated to be alone. I was pregnant and I'm not going to lie, I was freaking out a whole lot. This was all new for me, and he just left, which sucked. I hated him a little for that. Okay, I hated him a lot, but you get the drill. Preacher was merely happy to be there with me. Nothing was complicated with him. I liked that."

"You liked a world without complications."

"Yeah, I guess I did."

"Eat up. You're going to need your strength."

"I don't know if I'm going to be able to get used to this. You being all caring."

"I'm sure there's a lot you can take."

****

They stayed at the same hotel for another week.

Robin got her strength back. She finished taking her medication, and as soon as she was fit to survive, they were back on the road, journeying to the next hotel, apartment, or abandoned building.

Reaper didn't care where he stopped so long as there was access to food and water. Most of the time, they kept to old roads where they passed the odd minivan but mostly truckers.

The seasons changed from winter to spring, into summer.

Her time with Reaper wasn't bad. In fact, he gave her everything he heart desired. If she wanted to read, he'd provide her books. New clothes, she'd wake up or come out of the bathroom to beautiful new outfits.

Of course, nothing she could ever keep for long. The books always stayed in one place or Reaper burned them the night before they were due to leave.

She looked over at the clock on one of the walls which held not only the time, but also the date. Staring at it now, she realized she'd been with Reaper for nearly eight months. She'd missed her birthday and she was now nineteen. It was only by a couple of days, but she was now a nineteen-year-old, yay.

Returning her gaze to the fire, she tried not to think of her feelings when it came to Reaper. They shared a bed every single night. He never drank himself into a stupor. The meals they shared, the memories they talked about. He never spent time with any of the women he brought to the men. Even now, she looked across the fire to the three women who were drinking, snorting, and enjoying the attention of all the men. They were lavishing it up.

Loving it.

"I'm going to head to bed," she said, getting to her feet.

Reaper captured her wrist. He was sitting, talking with Trick, who'd come and given him a new tattoo.

Robin had been thinking of having another, but she hadn't talked to Reaper about it.

The chains around her wrist had started to grow on her. Where she once saw them as her prison, she now saw them as something more.

"Are you okay? Do you want me to send them away?" Reaper asked, looking toward the group.

"No, not at all. I'm tired. I've got to get some sleep." She needed to create distance. Whenever her feelings for Reaper blurred, her first and only instinct was to run. It was all she knew how to do. Trying to face the harsh reality of actually having feelings for the man who took her was too much.

Stepping into their room, she went straight to the shower, removing her clothes. They were all brand-new as her old jeans had gotten torn during one of their camping nights. Sometimes when the men got tired, they would find a spot and camp out in the open. It was dangerous, but she saw the men got a high out of trying to live on the edge. For her, she didn't get any kick out of doing anything that could get her mauled by a large grizzly bear.

Stepping beneath the warm spray, she closed her eyes and let her worries melt away. There was nothing here that could hurt her. She had to remember she was in charge of her own fate.

Reaper wouldn't touch her.

She opened her eyes.

What if she wanted him to touch her?

Shaking those thoughts and feelings aside, she felt a little sick to her stomach, and she wasn't about to even acknowledge her growing feelings for a man she didn't know.

Preacher was back at home and even though he hadn't been able to find her yet, she knew deep in her heart it wouldn't take him long.

Nine months.

He's supposed to be one of the best bad guys and he can't even find me.

She clenched her hands into fists.

There was no way Preacher would ever be able to find her. Not with how Reaper moved. There was no way for him to find her. Reaper always made sure to be the last one into any hotel room.

All of this was for nothing.

She turned the shower off and climbed out of the stall. Reaper liked to play a certain role, and when they were near the cameras, she'd come to see a pattern. He'd grab her, and to anyone looking, it would appear as if he was hurting her. His men would always play the part, but Reaper never hurt her. She no longer fought him, and she didn't know how that looked to the cameras. She hoped if Preacher was ever close and he saw her in those cameras, he'd see the lie for what it was and know she was in fact perfectly happy and healthy.

Well, not happy.

She had failed to graduate, which pissed her off purely because she'd spent all that time studying. One day, she had hoped to go to college, but it would seem her dream was never going to come true. Then of course there was the chance she would've never gotten free from the club to even go to college. Bishop had always acted like she'd be his wife for eternity with no life for herself. Her only job on the planet would be to please him.

Even after all this time, thinking about Bishop angered her beyond comprehension. She hated him. When she saw him again, she was going to hurt him.

Pushing those thoughts to the side, she instead focused on just ... being. She wrapped a towel around her body and dried herself off. She didn't look at her reflection. There was nothing she wanted to see right now. No pain. No fear. No feelings.

She was too scared to even give herself a chance to think about what any of this meant to her.

After pulling on a large shirt, she ran a brush through her hair and climbed into bed. She lay down beneath the blanket, even though it was too hot. She stared toward the window and saw the outline of Reaper as he came back home.

He opened the door then closed and locked it. He didn't say a single word as he left, going into the bathroom. Reaper always slept naked and nothing would stop that.

She stayed perfectly still as he returned to her. He no longer wore a towel and the bed dipped as he joined her. She waited. He lay flat on his back, looking up at the ceiling.

Normally, she would turn away from him and try to keep them both separate.

This time, she stared at him.

"You keep on looking and it's going to give me a complex," he said.

"I don't think it's possible for you to even get a complex."

He chuckled.

Instead of looking at the ceiling, he turned toward her, giving her his full attention. "Is this what you want?" he asked.

"I don't know what it is I want." She was only trying to be honest. "How are you feeling?"

"You're asking me quite a few personal questions there. Should I be worried?"

"No. It's fine. It's nothing."

"Talk to me, Robin. What is going on in that head of yours?"

"Nothing."

"I don't know. It doesn't look like a whole lot of nothing to me. Tell me what is going on in that little head of yours."

"Little?"

"You know it's a lot more than that." He winked at her.

She lifted her hand and without thinking, she cupped his cheek.

Reaper's smile disappeared.

Tears filled her eyes as she leaned forward and kissed him.

Reaper pulled away. "Don't cry. Don't kiss me if you're going to cry about it. You're going to give a guy a complex."

She laughed. "I'm nervous."

"Why?"

"What if … what if you're going to use this against me? Hurt me? I don't want to be hurt. I want to believe in this. I'm crazy. How can I even be thinking of this? You only took me to hurt someone I love."

Reaper kissed her. He ran the back of his knuckles across her cheek. "I won't use this against you. I won't ever hurt you. This, right here, is between us. I won't break your trust."

"I really wish I could believe you."

"Why doubt me?" he asked. "I'm not going to lie to you. In fact, I haven't lied to you once while you've been with me, have I?"

She looked into his eyes and knew he spoke the truth.

There hadn't been any lies. Whenever Preacher has been close, he'd told her. Reaper had been completely and openly honest with her every single step of the way.

"I…" There were no words.

Instead of pulling away and fighting these feelings, she leaned in close and kissed him, this time a little harder than normal.

He looked up at her, stroking her cheek.

Sliding her tongue across his lips, he opened up, and she deepened the kiss. Moving out from beneath the blankets, she got as close to him as was possible. She wasn't wearing any panties as she straddled his lap and she felt the hard ridge of his cock pressing against her core.

There was no fear.

No pain.

Nothing.

In fact, she felt nothing but pleasure.

An overwhelming need for release, to feel his

hands all over her body.

After lifting the bottom of her shirt, she pulled it up and over her head, throwing it across the room, not caring a single bit where it landed. Cupping his cheek, she leaned down, brushing her lips across his as he sat up. His large hand held her back, sliding down to grip her ass.

She released a moan, wanting him even more.

"Is this what you want?" he asked.

"Yes."

"I don't want you to regret this."

"I won't. Touch me, Reaper," she said.

He gripped her ass and rocked against her. The way his cock rested, she let out a moan as he touched her. The tip of his cock grazed her clit.

Within seconds, he turned her, putting her to the bed, and she stared up at him. He kissed her hard, bruising, and she moaned his name, not wanting him to stop. He didn't.

"Please," she said.

"Do you want my mouth and hands on your pussy?"

"Yes."

He kissed her again before trailing his lips down her body, going to her breasts. She gasped as he licked over each tight bud before moving to the next. He bit down, making her cry out, but he soothed it. The pleasure went straight to her clit and she spread her thighs even wider, desperate.

Reaper slowly moved past her stomach, then between her thighs. His large hands held her open.

She lifted up and watched as he used his fingers to keep her open. As his tongue slid between her slit, she gasped. The moment he grazed over her clit, she screamed his name.

"You taste so fucking good."

She arched up as he took her clit, sucking on her nub. His fingers teased over the entrance of her pussy before he added a finger. He fucked inside her, licking her clit, then added a second finger. He spread them out and she rocked against him, feeling the beginning of her orgasm.

Her body tightened.

She couldn't think.

There was no thought.

"Please, please, please."

Reaper brought her to orgasm, and she screamed his name, not wanting him to stop, feeling him in every single part of her. She begged for more, hungry and desperate, and Reaper didn't stop licking and sucking at her clit until she came with a second release.

This time, as he moved over her, she was more than ready.

He paused.

"Why did you stop?" she asked.

"Are you sure?"

"Yes, please, Reaper, I want you."

He placed the tip of his dick inside her, and she stared into his eyes, as inch-by-inch, he took her.

He held on to her hands, putting them at either side of her head, holding her in place as he started to rock within her. She cried his name and as he got to the last inch, he slammed inside, making the ache within her pulse back to life for more.

At first, Reaper was slow, taking his time, but he built up a pace, rocking deeply within her, making her scream and moan for more.

"Please," she said.

"You're so wet and tight. Fuck, I can feel you. You feel so fucking amazing." He growled her name, not wanting to give up, but to take her all the time. Over and over, he pounded inside her, fucking her harder than ever before, and this time, Robin loved it.

When he came, she watched him, feeling his dick as it pulsed within her, and knew she was in big trouble.

Chapter Fourteen

Her time with Reaper

The following morning, Robin opened her eyes, feeling the ache between her thighs. She turned, reaching out for Reaper, only to discover the bed empty where he should have been.

"Reaper?"

She sat up and the hotel room was empty.

After sliding out of the bed, she quickly pulled some clothes on before heading to the bathroom. She used the toilet before washing her hands. After her hands, she brushed her teeth, ran a comb through her hair, and then left the hotel room.

Several of his men were already downstairs, enjoying a breakfast around the dull fire.

There was no sign of the women from last night, but she imagined they were either long gone or in one of the bedrooms where they'd spent the night with one of the men.

Nibbling her lip, she didn't see Reaper, and now she was starting to feel a little unnerved. She didn't try to talk to any of his men. There was no reason to, and besides, most of his men liked to ignore her anyway.

She picked up one of the cartons of breakfast. She never knew who went to get food, only that there was always an abundance waiting to be eaten.

Sitting down in one of the chairs, she waited, looking around, hoping to see Reaper. This wasn't what she expected after sleeping with him. She opened the carton to see waffles were steaming.

Her stomach was in knots and after attempting to eat her food, she gave up, heading inside to the hotel room. She made the bed, sitting on the edge of it, and waited.

The day passed.

The only time she got up was to use the bathroom.

Each time, she came back, sitting in the same spot, waiting.

When nightfall came, she didn't go outside even though she knew dinner had arrived. She was too upset to even eat.

When Reaper did return, she saw. The room was in total darkness, so she saw when he arrived.

He was happy. Laughing and joking with his friends. He looked back toward the hotel room but he didn't come to her. He grabbed a bottle of beer, sat down, and drank. She watched him and finally decided to just be done with him.

Getting up, she left the hotel room and decided to take off for a walk. She didn't get far before Reaper came after her.

"You better not be running."

"What are you going to do? Run away and not come back, acting like an asshole?" She hated herself for even caring and wanted to curse him out even more. No, she wanted to hurt him. To really hate him.

"What's this about?" he asked.

She stopped walking and looked at him. "Where were you this morning?"

"Out."

"Wow, you really know how to play the part of a jerk, don't you? This was all a big game to you. Congratulations. You won. Go ahead, call Preacher. I'll even tell him myself that I fell for you. That I wanted to sleep with you. We could do a whole big selfie for it. If you want, that will really drive the wedge in deep." She shoved him in the chest but it was pointless. He didn't fucking move. She growled and stormed off.

"I'm not going to tell Preacher," he said.

"Whatever, I really don't care what it is you do. You're this big, old, powerful man. You can do what you want to, right? You don't have to worry about me. No, I'm just part of some stupid revenge plot. I'm the asshole for even giving a shit!" She screamed the words at him, not caring which of his men heard.

Reaper grabbed her arm, and before she knew what was happening, he hurled her up over his shoulder. She started to slap his ass, screaming at him to let her go. He didn't budge.

She tried to bite his butt but the jeans he wore stopped her from even breaking through to get directly to skin. She wanted to keep on hurting him, but she finally gave up and just slumped. It was useless to even try.

Reaper carried her back to the hotel room. He closed the curtains, locked the door, and sat on the edge of the bed. She scrambled up, wrapping her arms around her knees, and glared at him.

"I wasn't trying to ignore you today."

"Please, you were gone when I woke up. You were gone all day. You think I don't know avoidance when I see it? Believe me, you were avoiding me. I don't want to talk about this. This isn't fun."

"I took you to hurt Preacher," he said.

She stopped.

"You know the reason why I took you and why I hurt you in the beginning. I've known about you all your life. I didn't care about you. Sure, when you turned up pregnant, I saw it as a perfect revenge. I was going to take you when you were pregnant," Reaper said.

This was news to her.

"I intended to make you have the baby, and we were going to raise it together."

"Why are you telling me this?" she asked.

"Then O'Klaren, he fucked everything up, and I refused to be his little revenge slave." He shook his head. "Then you lost the baby. I had nothing to do with that."

"I know Preacher took care of it. You still haven't told me why you're doing all of this."

"To be out in the open with you. To be fair. I took you to hurt you. I was going to break every single part of you. Crush you. I didn't want Preacher to ever get you back and if he did, you were going to be nothing more than a broken shell of who you used to be."

"Why did you change your mind?"

"You." He laughed. "You started talking and I don't know what the fuck it is you've done to me, but I can't get you out of my fucking mind. I care about what you think and what you feel." He shook his head. "Nothing is ever going to change that. Not after last night." He turned to look at her. "I've had my share of women, Robin. I've fucked plenty of women in my time. I've made them do dirty things just because I could, and they were that desperate for what I could give them, I'd make them beg. I'm not a good man. Last night, I don't … I don't want to hurt you, and I don't know what the fuck is happening to me."

Tears filled her eyes because what he was saying weren't lies.

This was … real.

"I went out today because after you fell asleep last night, I spent all night watching you. You're so beautiful, and I … I just wanted to be with you. I've never felt that about anyone. When the sun came up, and you were still asleep in my arms and I still didn't know what to do, I had to go for a ride." He ran his fingers through his hair. "Don't think my change of feelings for you is going to let me let you go. I can't let you go."

"I wasn't going to ask." As Reaper was spilling

his soul, leaving him was the last thing on her mind, which was crazy. This man wasn't a good person.

He was a monster.

So was Preacher.

Both men were monsters, and here she was ... falling for him.

Reaper looked at her and then averted his gaze.

She didn't know what to do or what to say. "I'm going to go take a shower." She climbed off the bed and walked back toward the room. "If you'd like to join me, you're quite welcome to do so."

She left him alone and stepped into the bathroom. She didn't close the door. After removing her clothes, she turned the water on, waiting for it to heat up.

When it was ready for her, she stepped into the stall, keeping it nice and warm. Tilting her head back, she ran her hands across her face before running them down her head.

She heard him seconds later. Opening her eyes, she waited.

The curtain opened and he stepped beneath the spray.

She tensed up, waiting.

He reached past her, getting the bar of soap. Whenever they went to a new place with running water, he always had soap with him. She hated using the soap in the hotels where they stopped. One of the first places they'd stopped at, there had been blood on the bar of soap and she freaked out.

Reaper always got her the soap she needed, and whatever else she asked for. He cared for her that much. Licking her lips, she closed her eyes as his hands touched her. They were lathered with soap, and he ran his hands down her body, going between her thighs then back up again. He never lingered too long in any one area. When it came time to her hair, she leaned back against him, feeling the hard ridge of his cock pressing against her back.

After he finished, with shaking hands, she took the time to wash him. Soaping up her hands, lathering his body. Heat filled her cheeks as she saw the length of his cock standing out.

"I won't bite," he said.

She burst out laughing. "I didn't think you would."

She smiled at him and wrapped her fingers around his length. Her nerves were back, but she pushed them aside, instead, focusing on giving him pleasure.

How her life had changed.

One moment, she was begging to go back home, and now she stood in the shower with her captor, washing his body. By the time she was about to get to his hair, Reaper didn't let her. He pressed her up against the shower, lifting her up, and sliding her down over his dick as he started to sink inside her.

She moaned his name, not wanting him to stop, to keep on going.

"Please," she said.

"I love how tight you are. I could be inside you all day long. It's all I've thought about all day."

He used the cold tiles as leverage, and she rested back against them as he cupped her tits, pressing them together.

His tongue came out, dancing across each nipple, flicking the tips, going back and forth across each mound. She cried out for more as the pleasure went to her pussy.

"Touch yourself, Robin. I want to see you come," he said.

He ran his hands down her body, stroking over

her clit, driving her crazy for more.

He bounced her on his cock and she was so close to release. Reaper kept her at the edge. She was at the mercy of his touch, and only when he said she could fall on over into bliss did she.

She didn't mind being under his control. They found their orgasm together and he pulsed inside her. Each wave made her aware that each time they had sex, there was an even bigger chance of her getting pregnant.

At that moment, in his arms, she didn't care. Reaper didn't let her go. She wrapped her legs around his waist, and he climbed out of the stall, taking her through to the bed.

Still deep inside her, he pressed her to the bed and stayed within her.

"When do we have to go back on the road?" she asked.

"Tomorrow. But we've got all night and I intend to make every second count."

He took her lips, and Robin didn't fight him. Against all the odds, this was what she wanted from him. This was what she'd begged for. She didn't want him to stop, or to let her go.

For Robin belonged to Reaper, and the very thought didn't scare her, it excited her.

****

"You've got to keep them closed."

"They are closed. You're being all mysterious here. I'm kind of afraid." Robin wasn't. When he'd put the blindfold on her, she'd been a little nervous, but now, she was thrilled and wanted to know more.

She and Reaper had been together now for a month, and during that time, she couldn't help but feel … different with him. He was still a monster and she knew he did bad things on a daily basis. He didn't stop being the leader to Slaves of the Beast. They were still part of him, and she couldn't deny that element of who he was, no more than she could Preacher. When he came to her though, there was no violence or anger.

They were simply together. It was hard for her to even understand what was going on.

He'd have these moments either during making love or fucking, and she did know the difference. She loved his hands on her body and the feel of his cock inside her more than anything else.

It was afterward, when he held her, stroking her head and promising her it was going to be okay. Part of her knew she could trust him more than anyone else in the world. It was that part, she followed, that part she had no problem being with. Like now, he'd placed the blindfold gently on her face and she trusted him not to hurt her.

The scent of the open air, dirt, and the sound of trees filled her senses.

"You're not going to kill me, are you?" she asked.

"Believe me, I wouldn't go to this much effort to kill you."

"Nice to know I'm not worth the time."

"You're always worth the time and the effort, you know that." He leaned forward, kissing her temple.

They came to a stop. Where, she had no idea, and so she waited.

"Right, sit down," he said.

She lowered herself to the floor, crossed her legs, and waited. "I've done it, Sir, what next."

"I think I can get used to you siring me." He removed the blindfold. "Open your eyes."

She looked out on a picnic blanket. Wine and an abundance of food were laid out. "You made me a picnic."

"Hey, I've told you before, all you need to do is ask and I will deliver for you." He winked at her. "So, enjoy."

"I can't believe you made me a picnic. You know this is romantic, right?"

"I know, and it's why you won't be telling any of the guys what it is I did today."

"You don't want them to know how sweet you can be?"

"They don't need to know. Sweetness is a weakness to them."

She tucked her hair behind her ear and couldn't stop smiling. This was real. All of it was ... sweet.

"You're surprised?"

"This is a really good surprise. I'll never forget this," she said.

"You haven't even tried any of the food. I'd be careful about judging it. You've got to taste it."

"It's a picnic. You can't go very wrong with picnic food." She reached out, taking a strawberry, dipping it into the cream, and tasting. "I have to wonder how you got this past your men, though. Wouldn't they have attacked you for this?" She'd noticed the men loved to have good food, and they weren't shy about pointing out their need for it.

"I'm the boss. I can come and go as I please."

"Must be nice," she said.

Reaper moved behind her, wrapping his arms around her waist and kissing her neck. "And what does that mean?"

"What does what mean?"

"Me being the boss and coming and going as I please."

"There's nothing to it. Just stating a fact."

"A fact you don't like?"

"You can do what you want. I don't even talk to your men on your orders. I guess I'm growing a little tired of doing nothing. Of being nothing. All I do is sit at the hotel or walk, or go wherever you want to go. There's no rest."

"You know I can't let you go anywhere else, don't you?"

She knew.

Staring down at the picnic, she didn't want to change the topic but also, she was afraid of the questions he'd have for her.

Preacher was still between them.

He wanted to know her feelings about him, and like so many other times, she was afraid of the answer. If she told Reaper she'd stay with him, her heart broke for what could have been with Preacher. If she said she'd go to Preacher, then Reaper was hurt.

"Let's forget about it. You made me a lovely picnic and this is all that counts as far as I'm concerned." She grabbed another strawberry, dipping it into the cream and feeding it to him. When a little dripped on his chin, she leaned forward and licked the spot right off.

"One day, I hope to give you a normal life."

"How do you think that's going to be possible with you always riding?"

"I've settled down in one place before," he said.

"To hurt Preacher. To piss him off. I don't know if I want to stick around somewhere for you to have an ulterior motive." She pressed her lips to his, silencing any dispute. "No more talk."

"You're telling me to shut up?"

"Damn straight. Anyone tell you silence is a good look for you?"

She let out a scream as he grabbed her around the

waist and pressed her to the ground.

He grabbed one of the strawberries and dipped it in the cream, like she'd been doing. Only this time, rather than feed her, he slid the tip of the strawberry down her flesh. She let out a gasp as his tongue followed the path. He easily opened the buttons of her shirt and pulled down the cup of her bra. He circled each nub with more cream and then licked it off.

"What if someone can see?" she asked as he removed her shirt and bra, exposing her to him.

"No one would dare. Do you really think I'd allow someone else to see what belongs to me?" He took possession of her mouth, and she melted against him, sinking her fingers into his hair.

Reaper broke from the kiss first, to trail his lips down to her neck. She moaned his name as he sucked on the sensitive flesh of her pulse, wanting more, but he moved. He got to her breasts and he sucked on each tip, flicking his tongue to dance across her flesh. Closing her eyes, she begged for more, but he didn't give in straight away, making her desperate and hungry for him.

"Do you have any idea how fucking hard I am for you right now?" he asked.

"So hard?"

"Yes."

"Good." She ran her hand down his chest and gripped him through his jeans. "I want you."

"Oh, you're going to get me."

For a month, Reaper had been teaching her just how much he liked certain touches, and his needs were always there for her. She'd had him in her mouth, her pussy, and he'd teased her ass. Each touch only enhanced her need for him. He'd become like a drug to her. In the mornings, the evenings, whenever she could get her hands on him.

He pressed her breasts together and teased over each nipple before letting them go and kissing down her body, going to where her jeans sat snugly on her waist. He popped the button open and she released a gasp as he pulled them down, kissing between her thighs. She wore a pair of lace panties, but that didn't seem to stop him.

His face pressed against her crotch and she gasped. He tore them from her body, and his tongue was on her pussy, sliding between her slit within the next second.

"Spread your thighs."

She was already opening herself up to him before he said a word.

He licked over her, tasting her, teasing her, and she wanted more of him, couldn't get enough of his touch. He gripped her ass, holding her still as he licked and sucked at her. Up and down, circling around before sucking her clit into his mouth.

She screamed his name, thrusting her pelvis up for more, and he didn't take more but gave more, nibbling on her clit before going down to fuck inside her.

"I want to feel you come all over my cock," he said.

She wanted to feel him inside her, working his magic.

He pushed his jeans down, grabbed his already-hard cock, and slammed in deep. She held on to his shoulders, closing her eyes, feeling the entire length of him as he fucked her hard. He didn't stop.

Reaper went hard and fast, and she felt every single jolt as he fucked her. Wrapping her legs around him, she met him thrust for thrust, but she was never one to be outdone, not anymore. She shoved him, and even though he was by far stronger than her, he still moved to where she wanted him.

Putting her hands on his shoulders, she smiled down at him, using his chest for leverage to work his length inside and out. He grabbed her hips and started to pull her down, riding his length. Closing her eyes, she gave him her all, and he reached between the lips of her pussy and stroked her clit.

"I want you to come all over my cock, baby."

It didn't take him long to bring her to orgasm. The moment she came, she did so screaming his name, begging for more, not wanting to let go. The ride was incredible. It burned inside her, melting her to her core, and before her orgasm had even finished, Reaper followed her.

His dick pulsed in waves, filling her up, and she relished it, giving herself to him, and him alone.

She collapsed on his chest, his cock still deep inside her, running the tips of his fingers across her flesh.

"This was amazing," she said.

"You can have this whenever you want to."

All she had to do was give up about heading home. That was all he wanted from her, but she didn't know if she could ever give up Preacher.

****

"It doesn't hurt?" Robin asked.

"No, it doesn't hurt," Reaper said. "Look at my body. Do you really think if something hurt, I'd keep on doing it?"

"I don't know what your level for pain is." She watched as Trick moved the ink pen slowly across Reaper's flesh. In the time she'd been with Reaper, this was the third time the man had paid a visit to them. This time, he was doing something on Reaper's back. With his shirt off, it exposed the heart tattoo, directly over his chest. Reaper had a lot of ink.

"Do you only do work by instruction?" she asked.

"Are you thinking of a design?" Trick asked.

"I don't know."

He lifted his pen and reached down into his bag, grabbing a book. "Here you go, take a look in this. They're all my drawings. Some stuff I've inked on flesh, others, I haven't. I like to doodle."

"You do?"

"Yes."

She ran her hand across the book, wondering what it would be like to have Preacher's work of art on her body.

Pushing those thoughts from her mind, she didn't want to risk being asked questions by Reaper. She hated to lie and if he asked her anything right now, she was liable to break.

At first, the ink work were some symbols and bird designs. Nothing really popped out at her. The deeper she got into the book, the more elaborate the designs became. The bird started to sit on a branch, which then developed into a tree.

Some of the designs were dark.

She couldn't help but think about Preacher's artwork back at the nursery. He'd been so beautifully creative. She missed that part of him so much.

Running her hand over each piece, she tried not to think about Preacher, not anymore.

Her feelings for Reaper, they were messing with her emotions when it came to everything to do with her love of Preacher. The man back home, he deserved a woman who wasn't falling for another man. There was more to Reaper than she had ever given him credit for, and it scared her. Every second of every single day that she was away from Preacher, it drew her away from the life she once knew.

What was her father doing?

Bishop?

Her mother?

Why did she even care?

The life on the open road offered a chance to forget, to leave all she'd known behind.

Finally, turning to the last page, she came upon a rose. It was so deeply red and traveled up a thorn. Several roses were on the same bush.

She traced her finger across each petal.

"Have you seen one you like?" he asked.

"This one. Can you do this?" She held the book up.

"I can do it but it's going to take more than one sitting. Where do you want it?"

Robin stared down at her body and then stood up, lifting her shirt to beneath her bra. "Here, can you do it here?"

"All from beneath your tit, down to the top of your thigh? Yeah, I can do it. Like I said, Reaper's going to have to stick around a bit for me to do it."

"Can we?"

"You're sure you want that one?" Reaper asked.

"Yeah, why? Don't you like it?"

"It's not about what I like," he said. "It's about what you like."

"Then this is the one I want." She tapped the book. "Can I have this one?"

"Yeah, sure."

Reaper moved. "Get started on her right away."

"But your ink?"

"Can wait. I want her to have what she wants."

"You're sure?" Robin asked.

"It's not every day my girl decides she wants to mark her skin. I'd like to be here for the process. At least where I'm not having to hold her down."

She refused to think about that. That was a whole other time, other world. Sitting down on the chair, she lifted her shirt while Trick did whatever he had to do in order to ink her body.

This was right.

She knew it was.

There was a deep sense of calm to her as he put the point of the ink to her flesh and started.

****

One week later

Robin stood in yet another bathroom. The new ink was already healing. The salve Trick had given her was amazing. She'd followed his instructions exactly, and now she stood with a beautiful design on her body.

Even though it wasn't completely healed yet, she knew she was going to love it.

"Feel like a rebel yet?" he asked.

"No. Why would you even think this makes me feel like a rebel?" she asked, laughing.

"I don't know. It's a good look on you, though."

"You like it? Do you think it's sexy?"

"I think you're sexy. Does that count?" he asked.

"A little bit." She dropped her shirt and walked toward him, kissing his cheek.

"I've got to ask."

"What?"

"Did you expect me to not give you permission or something?"

"I don't know. I guess so. You've kind of controlled every other area of my life, why not this one?" She shrugged.

"I'm doing this to keep you safe, you have to understand that."

"I do. Believe me, I really do. I'm sorry. I guess I'm just in a weird mood right now. It has nothing to do with you, I swear."

"What does it have to do with?" he asked. "You can share with me."

"I don't know. With the ink, it just got me thinking about before, you know."

"Your time with Preacher?"

She moved out of his arms, walking into the main part of a new hotel room. This one was crappy. The walls were a dull yellow, and it looked like there was damp in the corners. The beds weren't made and she didn't want to even think about the stains on the blankets. The reception worker was a young kid, who didn't really care, and he'd been playing some kind of videogame, not exactly dedicated. She went to sit on the edge of the bed and thought better of it. The floor wasn't even much better.

Wrinkling her nose, she turned around. "Do you want to go for a walk?"

"Let's go," he said.

They made their way outside. She wore one of the heavy jackets he'd bought for her, and she took it, grateful for anything to ward off the cold.

Reaper gave instructions to his men before they headed out. She stretched out her neck, lifting her arms and trying to loosen up her body. She was wound so tight right now, and she needed to focus on everything else.

"Ready?" he asked.

"Yes."

They left the hotel room. Reaper rarely used places near built-up towns or cities. He avoided places with a lot of traffic and cameras. He'd been staying off the radar for a long time.

"You want to talk?"

"Not everything I talk about is going to be about Preacher. I hope you know that."

"He was a big part of your life."

"Not really."

Reaper snorted.

"I'm twenty years his junior. You do get that, right? It's why I know I had a whole life before Preacher. You know, my time with Bishop."

"Do you really want to keep reminding me of the other men in your life?"

"Why not? You've had other women."

"And they're not still around."

"Look, I can't change my past for what it is. Preacher was part of the last year before you took me. The pregnancy, the responsibility, all of it, he was there. He didn't have to be, but he was by my side and I knew with him, I wasn't alone. Bishop, as you know, he was a dick. All he thought about was himself, and I couldn't rely on him." She waved her arms, trying to think of the right thing to say but drawing a blank in every single direction. "I ... I never knew what I wanted out of life."

"What do you mean?"

"The club was everything. I had my mom telling me constantly my only place was to be one of the women to the men. An old lady. There was no care about what I wanted or who I wanted to be. It was firm, direct, *you will be an old lady*. You're Bear's daughter, and your only place is now and will always be at the club." She took a deep breath. "Graduating, college, it was never a consideration."

"Did you want to do all of that?"

"I honestly don't know, and the reason I don't know is because I've never given myself a chance to want it. What was the point if the first time it was in reach, it was taken from me? Am I making any sense at all?"

"Yes."

"When I got pregnant, it was expected for me to have the baby, and I did want it. Don't get me wrong. Bishop was all about getting rid of it, but I didn't want to. Then of course, there was the whole guilt about having another man's baby, and he wouldn't … give. It was always about him, not about what I was thinking and feeling. The first time I got to see my baby, you know on the ultrasound, it was the most amazing … experience of my life. I loved it. I really did." She pushed some hair off her face. "I loved my baby and then I found out she was a girl, and it just, I was at peace."

"Then you lost her."

She let out a breath. "Yeah, I lost her, and I don't know, everything shattered then. Before I did lose the baby, Bishop had mentioned about Preacher keeping the baby but her not knowing I was the mother." She shrugged. "Once again, it was all about him."

"I could kill him, you know. It would be easy," Reaper said. "He's hurt you a great deal."

"I know, but when I confront Bishop, I want to stare him in the eyes to know he didn't break me. That all he is and all he'll ever be is a coward."

Reaper took her hand, locking their fingers together. "You know, this is all nice, you telling me all of this, but it doesn't exactly tell me what you want."

"I've told you. All my life, I've been doing what everyone else has asked of me. I can honestly say I don't have the first clue as to who I am or what it is I want." She still felt lost. It didn't matter where she was or who she was with, she would always be lost, she knew that now.

"Okay, well, let's start slow. You know you wanted to go on this walk, right?"

"Yes, I did." She laughed.

"Success. What do you want for dinner?"

"Pizza. I think I'm wanting pizza."

"I'll make sure the guys stop by at a pizza place." Reaper pulled her close, kissing her lips. "We'll take it one decision at a time, and you will only ever do what you want to do, Robin. I won't tell you what to do."

"And what if one of those decisions is to go home?" she asked.

"Then we'll have to see what happens when you ask. Are you asking now?"

She shook her head. "No, I'm not."

Chapter Fifteen

Present day

A birthday.

Twenty-one years of age.

Robin sat on the bench outside of the supermarket. She had a large list of items to get but she'd overheard Bear talking to know he'd purposely gotten her out of the house. There was going to be a nice big party, another one at the clubhouse to celebrate her birth.

Yay.

She didn't know if she wanted to celebrate a life she didn't remember. A date that was merely a date to her.

Staring up at the large building, it offered her no solutions. Just a day spent wandering up and down the aisles. She'd made a joke to Preacher about how long it took her to shop nowadays because she didn't know what it was she liked or disliked. She could hold a can of canned peaches, and she didn't even know if they were worth putting in the cart.

Bear had given her a lot of cash and told her to enjoy the day.

She hadn't admitted to either Preacher or Bear that she was restless, or there was something she felt she needed to do, because the truth was, there was nothing she could think of. This was her life now. There was no returning memory for her. Just odd voices that wouldn't come back or make her life any clearer. She didn't want to talk to Preacher about her worries either.

He had this whole view of her life away from him, and part of her was afraid what he said was right. What if she did have a horrible time filled with death and torture? She had no way of knowing if it was true or not.

In fact, there was nothing she knew for certain.

Not of her life, not of her time here, nothing.

Getting to her feet, she decided she'd done enough moping for one day. There was going to be plenty of time for her to feel sorry for herself. It wasn't just for herself, though. She felt sorry for Preacher. He expected something from her, and she had yet to deliver. Every part of her life felt like a lie and she knew it was because of her.

With a cart in front of her, she put her bag inside and pushed on through the doors. The crowds weren't fun. She hated being in any crowded place but she needed to get used to it, especially if she was expected to attend a party.

Yay.

She had to start practicing her surprised and happy face.

More lies.

Starting at the produce section, she looked at the abundance of colors. Onions, eggplant, zucchini, tomato, so many varieties to choose from. Was there a time she knew what she was doing? Did she miraculously pick the right kind of fruit and veg or did she suck at this?

Picking up a sack of onions, she placed it in her cart. Rather than think about what it was she liked or didn't like, she decided the best way to survive was to stick to his trusted list.

She walked through each section, marking off each item she placed into the cart. By the time she got to the canned items, she was exhausted. She'd been stopped by five people so far, all of whom she had no idea who they were but they knew her. They wanted conversations and one of her favorite questions: do you remember when…? Tact was clearly not on everyone's minds, seeing as she didn't remember jack shit.

Her anger was coming out and knowing all new

levels. How the fuck would she be able to remember anything if she didn't even know her name? The only reason she knew her name was Robin was because people told her. There was no magical person around to give her memories though.

By the time she had finished at the checkout, she had a headache and wanted nothing more than to lie down. This had already been too tiring for her.

Pushing the cart outside, she pulled out her cell phone, ready to dial her dad or Preacher to come and pick her up.

"It's okay, sweet girl."

She turned toward the voice to see a large man. His hair was short and his beard thick and full. He was struggling with a baby.

Leaving her cart, she rushed to his side, holding the cart. "Here, let me help."

"Thank you," the man said.

She offered him a smile. "She's a wriggler."

The baby in his arms wasn't happy.

"Tell me about it. It's okay, sweetheart." He put the baby in the cart.

"How old is she?"

"Just over one now. She can hold her head and sit up," he said.

"She's beautiful."

"Her mother tells her that as much as she can."

"What's her name?" Robin asked.

"Bethany."

"Beautiful name. Anyway, I better let you get back to your shopping."

"Thank you so much for your help." He held out his hand and his shirt rode up. She got a look at his ink and there was something about him.

"Do I know you?"

There was a pause.

"No, we don't know each other."

"Oh, right. Sorry." She shook his head. "Forgive me. I'm not usually, you know, so … weird."

"It's fine, Robin," he said.

"I'll let you get back to your shopping." She held up her cell phone and stepped away. She was just about to call Preacher when he suddenly pulled up into the spot. She looked behind her to say goodbye to the man she'd helped but he must have already gone inside. There was no sign of him.

"Did you enjoy shopping?" Preacher asked.

"No, but I got everything on the list." Preacher returned the cart as she climbed into the front seat. Just as she did her seatbelt, she frowned.

The man had called her Robin.

If he didn't know her, how did he know her name?

"You okay?" Preacher asked.

"Yeah, yeah, I'm fine." They pulled away from the supermarket, and she rubbed at her temple.

"I'm going to have to ask again if you don't start talking."

"I've got a headache. It's nothing. I got tired with everyone trying to jog my memory."

"Sorry."

"It's fine." She waved her hand in the air, not really caring about the supermarket anymore. No, her thoughts were on the man with the young girl. Bethany. "Slaves to the Beast."

Preacher jerked the car to a stop. People went past, pressing on their horns.

"Rather rude."

"What did you say?" he asked.

"I have no idea what you're talking about."

"Did you remember something?"

"No."

"You must have remembered something."

"Why?"

"Slaves to the Beast," he said.

"What about it?"

"How do you know the name?"

"It was on a guy's arm. He had it inked near his wrist, why?"

"Where?"

"Preacher, you're scaring me."

"Slaves of the Beast is run by Reaper. The guy who took you. You spoke to him. Where?"

"Back at the supermarket." Before she had even finished, he spun the car around and she cried out. "Preacher, please, what is going on? I asked him if he knew me and he said no. Why would he lie?"

"Because you're here with me. That's fucking why." He had his cell phone out and she heard Bear answer. "Reaper's here. I need backup. Get the boys."

"Preacher, I really don't think this is necessary."

"I'm not asking your fucking permission."

They pulled up outside of the supermarket. Preacher unbuckled his seatbelt and she grabbed his arms. "Don't do this."

"I'm going in there and taking care of the son of a bitch who thought he could have you."

"He had a kid with him. A young child," she said. "Bethany." Her heart raced. "What if I got it all wrong? You can't just kill a child's father."

"No, there's no way Reaper would have a kid. He hates kids."

"The man I spoke to, he had a fucking kid with him." She didn't want to cause a scene or have a man hurt because of her. She felt sick to her stomach, scared, angry, and worried. All she wanted to do was to be free of all of it.

"You've got to be mistaken."

"I know what I saw, Preacher, and I'm telling you, he had a kid."

She turned to look behind her when bikes approached. She saw her father along with a couple of the men arrive.

"Please."

"I'm sorry, Robin. This is the closest we've come to finally ending this, and not me or one of my boys are going to walk away from this opportunity."

"Even when I ask you to?"

"Even then."

He climbed out of the car, and Robin refused to be part of this. Unbuckling her seatbelt, she got out of the car, but instead of following after Preacher, she walked away.

There was no way she was going to let him think for even a second she would accept this. She had asked for him not to pursue this man, and he'd done so anyway.

She left the supermarket and started the long walk back to town. She was pleased she wasn't wearing heels. Most of the shoes within her closet were flat pumps or walking boots. Her past self was a practical woman, and she liked that about herself.

Robin didn't know how long she'd been walking until Preacher finally decided to catch up to her. He rolled down the window and called her name.

She ignored him.

"You're pissed at me, I get that. But I care about you."

"You know, a lot of people keep throwing those words out at me as if they actually mean anything to me anymore. *I care about you, Robin.* What happens to you means something to me. Yet, no one is ever asking about what I want. What I'd like you to do. All of you are doing whatever it takes to appease yourself but not to help me. I don't know who that man was but you were going to go after him. He had a young child."

"If that was Reaper, aren't you curious as to how he got the kid? For all you know, he could have kidnapped her."

"Or maybe it's my kid. You ever thought about that? What if during those two years I had a baby, Preacher? You could be killing my child." She felt sick. She stopped walking, going a little light-headed.

"No, it's not your child."

"You don't know that."

"The man was gone. We couldn't find him and we didn't see any sign of a man walking into the supermarket. We checked the tapes."

"I know what I saw."

"Yeah, but did you see him go into the supermarket?"

"No."

"Then we will never know if he's the right man or not."

"Do you think I'm lying?"

"Robin, I don't know what to think." He got out of the car, rushing to her side. "Please, get in. You're clearly tired and need to lie down or something." He stroked some of her hair behind her cheek.

"What if I didn't speak to anyone?" she asked. "What if I'm seeing things?"

"You're not. You're exhausted. It's all the extra hours at the library. You're not sleeping well. You're having nightmares every single night. You think I don't know you're falling apart and trying to pretend you're holding it together? You don't have to be strong for me."

"I'm trying to be strong for myself," she said. What if the man wasn't even there? Was she thinking things up now? Trying to create a life where it was easy? None of this made any sense to her.

Preacher cupped her face, tilting her head back. He brushed his lips across hers. "It's going to be okay. All you need to do is rest and it will be fine."

"Rest. Right. Rest. Then of course there's the party."

"I can cancel it. It was supposed to be fun but I don't want you stressing out about this."

"No, no. It'll be fine. It should be fun, right? I can handle some fun. Dancing. Drinking. I can handle it." She dropped her head to his chest and he wrapped his arms around her. "Please, Preacher, take me home."

She asked for home, but she didn't know where home really was.

****

"Is she okay?" Bear asked.

Preacher looked back upstairs and shook his head. "I don't know anymore."

"There was no sign of the guy she spoke of," Bear said. "I've called Randall and he doesn't know of anyone who manifests dreams like this. You're saying she has dreamed about this and told you about it."

"No. She has spoken within her dreams of Slaves to the Beasts and of a girl, Bethany."

"You ever thought it might be her wish to have had a baby girl with you who she hoped to name Bethany?"

"No. I don't know. Fuck. I … I thought we had him today."

"Preacher, let's say he was there. He didn't go into the supermarket and disappear. Reaper's not stupid. We keep treating him like he is, but he knows where all these cameras are. He knows everything there is to know about all of this. What if he and Robin had a daughter?"

"No, I won't accept that. There's no way she had a fucking kid with him. Not ... not willingly. I won't accept that." He didn't want to even think about her and Reaper together.

"Two years is a long time."

"Don't you think I know that? I've lived those two fucking years every single day. I know how long it is. I know how useless each fucking lead has been, and Reaper, he's not clever."

"We haven't caught him."

"Because he has always been one step ahead of the game. Bishop. For two years, he fucking played me. The little prick. When I get my hands on him, I'll kill him."

"Has Reaper called you since?" Bear asked.

"No."

"Think about his message."

Preacher didn't want to think. "I thought you were on my side."

"He said Robin may not have been running away from him. We've all been acting like Robin is the victim, but what if she isn't? What if she really likes Reaper?"

"No. If she liked Reaper and wanted to be with him, she would only do it to make good out of a bad situation." Preacher ran a hand down his face. He was wound so tightly right now, and he couldn't think.

Robin was passed out upstairs.

Reaper was out there somewhere.

Bishop was as well.

Yet the key to finding both men was locked within a woman who didn't know shit.

"When I find the both of them, I'm going to hurt them in ways they could never imagine."

"I hope you're right." Bear stood. "What will you do if Robin is in love with Reaper?"

"Not going to happen."

Preacher stared at his friend and Bear looked sad. "I hope you're right, for your sake."

****

The party was in full swing.

Robin had smiled where appropriate. Accepted hugs and kisses. She'd done the good-girl routine, and now she sat outside, enjoying the cold night air and sipping at a bottle of beer. Since her and Preacher's disagreement at the supermarket, it had been tense between them. He hadn't come to bed, and part of her hadn't wanted him to. Things were a mess and she didn't have a single clue as to how to fix them.

People kept looking at her, waiting for those precious memories to just fall from her, and like so many times before, she had failed. Failing was something she should be used to.

She drank her beer and took a second one. It was her birthday. She only got to turn twenty-one once, and she was going to celebrate it in style.

"I've got to say the beer thing is a new look for you," Joanne said, approaching the bench where she sat.

"The beer?"

"The beer, the hair, the makeup. The old Robin wouldn't have dressed up. Not after what Milly did to her." Joanne slapped a hand across her mouth. "I'm so sorry. I'm not supposed to talk to you about those kinds of things."

"Are you even supposed to be talking to me at all?" Robin asked, feeling bitter.

"I can go."

"No, no, I didn't mean … sorry. I sounded like a bitch then and it really wasn't what I meant." She'd reached out to stop Joanne from leaving.

She didn't want Bear or Preacher to approach or one of the other men to ask her how she was feeling. "I'm used to people avoiding me, or looking out for Preacher and my dad, and you know, not really giving me the whole truth. I didn't know if people had been ordered to stay away from me. I didn't mean to upset you."

"Wow, if I didn't know any better, I'd say Robin is closer than you think."

"She is?"

"Robin is a nice girl. She's considerate and kind. It's why she was the complete opposite of Bishop. Even when he was sleeping around. You didn't care. You've always been a nice girl, Robin."

"Robin. That name again." She breathed in deeply. "Sorry, I'm struggling with a lot these days. I think I just want to forget everything."

"Drinking does help, but I will warn you, the day after, not such a good idea. You will regret drinking so much."

"Were we friends?" she asked. "Is that why you're so nice to me?"

"No, we weren't friends. We weren't even close. Your mother didn't like me but that could be because I was sleeping with your father whenever he was looking in my direction."

"I'm sorry, but ew."

Joanne laughed. "It's fine."

She had tried to set him up with Anne at the library, but Bear wasn't budging on dating. He didn't want to be with anyone and Anne still had her cheating ass of a husband, whom Robin had gotten to meet when he came to the library.

He was a good-looking man, but she didn't see

the appeal all the other women clearly did.

"We weren't close, but we weren't enemies either. I wish I had looked out for you more. You've never been a horrible person so when you got pregnant and then lost the baby, I was always sad for you. After the baby, you looked so lost, so miserable. I remember wanting to just give you a hug. Everything had returned to normal around you, but you, you were lost."

Robin sighed. "I don't remember any of it. I don't know at times if not remembering it is even better than remembering it. It sounds so … horrible."

"It was," Joanne said. "It really was."

She finished her beer. "I need to go use the bathroom."

"I'm going to see if Bear wants any of my company tonight." Joanne winked at her and Robin winced. This was the kind of information she really, really didn't need to know. Her father getting action wasn't on her list of priorities.

Getting to her feet, she put the empty bottle in the trash can on her way past, heading inside the main clubhouse.

It was so busy, and she saw the bathroom was full. She left the main room and headed up to the living quarters. She came to a stop outside of Bishop's old room. She couldn't remember if he had a bathroom in his room or if it was just Preacher's room.

Putting her hand on the door, she paused, feeling a wave of sickness wash over her. She needed to use the bathroom, and being afraid of a room was pointless.

She pushed on the door, stepping inside.

The heavy scent of leather, dust, and something else. She stood frozen, looking around, and like flashes coming through her mind's eye, Robin stopped.

Her life coming together as she remembered the

argument in his room. Bishop sat getting head while she watched, not long after she lost the baby. Touching her stomach, she saw Preacher, smiling down at her as he made love to her. The anger in his eyes at Bishop. O'Klaren. The night she was taken. The rape. The beatings. The ink. The falling in love.

All of it. Past Robin and present Robin coming together to form herself again.

Tears filled her eyes with the memories. They had all been locked inside her, trying to get out and now that they were, she was scared. She swiped the tears as they fell down her cheeks.

Bishop's room never had a bathroom. He was never allowed an en-suite.

Bishop. That traitorous, fucking bastard. Even without her memories, he'd been trying to hurt her.

Turning on her heel, she made her way downstairs. Just moments ago, the crowd had been too much, but now, it was like old times.

Opening the door, she looked around the room, focusing on each person. There were a couple of new faces, but she was searching for Preacher. He wasn't there.

Pushing her way through the crowd, she made her way outside. Joanne sat on Bear's lap. Preacher sat beside him, beer in hand, laughing at something one of the men had said.

Without thinking, she walked over to Preacher, straddled his lap, sank her fingers into his hair, and kissed him, hard, passionately, desperately, filled with hunger, shame, and guilt. For a long time, she'd craved this man's touch, wanted him more than anyone else, but that was all mixed with another new feeling.

Pulling away, she looked into his eyes. People had grown silent around her.

"Robin?" Preacher asked.

That was right. The old Robin would never have gone up to her man, kissed him passionately in front of his club. She didn't have the experience the new Robin did.

"Hello, Preacher," she said. "Miss me?"

"What?" Bear said.

She turned her head, smiling at her dad. "Hey, Dad. So, you finally killed Mom. What did she do this time?"

"Your memories?" Preacher asked.

She got off Preacher's lap. "They're here. They're all here." She touched her head. "Every single one." She licked her lips.

Today, she had seen Reaper. He'd been at the supermarket, and so had … their daughter. She couldn't let her anger or fear ride over this.

Staring at the man she loved, she forced a smile to her lips.

"How did this happen?" Preacher asked, getting to his feet.

"Bishop's room. I don't know what it was about the room, but it clearly triggered whatever I needed because they're all back. I remember everything. Milly, the baby, Bishop, O'Klaren, all of it. I remember being taken, and … I know what happened just before the car hit me."

"Wait, you haven't forgotten the last year as well now, have you?" Joanne asked.

"No, that's still there." She pushed some hair off her face. "We need to get to Bishop. There's a lot he knows and it's time for him to know that I remember what he did."

"So, he did have something to do with you and Reaper?" Preacher asked.

"Oh, he made sure I was taken, and I know for a fact he gave Reaper clues when you were close." She looked at Preacher and was torn. "We ... we need to talk."

"Sure, yes. Now?"

"Why not? It's my birthday. We really need to figure things out. Too much time has been wasted already."

****

Preacher saw the nerves filling up Robin. He couldn't believe she remembered everything and yet, was still standing. Still being able to function.

They entered his office and she looked around.

"Do you want to tell me what's going on and why you haven't collapsed into a heap, scared and upset?"

"It's because I'm not. There's a lot you don't know."

"And you're going to fill in all the blanks for me?"

"First, I want to tell you that I do love you. I also know you shared a lot with me when I didn't remember who I was and for that, I'm grateful."

"Cut to the chase here, Robin. You're not exactly behaving how I imagined you would. If you've remembered everything, where are the tears?"

"I'm not broken, Preacher. I haven't lost myself. For two years, I was able to deal with the pain. I can focus and get past whatever I've been through to move on." She pressed her lips together.

"It's exactly my point. You were a mess when you were in the hospital. Broken bones, beaten up. You were gone for two years from my side, and you're acting like nothing was wrong."

Tears filled her eyes and something twisted in his gut. He didn't know what to do.

"Because, Preacher, I didn't have the worst two years of my life." The tears fell but she didn't make a move to wipe them away. "I ... I fell in love."

Chapter Sixteen

Her time with Reaper

"We're going to a nightclub?" Robin asked, looking at the long line. Only a couple of men from Reaper's club were with them, and Reaper had also removed his leather cut. He only ever did that if they were moving through towns that were known to Preacher or with potential contacts.

"We sure are."

"Why?"

"Because I want you to experience as much fun as possible," Reaper said, placing his hand on her stomach.

She couldn't help but smile. "And a nightclub will do that? I can't even drink."

"No, but we can have some fun."

Reaper took her hand, leading the way to the front of the line. She was nervous as she heard grumbles from the men and women as they passed. She didn't want Reaper to get into a fight.

He paid the man at the front and they were in the club without a single fist thrown. She felt a little more relaxed as they made their way inside. The music was heavy, thick. The bar was crowded. There were so many people all around, but Reaper didn't just lurk, he took her straight to the VIP section, paying the guard once again, gaining them access. His men were already off searching for women, so it was just her and Reaper looking down over the dance floor.

"I figured you'd prefer to watch for a little bit before we went and joined in on the crazy."

Reaper held her chair out for her and she sat down, laughing as she caught sight of Reaper's men dancing, but it wasn't a sexy dance either.

"I love to hear you laugh," Reaper said. "Since we've found out about the baby, you've been … quiet."

"Oh, it's nothing."

"Are you thinking about Preacher?" he asked.

"Yes, no, not in the way you think. The last baby, I didn't … I'm worried is all."

"You know I won't let anyone hurt you, right?"

"I know. Preacher promised the same thing, so forgive me for still being a little on the worried side." She put her hand to her stomach, not even a little surprised she was expecting. The warning signs came with the morning sickness and tender breasts. There was no other indication, but it wasn't like she and Reaper had been using condoms.

"O'Klaren has been taken care of," Reaper said. "I'll never leave your side."

"You'll be a permanent fixture."

"I'll be whatever you need me to be."

"What about a dad?" she asked.

"I'm going to be here."

"Yeah, but we move all the time. I … unless I'm sick, we're constantly moving around. One hotel, empty abandoned building, or something else. There's never any stability and I don't think this is very good for the baby." She put a hand on her stomach.

"You're wanting to settle down?"

"I don't want my baby to be screaming for a feed if we're having to keep on riding." She ran her fingers through her hair. "I'm sorry. I guess the excitement has worn off, and now I'm at the stage where fear and worry have settled in."

"You don't have to be afraid."

"I don't? We don't stay in one place. Raising a child, a baby like this, it's not practical. I want to be happy and positive, but how can I be? Especially when all of this was for revenge."

"I love you," Reaper said.

This made her drop the glass.

Several waiters came to assist with the broken glass, and she was still shaking from his revelation. She thanked them all for their help before turning toward Reaper. "What?"

"I'm in love with you. I know this started out as … revenge. I wanted to hurt you and I did. You have no idea how much I regret harming you. You didn't deserve it. I'm in love with you and there's no way I would ever want to hurt you." He took hold of her hand. "This baby, it's a chance for us. I never thought I wanted to be a father, but with you, I want it all. It's why I'm looking into buying a house, settling down. We'll be surrounded by the club, and I'm already making contacts to secure our life. I want you to be happy."

"What about you?" she asked.

"What about me?"

"The road. The club. Never settling down. I don't want you to give up all of this for me."

"I'm giving it all up because you're worth more than a few stretches of open road. Robin, you've given me a chance to feel something I never knew existed. I'm in love with you, and that's not something I'm ever going to find alone on the open road. I want to share the rest of my life with you. I want to marry you."

"You can't marry me. Not … not without getting a divorce from Bishop."

"I'll take care of that little shit. Don't you worry."

"It's kind of hard not to. He helped you."

"And he'll know what to do to deal with me. I can end his miserable existence, if you ask me to do it. It'll be quite easy to do as well."

"No, I don't want him dead. At least not yet." She

looked down at her lap before returning her gaze to his. "I think I'm in love with you as well."

Reaper pulled her onto his lap, sinking his fingers into her hair and kissing her hard. "I know you're not over Preacher and will probably never will be, but I love you and I'll take whatever it is you can give me." He kissed her again. "Come on, let's go and dance."

****

Present day

Telling Preacher the truth was one of the hardest things Robin had ever had to do. The look on his face, no matter how much he tried to mask it, she would never forget it. He'd been hurt by her revelation, and it killed her inside.

Knowing everything now, and especially with all of his honesty during her time of not knowing who she was, made it all even worse. Preacher loved her and she knew it, felt it right down to her core, only, she wasn't the same person. Not even close, and he had believed she was hurt so badly.

Robin hadn't wanted to escape Reaper. Even now, knowing he was close somewhere, she was desperate to see him, but first, she had to take care of another little problem. Preacher hadn't known how to contact Bishop to bring him out of hiding, but she had. All it had taken was a single text. She stood alone in the park, waiting. Bishop had a problem when it came to his father and his own ego. He liked to believe he was this big, tough guy who could face anything, who could do whatever the hell he wanted because people feared him.

What Bishop refused to believe was he was no one without his father. He would always be Preacher's son, and now that she'd seen what real men were like, she had come to realize Bishop was just a cowardly bastard.

She shouldn't have given in to his needs and his belief he could have anything he wanted was her fault. Rather than beat the crap out of him, she'd pacified him. She could have started in the creation of a monster, but no more.

"One of our many old hangouts," Bishop said, coming out from behind one of the trees.

"Hello, Bishop," she said.

"You want to tell me what all of this is about? I already see my dad's truck over there. I'm guessing he's got a whole load of men waiting for him to take me in. Huh?"

"Why did you do it?" she asked.

Preacher hadn't wanted her to stand alone, but she had to face Bishop, especially now. He'd tried to manipulate her without her memories. He'd wanted her to forget, but there were even factors that had happened during her time with Reaper that Preacher didn't know.

"Do what?"

"Give him the divorce."

Bishop froze. "I have no idea what you're talking about."

Each and every moment where Bishop was lying flashed across her mind's eye. The women, the pain, the constant nagging to be her first. The way he treated her when she was pregnant, the final death of any love she might have for him by handing her over to Reaper. It all came to the forefront of her mind.

"You fucking piece of shit!" Robin slammed her fist against Bishop's face. It was so unexpected that he didn't do anything. She hit him again, wanting to break something. To hurt him. To do whatever it took for him to feel even a shred of the pain she'd felt. He grabbed her arms, throwing her away.

She reached into her jeans pocket, retrieving the

pocketknife she'd been carrying since she had gotten her memories back. It had only been two days, but Reaper, during her pregnancy, had shown her how to take care of herself. Even after their baby was born, he'd continued to teach her every single technique to always be able to take care of herself.

"What the fuck was that for? You crazy bitch."

"You're a traitor. A dirty fucking rat. A piece of shit!" She spat the words out as she stared at the man who'd helped to ruin her life. Who had set out to try to ruin Preacher's and Reaper's lives, pitting one man against the other. "Do you know what you did? What your actions did?"

"If you're going to use it, use it, but don't keep on spitting all over me, cursing. It wears a little thin."

"I want to do more than cut you. I want to kill you and believe me, Bishop, you will die."

"I don't see my dad killing me." He looked over her shoulder and gave Preacher a wave. Bear held him back as she'd asked her father to. They were supposed to stay in the car, but she was guessing from her actions, they didn't want her to be alone. "I'm guessing he knows the truth of what happened and if he knows, that means your memories have come back."

"Bingo."

****

What happened the night Robin was taken

"You can do this the easy way, kid, or the hard way. I really don't care. That bitch is coming with us and you're surrounded. There's no way for you to stop what's happening."

"I'm not letting you get her."

"Then it's your funeral. I did warn you." Reaper held his hands up and smiled. "Unless, you and I can come to some kind of arrangement."

"I have no idea what the fuck you're talking about. I will never help you."

"Really? You see, you being Preacher's boy, I imagine it's not easy living in his shadow."

Robin didn't like this. "Don't listen to him, Bishop. He's trying to get into your head."

"And it's working, isn't it, boy? You know what I'm talking about. No one takes you seriously because you're Preacher's son. You're just the little pest that gets in the way. They don't care 'bout you. They certainly don't respect you. You're nothing if not in the way. I mean look at Robin, beautiful, sweet, Robin."

She shook her head. "Bishop, come on. You know he's dangerous. He's trying to use you. To get you to do what he wants."

"I'm not using anyone. I'm merely stating some facts your boy here doesn't know."

Her heart pounded as Reaper kept on digging. Bishop was a strong guy, but when it came to his dad, he wasn't mature enough, not to deal with whatever this asshole was throwing his way.

She looked at Bishop, trying to reach him, but he was drawn too much by the power of Reaper's words.

"You're going to have to watch your father be happy with the woman meant for you."

"This is crazy, Bishop, don't listen to him."

"All you will ever be is Preacher's son. No one will ever look at you with respect. They will always be wondering where your father is. What he's doing. Where he's going. You will constantly be in his shadow. Even if Robin were to fall in love with you, what do you think that's going to achieve? Do you think she'll come to you with open arms? Do you think she'll fall in love with you? No, she will always be wondering what Preacher was doing. You'll be compared to him all the fucking time and you will fall short."

Bishop looked at Robin and she knew it was useless.

He was too weak.

He'd fallen into Reaper's trap.

"Please, Bishop, you're my best friend."

"It didn't stop you from falling in love with my father though, did it? No, it didn't stop you from being with him. Looking at you, Robin, makes me sick to my stomach." Bishop looked at her and she saw the disgust. "What do you need me to do?"

"I'm going to need you to stay here. To tell me when Preacher's got a lead, let me know so I can get her out of the way."

"I'll do it. I don't want him to have a single moment of happiness. I want him to keep on waiting. To know she's being hurt because he was too damn obsessed with his revenge to even know what the fuck hit him."

"You don't think he's going to know you let them take me? You're a fucking coward, Bishop. A piece-of-shit coward."

"The lady's right. I'm going to have to hit you, make it real."

Reaper passed her into the arms of another man, and she tried to get away, but she was caught up in their tangle of a web with no way to escape.

She gritted her teeth, wanting to be free. Wanting to be cut loose. When Reaper's fist hit Bishop's face, she smiled. She couldn't help it. If she couldn't hit him, then she was more than pleased someone else had gotten the pleasure she couldn't have.

****

Present day

Bishop shook his head. "So all of your memories are back and you're coming to me. Why?"

"I know you're a cowardly bastard, but I need you to get a message to Reaper," she said.

He burst out laughing. "You really think I'm going to help any of you?" He raised his voice so Preacher and Bear could hear.

She glanced behind her and nodded for them to join her.

"What the fuck are you doing?" Bishop asked.

"You know, you talk the good talk but we all know you're a terrified little boy. I'm surprised you haven't pissed yourself yet."

"Robin, what are you going to do?"

"Oh, what I usually do. I take care of people, it's what I do. I talked with Preacher and Bear. They've been looking for you and well, I knew how to bring you out. Now I've got an agreement in place. You help me locate Reaper, and you get to live. You don't, then you die."

"Seriously, what the fuck is this?" Bishop asked.

Preacher and Bear stopped by her side.

Bishop went to leave. Frost, Rider, and Cheeky were there, waiting. They had all the exits covered. She had to keep him distracted long enough for Preacher's men to be in place. Robin was shocked at the lack of love and compassion Preacher had for his own child. She didn't know what had happened in her absence, but she was guessing he was pissed at the betrayal and lies.

Child or not, Bishop would pay for what he did.

For now, she needed him to live.

"You ask what is this? This is the deal I got for you. Tell me where Reaper is. How to get to him, and they will let you live. Of course, it's reliant on you only caring about yourself. I figured it's the kind of man you are, so you wouldn't disappoint me. I'm getting a sense here, that you're going to do what we ask, especially if you want to live."

"What happened to you?" Bishop asked.

Robin stepped forward.

Preacher and Bear were nervous for her, but she wasn't. Bishop had been her best friend, and a part of her believed he was a soulmate. She knew him inside and out. Their time apart hadn't changed that. Bishop hadn't changed. He only ever cared about number one, himself. Everyone else was always in the way. When he'd allowed Reaper to take her, he'd destroyed her love and a part of herself because of it.

"What happened to me? You're really going to stand there and ask me that question?" She looked around her. "I'm twenty-one years old. You were so angry that I loved your daddy more than you, you gave me to his enemy. Do you know what happened to me?"

"I saw the pictures," Bishop said.

"There were so many times you could've helped, but I'm not talking about the beatings." She laughed. "They actually stopped. No, I'm talking about the fact Reaper made me care about him, Bishop. I guess you were right. You're not much of a monster for me, after all. I'm married, Bishop, to Reaper, and we have a kid together. I need to find him."

"Then all you had to do was ask," Reaper said.

She spun around and there was Reaper. His men were behind him but on his chest, in a baby carrier, was her little girl, Bethany.

"Hello, Robin, I was hoping I'd get the chance to see you again," he said. "Bethany has missed you. Say hello to mommy."

****

Her time with Reaper

"Well, what do you think?" Reaper asked.

"It's quiet, quaint. We're near a small town, but far enough away they have to get to us by car. Set back in a woodland, what's not to like?" Robin asked.

"Okay, so why am I getting a sense here that you're not happy?" Reaper asked, coming to stand behind her. He placed his hands on her very swollen stomach. "We've already found an abandoned warehouse. I've got a down payment put on the land, and I've got the boys working on everything else. Tell me what I'm missing," he said. "You know me. I like to make sure you have everything."

"I know. I … I'm worried."

"Why? Because you're nine months pregnant and about to drop?"

"Not just that. What if I go into labor and the power goes out? The car won't start? I'm … scared." It had been a long time since she'd been scared of anything. Reaper, he'd … helped.

It always seemed kind of ironic that the very man who had taken her and threatened her life would be the same man to make her feel secure. Thinking back to the time Reaper took her, it was like a whole different lifetime. A time she couldn't even begin to grasp as the same. Reaper kissed her neck, sucking on her pulse. She loved it when he did that, especially when he had some facial hair, as the scratchiness tickled against her flesh. She enjoyed it when he made her squirm, begging for more.

"I can't wait to have you riding on my cock."

"Your mind is always in the gutter."

"Only when it comes to you. It seems I can't think straight when I'm imagining all the dirty things you want to do to me."

She giggled. "You're crazy. You want to do a hell of a lot more crazy things to me than I want to do to you."

"Is that a promise?"

"I'm the size of a tank, Reaper. I can't do anything."

"I don't know. I think I could get used to this big belly filled with my kid."

She gasped as he bit down on her neck, and it was just the right spot to make her ache for more.

She heard the unmistakable sound of water, and when she looked down, she saw the puddle beneath her feet.

"My water just broke," she said.

"I'm calm. Are you calm?" he asked.

"Reaper, my water broke. The baby is going to come and we're here. I need to be in a hospital."

"Then let's go." He led her out of the new house and toward the car. He helped her climb inside but just then a contraction rushed over her body, making her scream in agony as it tore through her. She remembered a similar pain.

"No, no, no, no, I can't lose this baby."

"No, you're not going to be losing this baby. We're going to deliver this baby together. I'm right here, and we're going to make this work."

Once the pain had passed, he helped her into his car, and she watched as he ran to the other side. She cried out as another contraction came.

"They're too close together. This isn't normal," she said. "The baby is going to come."

He'd pulled out of the long private driveway and was on the road. They were heading to the hospital.

"We're not going to make it. The baby is coming, Reaper. I need you."

"Shit, fuck, shit."

She screamed. "I need to push."

"No, you don't need to push."

"I'm fucking pushing." She whimpered as she

started to push.

Reaper jerked the car to the side of the road and then he was there, in front of her. "I'm here for you, baby."

"The hospital?"

"We're not going to make it. We're going to deliver this baby together and then I'll get you to the hospital. Got it?"

She nodded her head, willing to do anything so long as it would get her out of this pain.

Reaper held her hands, watching as their baby was born into their world. She stared into his eyes, and when she heard the first scream of their little girl, she couldn't believe it. Collapsing in the car, Reaper lifted the baby into her arms. "I need to get you to the hospital now. They can take care of the rest."

"I got blood all over your car."

"And my hands, but we're all good." He was in the car and driving again.

She'd given birth. Her baby had survived.

Resting her head against Reaper's shoulder, she smiled, looking down into the face of her little girl.

"I love you, Reaper," she said, and she meant every word.

To be continued …

Note from the Author:

I know, I know, another *to be continued*, but only one more book, I promise. I'm so excited about this story, and I'm totally in love with it. Not long to go.

Book One: To Awaken a Monster

Book Two: Taken by a Monster

Book Three: A Monster's Beauty

www.samcrescent.com

TAKEN BY A MONSTER

BESTSELLING BBW ROMANCE
SPICY ROMANCE FOR REAL WOMEN

SAM CRESCENT

EVERNIGHT PUBLISHING ®

www.evernightpublishing.com